The Carterchronic:
Til Death Do Us..

You hold the key to life's most difficult problems! Let it flow from within.

Copyright © 2007 Bathwater Press, Inc.
All rights reserved
ISBN: 0-9789196-0-2

To order additional copies please contact us.
Bathwater Press, Inc.
www.g-natti.com
703-597-1373

GALUMINATTI

THE CARTERCHRONIC: TIL DEATH DO US..

2007

The Carterchronic:
Til Death Do Us..

I pay special tribute to my loved ones who no longer answer to the daily call of life. I sound a trumpet for the family members not acknowledged in my last book who have already departed this earth.

If I could say words to you that perhaps you could hear, I would tell you that despite how you may have departed this earth, your death was not in vain. We miss you in every way possible for a human to be missed.

With every publication I release, I will establish a memorial unto you -- the fallen. Your blood, sweat, and tears have all been captured into my quest. Therefore, my dedication is precisely a reflection of the love and support I have received from you. In essence, your inspiration has provided me the burning desire to take what God has given me to the highest plateau humanly possible.

Aunt Dunk, I miss you. For it seems like it was just yesterday when I was a little boy witnessing you give me, my brother and cousins money on frequent occasions. Your consistent demonstration of love back then is still remembered today. Back in the day, your very kind gesture was viewed as a lot of money, and we so graciously appreciated it.

Uncle Brinie, I miss you. I often think about how you would come home to grandma's house and have those life-changing conversations with her that I was too young to understand. Nevertheless, I knew the conversation was that of a son responding to the love of his mom.

Aunt Dunk and Uncle Brinie, both your generation of kids have been blessed and are living out the harvest that you have cultivated. May you boldly and proudly rest in peace!

PROLOGUE

Veronica's World

Veronica was adorned in a bright red, satin silk gown that showcased all of her curves. The color of the gown was such a beautiful contrast to Veronica's nice ebony dark complexion. I could not deny the truth. I missed that perfect body of hers.

When I saw Roni, my thoughts of her made me reconsider whether or not I married the right woman. I could tell that she had been working out since we last met, prior to my wedding. Her body was more toned, more refined and capital P FINE!!

Her lips were as juicy as ever in a very subtle way. Her eyes were so sexy and full of depth, sunken beyond those long dark eyelashes of hers. Her dark velvet-like hair made me want to rub my hands into that heavenly head as though I was a cosmetologist. Gloriously standing at five foot nine inches, Veronica had changed her hair style. She currently wore a low cut, boxed like fade that tripled her sexuality to no end, showcasing the beautiful features of her face.

In addition, my girl was endowed with swollen thighs and a jelly shaking butt that would almost have a brother releasing the hounds just by a lengthy stare.

Having said those words alone, any man could clearly understand why I had to have my date with destiny as I was about to break a sista off something proper.

We collaborated and planned our rendezvous for just an Alabama minute as Veronica managed to ring my phone at least one more time after we stumbled into each other that night at the club. Thus, we made a plan to rekindle the flames and make up for lost time.

Prior to my arrival to the hotel, I went and purchased me some strawberry dust (edible lotion) as I wanted to taste every inch of Veronica's body from head to toe. She would be both my dinner and my desert. I was so glad that she took the time to follow up and invite me back into her life after I saw her chocolate pulchritude at the club.

Therefore, we met and wasted no time because our desires were very basic. We just wanted to meet, delicately bite into each other physically and just hibernate for the weekend. The rules were very clear. We had planned to lie in bed all day for the entire weekend where we would make love, take a break and eat and handle each other's business as though we were completely there to satisfy one another. My goal was to get as much of Veronica as I could because I had been missing her tightness, her rightness, her softness, her naughtiness, and her amazing curvaceous body.

Since being married and having a wife who was pregnant and not craving a brother's love, my loneliness for love produced some weird sexual interests within me that were probably different from the normal male. For instance, Lord forgive me, but I found myself motivated to get to our church early on Sunday mornings so I could enjoy the praise and worship service.

Don't misunderstand me! My desire was truly for the wrong reasons. I mean, I was very devout at paying 12 percent of my tithes and everything, but that was probably my most spiritual contribution. You see there was one gorgeous sister who led the most awesome songs of praise. I would find myself overwhelmingly turned on by the way in which she praised God with so much compassion. She didn't even know that I existed, but I liked the way she represented in praising God and the way she hit those notes with her nice vocal chords. I treasured her just like she was a celebrity. That woman must have been every bit of one hundred pounds while standing about five foot tall.

On one Sunday, the preacher was talking about how Moses lifted the rod and parted the Red Sea. All I could think about was lifting my rod and parting her light brown sea. *Oh God, please forgive me! Those were just thoughts and I was just being honest about them.* That's right; I wanted to part those waters badly. That truly was my overwhelming thought whenever I looked into her eyes.

Matter of fact, on this past Sunday I had to repent for days, as that lovely sister was leading a song. She was wonderfully singing *Take Me to the Water.* For some reason, I felt like she was singing that song to me and heaven knows I did want to baptize her in such a righteous kind of way.

Come on now JR. You know you need to stop that. Repent of your sins and leave those lewd thoughts alone. Just focus on God and conduct your praise and worship with the Lord. Stop thinking that just because you been paying 12 percent of your tithes that you were alright with God. Those were the words I kept repeating in my mind.

But that was then and this is now. I was about to carefully peel into Veronica's tender parts. You see my wife Evelyn was doing well and she was out of town with her sister for a week. They were attending a Childcare Leadership Forum as she was trying to get herself and her wayward sister some education and training on childcare rules and regulations. Of course she was not that far away, as the course was being taught in Dallas, Texas.

Anyway, I was so firm as I was anticipating the melting

wetness of Veronica. She greeted me in the hotel with a real nice, stimulating wet kiss. Although her tongue was the aggressor, I was not reluctant at all towards nibbling that nice bra off so I could squeeze and caress that watermelon gold mine of hers. Then, all of a sudden, something beyond all expectations occurred and I was clearly not a happy camper.

"Mr. Carter! Mr. Carter! Are you okay? The meeting has just adjourned, but you appeared to be in such a long stare."

I finally came to my senses as I had dozed off at the city's real estate planning commission and John Caruthers had awakened me.

"Hey John, I'm doing fine. I just been thinking about all the work I have ahead of me, that's all."

Dang! I can't believe I was dreaming. It seemed so real. I really cannot believe this.

Chapter 1
It Ain't Easy Being Me

Life, as I knew it, had drastically changed. I was such a totally different person than I was over a year ago. For instance, upon my arrival here to Houston, Texas, my primary focus was to immediately place all my troubles behind me. I was able to accomplish that goal by becoming engrossed in my passion for the real estate business while also participating in a few extracurricular activities.

Not long after my emergence into the area, my social life exploded. I no longer had to chase women. Instead the tides had turned; women immediately chased me. Now, I could say the same regarding money. I no longer chased money from a hustler's perspective, but money instead, chased me.

Whoever would have believed that after a little over a year in Houston, I would be a married man and step-father with a child on the way to boot?

Jamie Randell Carter was my name. I had recently married Evelyn Sherree Lyles and immediately became a step-father to her son, Ricky Lyles.

Ricky was now 15 years old. He was a superstar-caliber basketball player who possessed all the charm and grace any top male super model would desire. He was highly sought after. In addition, he was on track to possibly become the first high school basketball player to join the pro ranks prior to graduating from high school.

Furthermore, my world was completely encircled with the likes of Julie; my bi-racial female boss, former lover, and top business partner. Then there was Loke; my true best friend, my dentist, and my ace partner in crime. I was happy at home with my wife Evelyn, my stepson Ricky, and a slew of people who helped maintain my estate. Last but certainly not least, there was my girl Jewel; my true confidante, my closest business partner, my attorney, and more importantly, she had my back regardless of the situation.

I no longer worked as a realtor for Julie at Star Top Realty. I was now her business partner in addition to being co-owner and CEO of real estate properties in Georgia, Virginia, and Texas.

Accepting that lucrative proposition from Julie literally lifted my financial estate to significantly higher income tax brackets. In essence, I still worked for Julie because she did own the properties in those three states.

Business was booming really well for me! I had begun to plant my monetary foot in the geographic locale of Houston, Texas. I would have never thought that leaving Ocala, Florida for Houston, Texas would have netted such a substantial return on my investment.

Once again, money was no longer an entity that I chased, but instead an entity that I possessed.

The life of a married man was a huge adjustment for me. I suddenly found myself in a situation where I was expected to really demonstrate this enormous transformation. Instead of this guy who loathed and entertained women, I was now this man who belonged to one woman...a man who was expected to be a loyal and committed husband.

The challenge was truly great, but somebody had to do the honors. Can I get an Amen on that? Evelyn was pregnant with my child and seemed to always be physically fatigued, mentally frustrated, and basically a bitter person. In addition, my pre-marital act of infidelity, which she was not yet aware of, still hovered over my head like I had just committed a crime. There I was living in a bed of roses, and to some degree, a happily married man. To put it mildly, my life was consistently filled with one challenge after another.

"Evelyn, I really don't understand why you're making such a big deal out of getting some home maternity support. I understand that you feel more comfortable with help from your family as opposed to a nanny helping you, and that's quite alright with me. Just go ahead and bring one of your relatives to the house. Everything will be just fine."

Evelyn and I were involved in a really heated discussion. Her body had begun to swell, and she was experiencing complications that she had not encountered during her first pregnancy. I wanted to hire a full-time nanny to be at her call, but she was simply not comfortable with the idea.

When she told me that she was seriously thinking of bringing a family member here, believe it when I tell you, that information was certainly news to me! I was very surprised on one hand and thought it was a great idea on the other. You see, all the time Evelyn and I had been together, she had never talked about her family or mentioned having them over to the house. It was as though her family members had been non existent, to me anyway.

Case and point, when we got married, for some reason none of her family members attended the wedding. At that particular time, I was really not overly concerned that they weren't there. As I recall the details back then, my family members threatened not to attend because they all felt that I was making such a big mistake.

I guess I was far too busy focusing on my own family scenario at the time. I was far too thrilled at the idea of marrying the woman who had totally swept me off my feet. In addition to dealing with the drama of my own family prior to the wedding and the foolish acts I did prior to the wedding, I just didn't have the time to concentrate on why Evelyn's family did not attend.

"J.R., I will probably have to send for my aunt. You know that my mom is too sick to travel and she doesn't really like flying anyway."

I had just arrived home from a very busy day at work. As I walked into the bedroom, Evelyn was standing there near the bed, and it was obvious that she was upset about something. She was going on and on about so many different scenarios regarding her pregnancy. For some reason, I felt that she was not being straightforward with me. I was tired and mentally exhausted. To say my patience was wearing thin was an understatement.

Despite the fact that my buttons were being gently pushed by Evelyn's emotional outrage, I still maintained my equable temperament.

"Okay Evelyn, by all means, go ahead and fly your aunt here so we can resolve this matter. That's quite alright with me. Besides, we have plenty of room in this house and another person will not make that much of a difference at all."

Evelyn stared at me as she walked alongside the bed. Directly across the room stood a full length mirror centered perfectly against the wall which is where Evelyn placed it.

As she strolled past me, she paused, stood there at the mirror for a moment, and posed this question to me.

"J.R., you think I'm fat don't you?"

She started looking at herself in the mirror. She totally took me by surprise with those words.

Now, was Evelyn fat? Heck yeah, but what pregnant woman wouldn't be? I mean, come on now. What kind of question was that? I'll tell you what kind it was. This was an age-old question that has been known to get many a men in trouble. But I was not falling for that! It was truly a test of my mental turpitude as a retired playa and happily married husband. Therefore, brotha man was not about to go out like that, as I had to represent in the greatest way.

"Sweetheart, I don't think you are fat at all. You are very much pregnant with my baby girl and you are the finest pregnant woman I ever seen in my life."

Now, I thought those words would capture me the crown of ultimate husband. Little did I know, Evelyn snapped the most ferocious look at me with the threatening words of a high school bully.

"Oh, so now I'm just the finest pregnant woman you ever seen? Whatever happened to me being the finest woman you ever seen? At least that is what you used to tell me before I got pregnant with your child. Yawl men are all alike. How a woman looks rule you guys' heart as well as infect what little common sense yawl might have."

I had to immediately respond.

"Evelyn, baby, you know that's what I meant. You are the finest woman I've ever laid eyes upon."

"Laid eyes upon? What about the women that you have not laid eyes upon? You see what I mean J.R.? You must think I am fat. I went from being the finest woman in the world to just the finest woman in a certain category."

Evelyn pouted at the conclusion of her words and I knew that she was very serious by her tone. I also noticed that Evelyn's communication skills had drastically improved. Those English courses at the local college that I recommended she take were surely paying off.

"Baby, that's not at all true. I don't care how pregnant you are. You are still the finest woman in the world and you can take that to the bank."

I walked over to Evelyn and kissed her on the cheeks and also hugged her. Then, I started rubbing on her body. She quickly reminded me that I was not about to get any loving.

"J.R., don't even go there. You ain't bout to get none so you might as well tell the truth." I pretended to respond in righteous indignation, while looking down towards the floor and away from Evelyn.

"Evelyn, I really don't think you are being fair at all. You have not given me any loving for days and I hear other married men tell me that a pregnant woman has the best stuff in the world. Since you have been pregnant you have not even given me as much as a rub down. Somehow, that just cannot be right."

She pushed me away and put her hands on her hips; the hips that you would now not even notice because her stomach bulged to the point of looking as though she was carrying twins. The size alone emphasized the fact she had a very large baby inside of her.

Anyway, Evelyn stepped away from me and started waving her finger at me as she spoke while bobbing her head from side to side.

I had to suppress my laughter as she looked so funny

bouncing her head and snapping her fingers with her highly conspicuous, pregnant stomach swaying from side to side. She didn't even realize how funny she looked.

While holding my breath to keep from laughing, I retreated to sit on our bed. She made me think of Lil John's music video called Snap Yo Fingers.

"Oh! So that ain't right huh? Listen here J.R.! I'm carrying your first born and this baby inside me is much rougher than Ricky ever was. Do you understand me? This little girl is kicking my butt everyday so I don't want to hear you crying anymore about how bad I'm depriving you of some loving. Stop whining like a little baby because the only baby that's prevalent in my life is the one that I'm carrying. You should be excited that I'm taking all precautions to ensure that our baby girl will be welcomed into this world without complications. Do you hear me, Mr. I Got to Get Me Some Loving?"

I quickly walked over and rubbed her stomach and then I put my head right on the surface of her huge stomach.

"Move J.R.!"

She pushed me aside.

"I will see if I can get my aunt to fly in on tomorrow. If so, she will be staying with us for quite sometime and I don't want to hear any complaints out of you."

I pulled further away from Evelyn and said, "Sweetheart why would you get any complaints out of me? I have always encouraged you to bring your family members to the house. You're the one who has been hesitant regarding that endeavor for whatever reason."

Evelyn just stared at me as though she was hiding something or that she had deep thoughts that were imbedded within her mind. Sometimes I often wondered if she knew about my dark past with Doralee Mayberry. Then again, if she did, I am certain she would not be able to contain herself from cursing me out and probably opting to leave me. I think that was just the guilt-stricken thought that possessed my mind as that fateful, dreaded event with Doralee still hung over my head. The feeling was equivalent to a cloud about to drop down some burning rain.

I still could not believe that I slept with another woman just prior to my wedding. The more I looked back in retrospect, the more I became dumbfounded as to having ever committed such an act. To say that hindsight was 20/20 was definitely an understatement for me.

Then, all of a sudden my intercom sounded from my house maid Rosie, alerting me that I had an urgent phone call. I quickly walked over to the phone and answered, "J.R."

The voice on the other side of the phone was in a state of utter panic.

"Is this Mr. Carter?"

"Yes, this is Mr. Carter. May I ask who is calling?"

"Oh my God! Oh My God! Lord have mercy!"

The female voice on the other end of the phone was crying out loud for some reason. I was totally puzzled as to what this was all about. The woman was crying terribly loud and I was trying to find out what was going on.

"Excuse me Miss! Who am I talking to and please tell me what is going on?"

She was crying and gasping for breath.

"Mr. Carter, I'm calling on behalf of Mr. King."

"What? Ma'am, please slow down and tell me what

you are talking about?"

I quickly uttered. She took a deep breath over the phone while still crying as though she was truly hurt.

"Somebody shot Mr. King and the medics from the emergency ambulance truck just pulled a blanket over his face. I think he's been killed Mr. Carter. Oh my God! Oh my God!"

The words hit me hard, but I was still trying to understand.

"Hold up! Who shot who and who killed whom?" I said in a rage so quickly.

"Cynthia, is this you? Please take your time and tell me what you are talking about? Is Mr. King okay?"

"Sir! This is Cynthia, Mr. King's secretary."

"Okay Cynthia, please take your time and tell me what's going on, and what are you trying to say," I repeated.

"Mr. Carter," she was sniffing up a storm.

"Let me tell you what happened. I heard gun shot sounds from the office and I walked out to where Mr. King parked his car, knowing that he had just left the office. There, I found him slumped over the steering wheel and his head was leaning on the horn causing it to sound continuously. Blood was all over his face. Somebody shot him Mr. Carter and I tried to move him, but he would not respond. I called the ambulance and they came and took him away and they covered his face as to pronounce him dead."

"What? Oh my goodness! Heaven help us all! Cynthia, please tell me what hospital they have taken him to?"

I could not believe what I had just heard. Not my boy

Loke, as I was trying to digest the disturbing news. I was not about to believe the worst case. I started pacing back and forth as my boy, my partner, my ace boon coon, evidently had been killed. My mind was racing so fast and I began to get really nervous. To say the cards in my deck had definitely been rattled was not even a clear depiction of what I felt.

"Because of the proximity to his office, they have taken him to Houston Regional Medical Center. This is truly a travesty Mr. Carter. Can you believe somebody shot Mr. King?"

My heart, stomach, and mind all fell to the floor. I immediately became another person.

"Now Cynthia, I'll head to the hospital as soon as I can. Are you alone?"

I was all about business as I was clearly focused on getting to the hospital to check on my boy.

"No Sir! The Houston Police Department is here right now and they're investigating everything that happened. Also, my mother and brother are here. This is so sad Mr. Carter. Mr. King was loved by everybody and he did so much for so many people."

After I heard that Cynthia was okay and that she was with the policemen and her family, my ears became numb. I had to get in the mix!

"Okay Cynthia, be strong and please keep the faith."

What the heck was I telling her? I was the one that really needed to keep the faith with all the trouble going on in my life.

"Okay Mr. Carter, thanks!"

"No! Thank you Cynthia for calling me. I got to run now and check on Mr. King!"

I hung up the phone, put on my shoes and grabbed a jacket as Evelyn was trying to find out what happened.

"J.R., what's wrong baby and where are you going?"

Tears started forming in my eyes as I thought about Loke.

"Evelyn, apparently someone has shot Loke and they're rushing him to the hospital baby. I got to get there."

"Oh My God! Not Loke! Do you know what happened baby and was he fatally wounded?"

Evelyn placed both her hands to her chin and just stared out into space.

"Baby, I'm not totally certain. I don't want to think so, even though his secretary believes the worst has happened! I got to run and get to the hospital."

"J.R., don't go alone baby. Take one of the security guards with you."

I rushed right by Evelyn with my jacket and wallet, and then I stopped to head back her way.

"Evelyn, I'm fine. I'll call you from the hospital."

I gave her a quick kiss on the lips and frantically rushed out of the house. There must have been a thousand thoughts that went through my mind. The most dominant thought was that my boy was gone. As I began to straddle up in my truck, I became so nervous. I actually found myself nearly losing it mentally. I began to wonder how I was going to drive to the hospital. I stopped in my driveway and said a prayer.

"Lord, please don't let this be so. Don't take my boy Loke. Please hear my prayer God. I am praying for Latrell Oliver King (short for Loke, pronounced like coke). He is closer to me than anyone God. Please, spare his life. Please God! I need this one real bad Lord!"

I shouted out in my prayer and then I sped down the highway. As I was driving, I reflected back on the first time that Loke and I had met, back at that club.

I thought about how he sat down and talked to me and shared his life story with me. I thought about everything we ever did together and more tears were produced. My eyes were raining tears to no end.

I thought to myself that if God did not grant me this one favor, I would handle matters myself and avenge his death.

Those thoughts had to be produced from the dark side of me as I knew I should be focused on believing and not doubting. That's exactly what the preacher talked about on last Sunday. I wonder if the sermon was intended for me.

Finally, I pulled up to the emergency entrance of the hospital. I couldn't even park my truck correctly. I just jumped out and ran into the hospital.

"Sir, you can't park there," shouted this old man in a uniform who was standing near a security vehicle.

"Sir, please park my truck for me and I'll take care of you when I return. My brother just got shot and I got to check on him."

I ran into the hospital and almost scared the front attendant at the desk.

"Ma'am, I'm looking for Mr. King. He should have arrived maybe 20 minutes ago. I was told that he was fatally wounded."

"Sir, he is under critical care at this time and I don't have any further updates of his status at this time. The best thing that you can do is sit in the waiting room until we have more information regarding his condition."

This was really not something that I wanted to hear right now. I dashed beyond the double doors where they house the emergency patients and the attendant came running after me, shouting the words, I was not allowed beyond the doors.

As I ran beyond the doors, I came across a nurse. I urgently spoke to her and I asked her where was Mr. King. She proceeded to tell me that I was in violation of some hospital security code and I clearly spoke out at her.

"Nurse, I am not trying to violate any regulation or rules, but I just need to know about my best friend. Please help me if you can. I just heard that he had been killed and I rushed out here right away."

She immediately consented and pointed me to Loke's room. The front desk attendant caught up to me and stressed to the nurse that she told me I was not allowed in the area. The nurse just listened, but still led me to a room where the door was shut. She informed me that Loke was in the room with two surgeons as they were trying to figure out his condition. She did emphasize that he was still alive.

"But nurse, if he arrived alive, why did they cover his face as though he was dead," as I reflected back on the conversation with Cynthia.

"Sir, you can't always conclude death by that act. Bodies are sometimes covered up prematurely. Many medics do this to prevent the public from viewing graphic details of a victim who has visible gunshot wounds."

All I said was, "thank you Lord!" I was breathing so heavy. A few minutes later, the nurse finally told the desk clerk that everything was okay and it was alright for me to remain in the immediate vicinity. The desk clerk was obviously upset at my decision to blow her off and run beyond the restrictive doors.

"I'll definitely be sensitive to the situation," she said, "but next time Sir, you need to follow the hospital rules."

I shifted my eyes toward the clerk indicating my displeasure with her disposition, but I never said a mumbling word to her.

As soon as the door to Loke's room opened, I tried to look in the room, but could not see anything. This heavy bearded, overweight Caucasian male appeared from beyond the door. I bum rushed him.

"Doctor, I'm Mr. King's best friend and closest family member in the area. Please tell me his status."

The doctor took off his glasses and proceeded to tell me that I should not be in the emergency room area as I was interrupting other patients. I just quietly stared at him. Then I convincingly conveyed to him the essence of my emotions.

"Doctor, if you don't tell me what's going on with my brother I will break that door down and find out myself. I won't return to the front waiting room area until I know the status of my boy!"

He placed one of the armed extensions of his eyeglasses in his mouth. Then he proceeded to write something down on a clipboard and then removed the glasses from his mouth and further spoke to me.

"Mr. King has sustained two bullets to his rib cage. He has lost a significant amount of blood, and we must operate right away to retrieve those bullets. He is in a severely critical condition right now. Also, one of the bullets may have penetrated the aorta region of his chest. If such is the case, the operation to retrieve the bullet will be a very difficult procedure and highly risky. He is alive and we must proceed with extreme caution. Now, please return to the waiting room area because there is nothing you can do for him right now."

I was relieved that Loke was still alive, but I was certainly worried as to the dangerous state of his current condition.

"Thanks doctor! How soon will the surgery be performed?"

"Right away, in order for us to have a fighting chance to help him fully recover."

I immediately returned to the front corridor and then went outside and called Julie on my cell phone. I informed her as to what had happened to Loke and she was relatively calm throughout the conversation.

"J.R., I'm on my way to the hospital, but before I proceed I will have the number one surgeon in this region contacted and made available for this operation. Trust me! Loke will be fine. I'm on my way."

After I got off the phone with Julie, I called Evelyn and Jewel to tell them what had happened. I asked Jewel to track down Loke's relatives and inform them of the situation with Loke and his present condition. As usual, Jewel got busy without fail.

I went out to the parking lot where I left my truck and was greeted by the security guard who parked my truck. I paid him a casual fee for the inconvenience, obtained my keys, and returned to the waiting room in the hospital.

Julie showed up not long afterwards and informed me that her surgeon of choice did heed the call and was making preparations to lead Loke's surgical operation.

Julie asked me what happened and I quickly informed

her of everything I knew. She told me that she had a significant amount of guilt because she had not responded to Loke's phone calls over a two week period. She did not tell me why, but just stated that she never did. We waited together in the waiting room keeping each other company.

Sometime later Jewel arrived at the hospital. She told me that Loke's ex wife and kids had been notified and they were taking the quickest flight possible to Houston. Jewel had arranged reservations for them at a hotel near the hospital. Jewel was my warrior, my most trusted soldier in time of war, and she knew exactly how much Loke meant to me.

"Jewel! What about Loke's mom and dad?" She looked at me like I stole her money.

"J.R., Loke's mom and dad are both deceased. I thought you knew that already."

I rose up from the chair and walked away from Jewel. I turned around quickly with my right hand on my hip and left hand clasping my forehead.

"Jewel, Loke has never told me that both his parents were deceased." Jewel had a very confused look on her face.

"Well, I did a thorough check and his ex wife confirmed that fact," said Jewel with much assurance in her voice.

"The ex was the only relative I was able to track down under such short notice and she informed me that she would contact his other relatives."

I did not give much thought to Jewel's words. At that point, I was just glad any of his relatives were able to be contacted.

Furthermore, after a couple of hours, I eventually convinced Jewel to go home and get some rest. However,

I simply was unable to convince Julie to leave, and so we both spent the night at the hospital.

Chapter 2
Hearst Wheels Looming

I fell asleep, and while doing so, found myself in the bystander position from hell. I seemingly saw the whole event as to what happened to Loke.

Loke was in his office finalizing some paperwork well past 8 pm. His secretary, Cynthia, elected to hang around and ensure he did not need any secretarial services.

You see, prior to this tragedy, Loke had reopened another dentist office down in the hood of Houston, much to my disliking. For some reason he had in his mind that he would relocate dentist offices in economically challenged locations like Magic Johnson had done with his theatres. I highly encouraged him to expand his practices and open dentist offices in other locations.

Prior to this major business movement, I definitely invested in his strategic acquisition as well. Nevertheless, I had initially tried to talk him out of opening an office in a high crime district.

When he wouldn't listen to me, I insisted that he hire around the clock security. Loke always thought that his popular personality and charitable ways would dissuade anyone from wanting to really do any major harm to him or his offices.

On last night, Loke was about to leave the office.

"Hey Cynthia, I think the time has come for us to call it a day."

Loke sounded those words over his intercom phone to Cynthia's phone. She immediately came into his office and agreed totally.

"Sure thing Mr. King. I have one more phone call to make and then I'll be leaving."

"Now Cynthia, you know I don't like leaving you here in the office alone. I would hate for anything to happen to you."

"Mr. King, my mom and brother are both on their way to pick me up. They will probably be here in a matter of minutes. You sure don't have to worry about me Sir. I'm fine. I know this neighborhood like the back of my hand."

Loke looked at her and grabbed his briefcase, suit jacket, and proceeded out the back door.

"Okay Cynthia, I'll see you on tomorrow. I will only come through for half a day as I will be at my main office most of the day. Good night, and you be very careful my dear."

"I sure will Mr. King. I thank you once again for hiring employees that live right here in the area. You don't know what you have done to improve conditions for the people who live in this hood Mr. King."

"Well thank you Cynthia! I'm just trying to do my part. Right now though, I am too tired so let me get up out of here. Good night."

"Good night Mr. King! I'll see you tomorrow."

Loke left out the building and walked out his back door which was less than five feet to his personal parking spot. Just as he was about to open the door to his newly purchased Cadillac Escalade, a stranger walked up on him from the dark.

"Move away from the car mutha f…. right now or I will blast ya brains."

Loke looked at the potential assailant pointing a gun. As he stared with both shock and intensity, he tried to remain calm during this unexpected ordeal.

"Hey man, I'm willing to help you with whatever you

need, but please don't harm me now."

Loke proceeded to sit down in his truck as though there was no fear.

"I'm warning you one more time nigga! Get out the damn truck."

Loke noticed that the hand gun being pointed at him was a Glock and the young man was trembling while pointing the gun.

"Look man! What is it that you want? You need some money? I can spot you a few bills, but don't get trigger happy on me."

"You know what I want nigga. I want yo truck and yo money so get out right now befoe I blow ya head off."

Loke looked at the young man again and said with smooth words, "Look here my brother, I just bought this truck and if you jack me for it, you won't get any further than two miles because the cops will be all over you before you arrive at the chop shop. I suggest you let me give you a few bills and you go on your way and we will call it a day. Is that okay? Will that work for you?"

Loke thought to himself, *he is out of his mind if he thinks I'm giving him my brand new Escalade. That little punk done pushed up on the wrong brotha. Shoot! He gonna have to kill me.*

The young lad just looked at Loke and continued pointing the gun. Then Loke acted as though he was reaching over to get some money for the kid. He took out his wallet and grabbed a few twenty dollar bills and then held it out for the young man. As the young man reached for the bills, Loke attempted to knock the gun out of his hand, but he failed.

The young man, in fear, fired two shots to Loke's chest

and fled. Loke just sat in the truck at first with thoughts of unbelief. He could not believe that he had been shot. Then, he eventually started thinking words in his mind, as though he was talking out loud. *I can't believe he shot me. Oh goodness! He did something because I'm starting to feel the pain. Oh well, let me get up and tend to this pain. Oh no! Either my mind or my body is not cooperating. I can't move for some reason. I feel like I'm glued to the seat and my body feels too heavy to rise up. Come on Loke! Get up and stop playin man! I was breathing out oxygen much faster than my body could take it in. I started thinking about how all of a sudden I could not move and my body was feeling so wet. There was a heavy wetness that started staining my clothes. It seemed to be rapidly leaving my body and soaking into my clothes. I started fading in and out, reflecting back on how I became a dentist and how determined I was to make it out of the hood when I was a young teenager. I thought about my parents who were so proud of me as I walked across the graduation platform with my degree in hand. I immediately thought about my kids, how they would be raised without their natural father in their lives if I died. I somehow went all the way back to the first time I had sex and how it was such an unpleasant feeling for me. I thought back when I first learned that everybody would someday die. I was outside in the projects, about six years old, and I remember being so sad because I did not want to ever die. You see, I always thought I would live forever. I thought about my college days and how I was the man on campus and everybody knew it. Then, all of a sudden my thoughts became darkened. It was as though I could not bring myself to think any further. At that instant, my mind, body, and soul seemingly became one spirit that was departing from me. All of sudden, I seemed to realize that I was breathing my last breath. I was about to leave this earth as we know it and enter that proverbial hallway without a clue as to what path I was taking--heaven or hell.*

Loke's body slumped over the horn of his Escalade and sounded the trumpet to the public. While Cynthia was on the phone, she heard the sound of the gun shots, and then the horn blowing. She ran out back and saw Mr. King sitting in his truck slumped over the horn. She ran out to him.

"Mr. King, are you okay? Mr. King."

She saw the pool of blood gathered around his chest and began to shake him and then removed his head from the horn. She screamed out crying, "somebody help me...somebody please help me....oh my God!"

She screamed again to the top of her lungs, "Oh No! Please, please, pleeeaaaasse...somebody help me."

By now, her mother and brother had arrived in the front corridor and heard the sound of Cynthia's voice. They rushed out back to where Cynthia was located. After seeing Cynthia holding Mr. King in her arms and ensuring that she was okay, though she was crying out for help, they immediately called 911. Then, before I knew it, my reality had set back in.

"J.R., wake up! The doctor is coming shortly."

I awakened to Julie's voice. The time was about 7:45 a.m. and it seemed as though I was just talking to Julie as I recalled getting both of us some coffee at about 4:15 a.m. Julie looked as refreshed as she did when she showed up at the hospital last night. I felt like the victim of a boxing match, who had just gone 16 rounds with Mohammad Ali.

Less than five minutes later, the doctor appeared. He was clad in blue medical scrubs and apparently had just taken off his head apparatus. The doctor looked really serious, so I braced myself to receive what I felt was going to be disparaging news.

To my surprise, upon closer view, he was the same doctor who Veronica, a former lover of mine, had divorced. I said a quick prayer as he seemingly approached us in slow motion. Julie held my hand and I was so scared.

"Julie, Mr. Carter, how are you? Mr. King is still in very critical condition. He lost an exceptional amount of blood, but we were able to retrieve the two bullets. The operation was done without us having to penetrate the aorta region, but his left rib cage had to be repaired. He is still in a coma, and he is still in a very serious condition. We're doing everything humanly possible for him. There'll be someone constantly monitoring his progress."

Julie kissed me on my cheeks and hugged the doctor as those strong words of solace became an anchor for our souls. As I stood there, I was somewhat reassured at the news of Loke's condition, but there were numerous questions that my mind pondered.

"So doctor, is he going to be alright? Will he be the same?"

"Mr. Carter, Loke will be tender around the chest for quite awhile, provided he survives his current condition. He is still in a severely critical state, but let's keep our fingers crossed and hopefully he will be okay."

"Can I see him now?"

The doctor paused and took a deep breath slowly. He placed his hand on my shoulder.

"I recommend that you and Julie go home and get

23

some rest and perhaps come visit Mr. King on tomorrow. Please understand! He won't be aware of his faculties for at least a few days. His condition is much too grave to even have family members in the room."

"We will give him the time Dr. Clowers," said Julie.

"Thanks for answering the call one more time," Julie convincingly conveyed.

"You are more than welcome Julie."

I extended my hand to him again and said, "Thanks Dr. Clowers. Julie told me you were the best in the business and we really do appreciate the life-saving surgery you used to preserve our dear friend's life. Mr. King will be very pleased."

"No problem Mr. Carter! We did everything we could do for him and we'll monitor his condition around the clock. Now, please go and get some rest and we'll call you if his condition changes any whatsoever, okay."

The doctor returned through the emergency room doors as Julie and I prepared to leave the hospital.

Julie and I decided to stop for breakfast at a nearby restaurant. We talked quite a bit about Loke as we traveled together to the restaurant.

Then, while eating, Jewel phoned to tell me the exact time Loke's ex wife and kids would be arriving at the airport. I assured her that I would pick them up, take them to the hotel, and then to the hospital. Jewel wanted to come along with me of course and that sounded great to me.

Julie and I finished our breakfast, wrapped up our conversation, said our farewells, and I headed home to my family. When I got there, the first place I headed for was the kitchen in search of my wife. I saw Evelyn standing near the kitchen counter looking out the window. I went over and kissed her on the cheeks and said, "Baby, I am so tired. I'm going to crash for awhile because I have to pick Loke's family up from the airport in about five hours."

I walked away from Evelyn, and as I did, she turned around and quickly glanced at me. I guess I must have been more exhausted than I realized because at this point, I stopped immediately in my footsteps.

Hold on. I said to myself. I thought Evelyn was pregnant with my baby girl. Lord, what is going on now? Am I that sleepy or am I still dreaming?

I turned and looked around at Evelyn again. I stared at her. She continued to look out the kitchen window. Her hair was much fuller, hips were proportioned like the Evelyn before the pregnancy, and her breast accentuated the rest of her voluptuous body.

Wait a minute! Evelyn is not pregnant now. Her stomach is completely flat. What in the world is going on up in here?

"I see yawl have met already," Evelyn said as she walked into the room.

The woman who I thought was Evelyn turned around and said, "Naw, not really! I thank yo hubbie thanks I'm you," said this stranger in the room as she just stared at me.

Evelyn looked at me as I looked at her and then I looked back at this stranger in the kitchen. My lower chin went south as I opened my mouth wide and I just kept looking back and forth at the both of them. The stranger in the house had to be related to Evelyn; they looked exactly alike. This stranger had a smirk-like smile on her face as though she was enjoying the attention.

"J.R., snap out of it. Meet my sister Teralyn. I call her T, and Teralyn, this is my husband J.R."

I shook Teralyn's hand and she said, "Nice to meet-chu J.R.; heard a lot about-chu."

"Thanks Teralyn, I wish I could say the same, but I can't."

I looked at Evelyn with a, what in the world, kind of look on my face. Evelyn came closer to me and hugged me tightly.

"Honey, I tried to tell you about Teralyn, but you were too pre-occupied. We are identical twins. She flew in last night on the red eye. Baby, how is Loke?"

Twin sister? Evelyn never even mentioned to me anything about having a twin sister and I can clearly see why. The woman is finer than any woman I have ever laid eyes on before in my life. I could not believe what I was seeing. Nevertheless, I had to play the surprise off.

"Evelyn, they removed two bullets from Loke's chest. He is still in a very critical condition. The doctor thinks he has a chance, but cannot make any promises. I can't believe someone tried to kill him."

Teralyn responded, "Who's Loke and why did he get shot?" I told her that Loke was my best friend who was like a brother to me. I started to tell her what happened to him when I realized I didn't really know myself.

Evelyn bailed me out and said, "J.R., you go and get some sleep honey. I'll tell Teralyn all about Loke."

She kissed me on my lips and I quickly made an exit from the kitchen and to my bed. Evelyn did not have to tell me twice. I was completely tired, exhausted, done!

While I was asleep, Evelyn told Teralyn about everybody she knew that was affiliated with me. When I woke up, Evelyn told me that Jewel and Teralyn had met last night. From the manner in which she described it, I did not get the impression that they hit off that well at all.

Jewel eventually arrived and as we left the house, she shared with me the experience of meeting Teralyn. Jewel, I might add, was very sensitive to my feelings regarding Loke while driving out to the airport to pick up his family.

"So Jewel, what do you think of Teralyn?"

"What else should I think J.R.? She is a splitting image of Evelyn? I can't believe two people can look so much alike. I guess since you are married to one of the twins, I should be asking you what do you think."

Jewel stared at me without blinking.

"Well Jewel, I really have not had time to process Teralyn as I have been pretty pre-occupied with Loke. I agree with you though. I can't believe Evelyn has an identical twin and has never mentioned it to me."

While Jewel and I were traveling to pick up Loke's family, Evelyn and her sister were engaged in serious conversation back at the house.

"E, I don't care what-chu sayin, dat woman is screwin J.R. I can tell by da way she responds to him. I can tell by da look in her eyes. She is screwin da hell outta him and you da only one dat don't know." Evelyn got impatient with her sister.

"T, I am not gonna keep on talking about this. Now I told you that J.R. and Jewel were like brother and sister and Jewel is very much a dear friend of mine. They are not as you say, screwing."

Teralyn approached Evelyn again while standing near the doorway to her bedroom. Evelyn was positioning herself on her bed.

"Gurl, ont care what-chu sayin. Ain't no man gonna be hangin round a woman dat attractive witdout screwin her. I could see if dey were natural brotha and sistah, but E, dey not even related. You in denial gurl. I ain't stoopid."

Evelyn sat up in her bed as though she was frustrated.

"Now T, I'm gonna tell you one more time that I don't want to hear that kind of talk up in here. J.R. and Jewel are business partners that happen to be like family. Once again, Jewel has become a close friend of mine also."

Teralyn leaned forward with her left hand on her hips and her right hand waving her index finger in the air as she spoke.

"Gurl, I'll be yo darn friend too if it meant stayin up in dis big ole house to enjoy all dis. Why she gotta be stayin all up in dis house anyway? Ain't she got huh own place? You betta watch-cho back sis. All I'm sayin is dat-chu in so deep dat-chu can't even see da forest from da damn bushes. Gurl, you betta recognize." Evelyn got angry with a rapid fire response.

"It's forest from the trees girl."

"Whateva," responded Teralyn.

"T, I did not bring you here for this crap okay. Now, I refuse to continue this conversation with you. I don't need you analyzing relationships. What I need you to do is help me with this child I'm pregnant with. If you have a problem with that, then you let me know right now. I can always send yo pretty little butt back to Alabama, cause I ain't trying to hear this mess. Do you hear me?" Teralyn started clapping.

"Dat's what I'm talkin bout! I was startin to wonda if you'd been kidnapped cause you been soundin like a tight butt, stuck up cutie since I stepped foot in dis house. Dem last words were more like da ghetto fabulous hoe dat I grew up wit."

Evelyn quickly threw a teddy bear at Teralyn, but Teralyn ducked just in time. Teralyn laughed real loudly and then went off to a room in our guest quarters' area of the house.

Chapter 3
Oh No She Didn't

After arriving at the airport, I offered to treat Loke's family to a quick dinner, but they wanted to go directly to the hospital. As we were heading there, Julie called me and informed me that Loke's condition had taken a turn for the worse.

The doctor had contacted her and shared with her the latest update. I had the speaker phone on so they could hear the conversation. The kids heard the news and they started crying. Jewel, in a subtle way, had started crying as well. I signaled my limo driver to speed it up, and he obliged.

By the time we reached the hospital, Julie was already there. Shortly afterward, Dr. Clowers came out to give us the update. I was beginning to feel deep down inside that my best friend and partner was not going to survive his current medical condition.

The doctor came out from beyond the closed doors with a look of despair.

"Hi everyone, I'm Dr. Clowers. Mr. King's condition has taken a turn for the worse, but I must tell you, he is a fighter. His condition today is worse than it was yesterday, but he is still hanging on."

"Is my dad gonna die?" His 13 year old son uttered while crying. Dr. Clowers quickly embraced the family with these words.

"While it is not looking good right now, I still believe in his will to survive. I will be doing everything I can to keep him alive. I encourage everyone to remain positive. That is really all I can say for now. I recommend everyone go and get some rest and you will be notified of any further changes."

"We would like to see Loke Dr. Clowers, if only for a minute. I realize he may not survive the night," uttered Loke's ex wife.

"Okay Ma'am, but please be as quiet as possible and understand that he is not in a visitation state by any stretch of the imagination."

"Now Dr. Clowers, if he is in utter misery, we need to discuss measures to relieve him of such."

I listened patiently to every word exchanged between the doctor and Loke's ex wife. For some reason, I did not like the sound of her last words.

"What do you mean by measures to relieve him of such?" I uttered.

"Well J.R., if Loke is suffering under the current state and there is no further help for him, we need to pull the plug," replied Loke's ex wife.

At that point, I could simply not restrain myself, for my anger got the best of me.

"Pull the plug! You mean, facilitate his death? Don't you think it's a little sudden to be discussing those options?" Jewel immediately grabbed the kids and began to lead them to another waiting area in the hospital.

"J.R., I'm talking about doing the right thing if the need dictates. I recently lost an aunt who was suffering for weeks and we had to pull the plug to relieve her of such pain." I was literally furious at her words.

"Woman you done lost yo mind. We initially received an ounce of hope with the bullets being retrieved from his body. Ain't nobody pulling a plug up in here if I got anything to do with it."

"I really don't appreciate your tone and the way in

which you are talking to me." Loke's ex wife was completely heated over my attitude.

"We don't need any Johnny Come Lately up in here making matters any worse than they already are. You should be ashamed of yourself," were my provocative words.

"Look here Mister. You don't even know who I am and therefore you have no right to be talking to me like that."

"I know enough about you. I shouldn't be too surprised because your poor decision in the past is what led to Loke even being here. After all, you did forsake him for another man didn't you?"

"What? Your rude comments alone have raised my concern regarding your involvement of Loke's medical condition. I don't mean any harm, but you need to mind your own business because you don't know what you're talking about."

Jewel, Julie, and the doctor quickly separated me from Loke's wife. The doctor quickly took charge.

"Mr. Carter, please calm down. I understand your concern. Let's try and keep this civil."

Julie grabbed me by my arms and whispered these words into my ear.

"J.R., please don't prolong this mockery any further."

However, I was not about to allow this woman, who I viewed as an outside intruder, to decide the fate of my friend. I was outraged! I looked at Jewel while wondering what Loke's ex wife was talking about.

"My what? Oh no she didn't just call me rude, and telling me to mind my own business! Did she just call me a name?" I was not finished with her. All of a sudden without warning, I just blurted out these defensive words.

"Loke is my business, you high class acting bourgeoisie. If your creeping butt would not have been cheating on him, he wouldn't even be in this city, nor would he had gotten shot." She quickly interrupted me this time.

"Will someone please get this trifling lunatic out of my presence before somebody really gets hurt in here?" I continued to lash out at Loke's ex wife as though I had not been interrupted.

"Talking about pulling a plug on Loke, you better carry your fat, sophisticated butt back where you came from because you ain't running jack up in here. Besides, Loke being dead does not exonerate you from cheating on him with a white man."

Loke's ex wife immediately responded as though she was embarrassed.

"Somebody please get him out of here. He has lost his mind talking to me like that." Julie pulled me away from Loke's wife. Then immediately, I came to realize the words that were being lashed at each other could never be taken back. My thoughts literally arrested my tongue, as Julie took me away from the potential fight.

About 15 minutes later, Loke's ex wife and kids were allowed to go in and see Loke. Julie felt it was better if I remained away from Loke's ex wife, and so I did.

Jewel ushered Loke's family out afterwards and had the limo driver drop them off first at their hotel. She then headed back to the hospital to comfort me. Meanwhile, Julie had already done her part to try and settle me down. She had insisted on my going to the hospital chapel to pray for guidance and understanding.

I prayed so diligently for Loke. Sometimes your spirit provides words for such occasions; words that you never knew existed. The prayer I prayed that day was, by my standards, an amazing piece of work, if I had to say so myself. I told God that I realized that my prayer may seem somewhat selfish, but I desperately needed him to intervene on Loke's behalf.

The urging alone in my prayer forced me to confront my own fear; the fear of Loke dying and not being there for me. I even asked God to help us all recover from this travesty. I stayed in the chapel for about an hour, just praying and having a talk with God. Not really certain if anybody was listening, but I just kept on praying.

Afterwards, Jewel returned to the hospital! When she saw me, I was drenched in my tears. She hugged me. Her support meant a lot to me and you could tell it was authentic because she could not contain the tears that were welling up in her eyes. Then, Jewel and I rode home together…totally speechless until we reached the house.

"J.R., please get some rest. I'm gonna stay at my condo for awhile." I was ever so shocked to hear Jewel say that.

"Jewel, is this because of how I acted tonight? I apologize."

"No J.R.! I need to stay at my place. I don't think this house is big enough for your sister in law and I."

"What Jewel? What in the heck are you talking about? Did she say or do something to you?"

"No J.R., she did not. I'm just using my woman's intuition. I'll be fine."

"But Jewel, you have been staying at my house for sometime now. Plus, you are Ricky's agent?"

"J.R., I will continue to be Ricky's agent. I communicate with him nearly everyday. I'm anxious to see him by the way. I know he is still at the training site with the coach and his team, preparing for the state championship. I will continue to do my job. I just need to stay at my condo for awhile."

"I'm sorry Jewel. I have been so wrapped up with Loke that I didn't even think about the dynamics here at the house."

"J.R., you be careful. Don't get into anything that you have got no business doing. I know Teralyn is beautiful and a splitting image of Evelyn, but please remember she is not your wife. I got to run hun."

Jewel kissed me on my cheeks and rushed off in her car. I was somewhat confused as to what she was trying to tell me regarding Teralyn. Is there something I'm missing here?

Anyway, it was after midnight when I finally went into the house. Evelyn and I had an agreement that if I did not get home in time to go to bed with her, I would sleep in the guest quarters. She easily convinced me because of my own sleeping disorders I had seemingly been having of late. Anyway, I realized that my entering our bed room would wake her up and after doing so, she would be unable to go back to sleep.

Therefore, I would often sleep in the same room I initially used prior to my wedding which was located on the other side of the house. I was somewhat depressed over the Loke issue and very tired. I was also still in a state of disbelief about Loke.

I also reflected back on the comments of his ex wife which still made me angry. As I went into the house, I first went to my bedroom and saw that Evelyn had turned out the lights and closed our door.

Thus, I went straight to my guest quarters. As I got close to the room, I heard some loud music coming from that side of the house. I was very curious as to where it was coming from. I was shocked to find Teralyn in the same guest bedroom that I normally stayed in. The door was wide open and the music was extremely loud. She was thumping the sounds of Ciara's song *Promise*. Can you believe she was actually dancing and moving like Ciara as well?

When I looked in the room, Teralyn was doing a sexy dance as though she had practiced on the same *Promise* video with Ciara. She had on some red thong panties and a red sports bra, showcasing nothing else, but skin. Although I stood right in the doorway, I'm not exactly certain that she was able to see me; at least if she did, she pretended not to.

Her back was to me and she was dropping it like it was hot. I was simply mesmerized. No matter how I tried, I just couldn't take my eyes off her. Her butt cheeks had swallowed that thong that she had on. I mean her butt cheeks ran deep. She was rocking it up and down like stripper dancers do.

Teralyn had lips like Chaka Khan, breasts like Tyra, butt cheeks like Beyonce', legs like Tina, shoulders like Pam Greer, and the overall facial beauty and height of Ciara. She literally had the perfect body. Under normal circumstances, I could have stood in that doorway and enjoyed this show forever. However, since Loke's shooting, my mind was not the same. I was terribly overwhelmed at the huge similarity of Teralyn and Evelyn. However, there was one major difference. As a result of Evelyn's present condition, there was no contest as to who would win out in the body department.

I needed to go inside and get my power point presentation and some other personal items so I had to interrupt Teralyn. At first, I knocked on the door but she did not hear me. Then, I walked into the room and said, "Excuse me Teralyn but I need to get my things."

I tried my best to make sure I looked away from her while I was in the room. She stopped her routine, turned down the music, and just turned to talk to me as though she was fully clothed. There was clearly no shame to her game.

"J.R., did I choose da wrong room? If I did, I'm sorry. You want me to jest move to anotha room?"

"No Teralyn, not at all. I'm sorry to disturb you, but I need to get some personal items."

"You ain't disturbin me. I'm jest tryin to get my workout on cause I gots ta keep it real."

She talked to me freely while I continued to get all my belongings. For though I was extremely nervous, I was moving as quickly as I possibly could. Teralyn, however, was seemingly trying to detain me with more and more conversation.

"J.R., I jest want-chu to know dat-chu really made my day when you mistook me for E. I felt so proud."

"Hey, I really did make an honest mistake, awhrah, Teralyn."

I was quickly losing my concentration. While sitting on the floor positioned directly in front of me, she started doing wind mills with her legs wide open. I wanted to sneak a look and gaze between her thighs, but I knew better. That was not the right move for me and my thoughts confirmed that realization. *J.R., maintain your composure boy. Now see, that's what the preacher was talking about on Sunday; recognizing temptation and refusing to yield.* Thus, I rushed out of the room.

I had to take the next available room which was right next to the room Teralyn occupied. I was wondering why Evelyn would have Teralyn move into my room. She clearly knew that I used that room when I came in the house too late so that I would not wake her up in our room.

I was very much awake and my adrenaline was still riding high as I reflected back on Loke. I was really missing my friend, as I anticipated his death and I did not want him to die.

In order to release some of the stress built up within me, I decided to go to my indoor gym and work out by shooting some basketball. I changed into some shorts and a tee shirt, but I also realized that I had left my favorite basketball in the room that Teralyn had occupied. I was just gonna go to the gym without that ball, but I just had to return because that was my favorite basketball.

As I returned to her room, she was sitting on my basketball and twisting her waist by placing all of her weight on the ball and tilting her whole body left and right. I was still somewhat surprised and amazed over the fact that Teralyn would be so loosely clad around me, but I acted as though she was fully dressed. I returned to the room and asked for my basketball.

"Teralyn, I don't mean to disturb you, but can I get my basketball?" She turned around and once again had her legs eagle wing, widespread open as she sat on the ball.

"J.R., are you sure all you want is dis basketball? I mean, you sure you don't want nuttin else?"

I looked at Teralyn and quickly responded, "No

Teralyn, all I need is my basketball."

"What's da matter J.R.? You afraid of dis stuff?" She said as she started to put her hand down between her legs.

"Teralyn, please give me my ball so I can go to my gym and work out."

I acted as though I heard nothing she said. Also, in the back of my mind, having experienced what I did with Doralee, I wondered deep down inside if Evelyn was trying to test me or set me up. I mean, you do the math. Why would my wife have her twin sister in my alternate bedroom looking all fly and loosely clad?

"Come and get yo ball J.R.," she said as she removed the ball from underneath her buttocks and handed it to me.

I grabbed the ball and went straight to my gym. However, I must come clean about everything. I sniffed that ball real good as to capture every bit of scent that Teralyn's fine body may have left on it. It was clearly upon that realization that I knew on the other side of a man hurt by his best friend about to go on to glory existed one horny brother who was anxious to hit something in a very sexual kind of way.

Nevertheless, I ran up and down the gym doing full court lay-ups, while my mind was pre-occupied with Loke. I carried on for about a full hour, just running real hard and doing jump shots and even trying to dunk the basketball.

While I was busy working out on the basketball court, Teralyn, by now, was on the phone in the guest bedroom quarters with her best friend.

"Shaneequa, what-chu thank I'm gonn do gurl? You crazy if you thank I came all da way up to high society jest to take care of E and her baby. Chile Puhlease! As long as I'm here, I'ma find a way to get some of dis cheese too."

"But T, I thought E paid you for coming?"

"She did chile and dat's why I ain't leavin no time soon. Dem fresh hundred dolla bills felt way too good in my hand. Can you believe she paid me eight grand to come here for a month?"

"Stop gurl. You gots to be lyin."

"Not at all chile! She said dat she was gonn pay me two grand but J.R. insisted she pay me more. Nigh can you see why I like him and want to give him some?"

"I can clearly see why. If he paid me dat kind of money, I would make certain dat he was taken care of in every possible way. My mouth would be on full time alert for his crotch."

"I know dat's right. I don't thank he got nerve enuff to get all up in dis stuff dough. He acts like he scurred of me. I still plan to get me some mo of dis cheese dough. I plan to do a lot mo to get a lot mo."

Teralyn was up to no good and telling her best friend Shaneequa about how she was going to make the best out of her visit.

"T, hi you gonn do dat gurl? E just flew you in for a temporary period of time. Hi you gonn do anythang more dat fast?"

"Look playa, you outcho mind if you don't thank I'm gettin paid off dis trip as much as I can. I will find a way to sink my Alabama boots into dis Houston oil field some how or anotha. Aint' no jokin bout dat gurl. I might have to screw E's security guard or somebody wit clout. You see what I'm sayin?"

"You are so badd gurl! Hi you gonn do yo twin sista like dat?"

"Like what? Gurl, E knows how I be. She knows I do whateva I gots to do, to get mine."

"I know dat's right," said Shaneequa.

"If she foolish enuff to bring me here wit all dis, den she foolish enough to put up with whateva happens. No wonda nobody in our family got invited to da wedding. Chile you know I had to take care of Ricky's dad when E was last pregnant. I'm surprised she waited so long to call me dis time."

"T, I know you ain't saying dat E knew bout-chu sleeping wit Sam when she was pregnant?"

"Dat's exactly what I'm tryin to tell ya. She knew she won't takin care of dat nigga. He would tell me how E was so stingy wit her stuff. I can imagine how horny her husband gots to be, but I do thank he's screwin dis attorney."

"But T, you ain't been dere but twenty-four hours. Hi you know who he screwin?"

"Chile Puhlease! Game recognize game. I can tell by da way dis hoe caters to him and by da way he takes care of her. E is so naïve. She had da nerve to tell me dat dey like brother and sister. She out her blown up, pregnant mind."

"Wow gurl! I hope you don't screw thangz up. Sometimes you can be wrong. Don't mess up a happy home."

"I ain't messing nothin up dat ain't already messed up. I plan on figurin out a way to stay here, but I'm not fa show how. I thank J.R. could be an avenue."

"But T, what if J.R. don't fall for it?"

"What? Trick I'm bouts ta hang up on you. You name one man dat has eva turned down my tight sugar walls.

41

You gettin me mixed up wit-chu," said Teralyn as she started laughing.

"Oh no you didn't even go dere. You knowz my stuff be pullin all da niggas, so don't even try it. All I'm saying is what if J.R. don't play?"

"Shaneequa, if he don't play den he don't play, but I'ma make him play. If he don't play, I'm screwin da gardener, da security guard, his friend, da cook, da attorney or whoever. Hell, I'll even screw Jewel or my nephew Ricky if I gots to. Den again, alldough my nephew is fine as anythang, I don't think I'll stoop dat low. I'ma screw somebody up in dis mutha f…. because I'ma get paid somehow or anotha. U feel me?"

"Gurl, you know you wrong for dat about-cho nephew. If anybody should get dose honors, it should be me cause I ain't related to him."

"Trick Puhlease! You know I waz jest jokin. You ain't bout to get no parts of my nephew. You ought to be ashamed of yoself. He ain't even sixteen and legal yet."

"Look Gurl, I was jest sayin if anybody should do dat between da two of us, it should be me and not you. I know he still a child."

"Yeah right hoe! You know if you had a chance to screw my nephew you would be all ova his butt. Don't front. I know yo horny butt."

"T, who in dey right mind wouldn't want to screw dat boy, as fine as he is? Anyway, I feel you gurl on dat otha stuff. Nigh, maybe you can hook me up and help me get dere?"

"O---Kay! Dat's what I'm trying to tell you trick. We can run dis mutha like it's ours. All I need to do is get my foot in jest one doe and den, dat's all she wrote."

"Nigh T, I'll be honest wit-chu! I ain't tryin to cross E by any means. I know she can be one mean tail b---h when she wants to be."

"Gurl, E talkin proper and everythang now. Act like she ain't never been in da hood. Can you believe dat?"

"Well, I can understand dat! She gots to be who she gots to be. You need to do the same. If it means being proper and all dat, gurl, you better get in dere where you fit in or else you gonn be back in Muntgumery wishing you woulda done right."

"You right playa! I guess I could improve my talking skills because my looks are already dere."

"Look, you need to have a scrategy gurl. All you gots to do is talk how dey talk. I do it all da time when I'm around smart folks. Sometimes all you gots to do is say what dey say and act like you know what da hell it meant. It's easy gurl. Nigh, you need to take care of E and stay on her good side, and den do what you gots to do to get in wit everybody else. Don't make no enemies T. You know you got a track record for dat."

"Look hoe, you da one wit dat criminal record not me, ahahaha."

"Nigh T, dat's what I'm talkin bout. You didn't have to go dere."

"Oh shut up hoe! You knowz I be jokin."

"Naw...naw....some thangz don't need to be joked about. You knowz I'm still hurt over dat stoopid undercover cop pretendin to want some."

"Get ova it gurl, you know I'm jest playin. But anyway, give me bout 2 weeks and I'ma be rollin up in dis joint."

"I hope so gurl cause you might not get dat chance again. Let me know when you can send for me too."

43

"You know I will chile. Jest keep yo legz closed and save em for H-town. U feel me?"

"I don't know bout all dat. You know I don't keep dese legs closed for long. Gurlfriend gots to get hers."

"I feel ya playa. All I'm sayin is hold it down and keep it clean cause when you get here, we will be hoeing."

"Nigh T, one last thang. Don't be stressin wit J.R. and dis attorney you thank he screwing. Don't be a threat to anythang going on, but be a friend so yo butt can get in good. You understand playa?"

"I feel ya hoe, but I might have already pissed off dat attorney. I hardly spoke to her when E introduced us."

"Well gurl, yo butt needs to get busy and make up for dat. Do you thank J.R. is gonna want to keep you around if you all up in his bizness. I don't thank so. You need to come correct wit dat. Remember, you jest tryin to get in and start rollin some dough yoself."

"You know Shaneequa, sometimes you make a lot of sense. I will try my best to rememba dem words. I must admit, I already got some making up to do to dat darn attorney."

"Hey T, do what-chu gotta do. It will make it easy for me to get dere quicker."

While Teralyn was still plotting a way to establish her foot in Houston with no intentions of going back to Alabama, I finished my workout and returned to my room, took a quick shower and fell asleep. I had a very good workout and I was feeling pretty good for the moment.

Chapter 4
Brownstone

Brown, thick, and juicy lips that curved out and opposite one another. Her upper lip curved out and upward towards the sky and her bottom lip curved outward and downward towards the ground. She was much bigger than the women that normally caught my eye. She was phat and tender looking. Her dark brown complexion reminded me of a brownstone.

She was probably a size twenty-two with a bathtub size backyard that had a very high, tick, tick, boom like curve, while standing out like a woman of another era. Her hair was nice and short and very rich in color, while maintaining a nice part down the middle. She was so sensual, so sexy, such a turn-on whenever she spoke.

I met her at the city real estate council meetings. She was a corporate administrator for the Mayor.

Despite being in over twelve business meetings with her, we rarely spoke. However, when we did, it was always courteous and professional words to one another.

So tell me! How did I just wind up with a plan of meeting her at her upscale, suburban house on the west side of town?

I'll never understand but you can best believe that I drove fast as I arrived at her house as though I knew exactly where she lived. Being a realtor afforded me the opportunity to know the location of practically every subdivision in town. Upon my arrival, we conversed like we had known each other for years.

"What took you so long? I was beginning to wonder whether or not you had chickened out," she said as she answered the doorbell.

"Well honestly, I stopped making house calls a long time ago." She had on a tan silk house coat and she was all smiles. She left enough gap in the house coat to showcase the nicest set of 44 triple D's I ever seen in my life. I mean, they were pointed outward and appeared to be a bottomless pit that seemed unbelievably deep.

"Oh really? Then I wonder why I am so special to be getting all this time and attention."

She closed the door to her nice house and for a moment we just stared at each other. I saw that special look in her eyes. You know the one that potential lovers share just before they tear each others' clothes to mere shreds.

"You are special because your intellect and intelligence really turn me on. That coupled with your bodacious body had me observing you like crazy at the executive council meetings. Your subtle, very businesslike persona really captured my attention."

I stood just past the doorway and I was anxious to no end to taste those huge triple D's with protrusive nipples the size of a ping pong ball. I had to make my presence known.

"Oh really! I bet you tell that to all the women, don't you?" She began to slowly pull the drawstring that kept her house coat closed.

"Not really! I only say that to one woman now, but she doesn't seem to acknowledge my words because she keeps holding back on me. Every since she's been pregnant, I haven't been able to put it down like I'm accustomed to doing. I'm presently at the closest avenue to celibacy that I have ever experienced. Sometimes I think I'm about to dry up from not being able to perform any lube jobs. So, you can best believe I am full of lust and sexual fervor."

I drew myself closer to her, anticipating a collision with both our bodies.

"That's okay baby! I'll have you lubricating all over my house before it's over with."

"You promise baby? Don't start nothing you can't finish now."

She lifted up her thigh and I immediately stared at the thickness and richness of her body real estate. Then, she further teased me with words.

"Don't be so slow to start the lubrication process because I'm slightly overdue for a lube job myself. I'm definitely going to start something, Big Chocolate, and I don't know if we will ever finish. I might want your loving over and over again."

Her words got lower and lower as I drew in closer to her. I mean, let's face reality. I was clearly overdue. I had not been wet from a woman's southern border since Evelyn found out she was pregnant and went on total lockdown. She acted as though lovemaking was suddenly against her religion.

I needed to feel that sensation, because as my business coach Julie once told me, regular sex helps the mind flow freely. It's an investment that we all must make in order to reach our high, professional performance state. *That's right J.R.! Fix it to your advantage* was the sound of my inner self.

Brownstone lunged forward with her lips and pressed them against my lips. I eagerly returned the kiss and then raised my hands to massage her head as I begin to ease my tongue into her mouth.

Her tongue met my tongue half way as she was good at multitasking. While kissing me, her hand had no problem finding steel water which stood up in a rare form of hardness. She rubbed the exterior of my pants which was bulging up a storm from steel water's imprint. Then, I used my hand to rip that robe off her, exposing her nude body and causing those triple D's to bounce around like the head of a clown ejecting from a toy dummy box.

Then the J to the R got busy like old times. Feeling a need to be both gentle and rough, I pulled her tongue from her mouth with my tongue with a subtle tease suction that seemed to increase her stimulation. At the same time, I gently grabbed those melons of hers and slowly and gently rubbed those tips in a slow circular motion that seemed encased around fifty cent diameter brown spots. I must admit those melons reminded me of a tasty desert perfectly prepared for a sexually starved brother. I gently sucked them, used my tongue to firmly stab into the center most portion, and then let it reside there for a minute while pushing to the core. For some reason, I was reminded of Rick Ross's song, *Push It To The Limit.*

Afterwards, I shifted back to her mouth. I gradually kissed her more passionately, while caressing her tongue with my tongue, licking her top lip then her lower lip, and then proceeded to gently suck her neckline.

"Wow! I forgot all about this type of sensation! Oh My! That feels so good baby! Take me and screw me like I'm a slut, please! It's been such a long time for me!"

She gently whispered in my ear. My mouth slowly and gently massaged her neckline with my tongue pressed up strong against her most defined vein. I then gave her gentle bites as I made my path back to her chest to taste

48

those melons again. Tips that now plunged forward about an inch from the brown circle spots met my aggressive tongue. I initially swished my tongue back and forth over the right tip with lightning quick movement while it was housed between my lips.

"Oh Mercy! Oh my goodness! That feels so good baby."

She was breathing loudly as though she was losing her breath and I quickly shifted to the other tip and repeated the action. Bingo! That left tip was a sexual center of gravity as she began to collapse in my arms. It was as simple as clockwork, as simple as a mathematical formula, as simple as a lion placing his jawbone across the neck of a deer and the deer totally submitting it's life. She quickly started trying to pull my belt off so she could get to steel water.

"MMMM! I can't wait to get you inside me. Take it all baby. Please!"

Her voice began to squirm like a person sounds just prior to going into a low pitch tone of begging. She pushed me back and firmly grabbed my hand and led me to her bedroom.

While traveling to the bedroom, she turned, pulled me to her, ripped off my shirt, removed my tee shirt and then she rubbed her hands on my chest like she had just discovered solid gold.

Next, she gently pulled the hairs on my chest with her finger tips and then pulled my head down and stuffed her tongue in my mouth. Then, she pulled me further as we went through her hallway and found the bedroom. She was already butt naked, so she sat on the bed and quickly pulled down my pants and removed my underwear.

"Oh yes! There must be a god somewhere."

She shouted out after gracing her eyes on steel water, before she literally dropped to her knees and slid it between her juicy lips. She dipped and pulled and sucked and pulled and then she would just look at it as though her mouth and steel water already had a relationship. Then, she would stare intensely and gently laugh. I mean, home girl looked at steel water like she knew him for a lifetime, although that was the first time she had ever seen him.

She even chuckled to herself again and then she put steel water between them 44 triple D's and she literally smothered and sandwiched steel water while moving her chest vertically up and down, up and down. It felt so good, so unique, so stimulating.

Then, she grabbed steel water and chuckled again and started devouring him like there was no tomorrow.

"Where have you been all my life?"

That was the question she kept asking as she kept taking her mouth up and down my southern pole like she was a programmed robot. She got quicker and quicker, faster and faster, up and down. She even tried to put all of steel water in her mouth. I was just standing there and letting her enjoy every inch of me.

All of a sudden, she stopped bobbing and just started nibbling, sucking, and slowly drenching steel water's head. I had to admit, that slow and intense caressing literally drove me wild. Then, she jumped on the bed with her legs wide open. Before you knew it, she reached down and started pulling me forward as though she wanted me to just dive in.

However, she didn't know the J to the R. I grabbed her feet and started licking between her toes and then I started sucking each toe on her right foot and afterwards I did the same on the left foot. The sexual touch was literally killing her. I finally started making my way up her leg while leaving a wet trail from her feet all the way up to her deep inner thigh. I occasionally paused at her calves and gently bit those muscles while swishing my tongue across them. I gently bit her inner thighs and my tongue cleaned up after the bites with a sensation of a stimulating whip across those juicy thighs.

Then, as I got closer and closer to that bathtub of glory, she trembled and shook like someone was jerking her.

"OH! Oh! I'm coming baby! Lord have Mercy, this is a big one."

Her parts were vibrating and her body had a rhythmic movement like she had been hit with electricity. Can you believe that? She came before I even tasted her sweetness, before steel water even got a chance to throw down, before the J to the R was about to literally break her off something proper. Nevertheless, I proceeded on because I was not about to be denied.

"That was so good honey! I don't think I came like that in years. I know I haven't with a man. Those toys just get old after awhile. Baby please! Don't delay any further. Get on up in here. I want to feel you inside me right now."

Although she rushed me a bit from my desire to taste and bite more of her body and before steel water went to town, I wasn't mad at a sista.

However, this was my show and I was running this mutha up in heeerrre. I dove between those ever-so-rich thighs of hers and let my lips and tongue do the dialing. They dialed up to the elevator floor and my tongue found that unique part that would drive a woman crazy from the most accurate degree of stimulation.

After I found Elvira, hiding beneath the folds, I crept up on her with my tongue like a hunter was sneaking up on a rabbit in the forest. I gently touched Elvira with my tongue at first. Then I begin to conduct circular sweep activity with my tongue that seemed to drive Brownstone crazy as she could not contain herself. Thus, I had to hold her down because the J to the R was about to put it down. As my nice and thick lips made their way between her folds, I used my tongue as the frontal assault of the attack. Her body was responding like a tidal wave in the ocean. I just knew that I was about to cause some havoc. My strategy was simple. Caress her down with my tongue and then gently stand her back up and spoil her with my thick lips, as she felt the security of my support. My mouth practically worshipped her insides as though I loved and treasured every inch of her body. She started coming again, but I was still not done.

Without delay, I let steel water rip into her and do what he does best. Like a dead bolt lock going into its designated slot was how I drove into her. After steel water found his way home, I was determined to rock her world like I would never get this chance again. I had not been inside a woman it seemed for years and I was show nuff gonna enjoy this stuff with all I had. I stroked her back and forth as she was sliding up and down on the bed from my muscular hip movements and rhythmic motion. I increased the intensity and went fast and hard as she started calling my name like she was in a deep sea of ecstasy.

"Oh yes baby! That's my spot! That's my spot baby! Give it to me daddy! Give it to me, please."

The more she spoke the faster I moved and the harder I hit it. I felt myself going deeper and deeper. It felt as if I was passing through different layers of walls.

"Don't stop daddy! Please don't stop! Oh please, don't stop!"

I finally reached that last wall and that was all she wrote, as I hit it repeatedly. I was determined to bring down them Berlin walls. I positioned both my hands underneath that bathtub backyard of hers and I tried to tear that wall down. Just like President Reagan years ago told the Russian president Gorbachav to tear down them Berlin walls, I had to bring them down. She started screaming with a mixture of excitement, joy, and a little crying in her voice.

This is yours daddy! Oh! You can have me for life! It's yo stuff anytime daddy! Oh daddy! Oh..Oh..Oh...Oh!"

I knew I had her on the final stretch as she was done for the count and thus I started facilitating her arrival by talking strong, low, and nasty as though I was dishing out threats of death.

"You betta bring it gurl. I want you to screw me like you never screwed before, you hear me?" I raised my voice with a rich, deep, bass like tone.

"Stop holding back and gimme all this juice....you hear me...GIVE IT TO ME like you owe me. You sophisticated slut. This is the J to the R baby! The J to the RRRRRR baby."

My words went from low to loud and the louder I got the louder she got as she seemed to be crying more than anything.

"Oh yes! Call me more names daddy. You turn me on more when you call me dirty names. It's yours daddy. This kitty kat is all yours baby. Oh! Please f..k me anytime daddy, anytime daddy, anytime, anytime."

"You better give it to me you high class hoe! Gimmie that big, phat, juicy butt of yours right now, right now baby, right now. You better not hold back girl. You better not hold back. Gimmie what you promised me you horny slut. Toss that booty girl. Toss it! You good for nothing hoe!"

If someone would have heard me, they would have thought I was about to literally rape a stranger and kill her. I was shouting so loudly.

"I'm coming again daddy. I'm coming on home baby. Oh god! Oh yes! Yes! Yes!"

She came all over the place and I felt her as she shook the bed and I think damaged a portion of the headboard, but we didn't care. I went in for the count. I tell you I was firm, I was direct, but more importantly, I was erect! I had never before experienced a woman with this stamina and appreciation for the art of making love.

Then it happened! I was trying to control myself but I couldn't any longer. All of a sudden, I found myself squirming, writhing, and literally screaming out her name. Talk about some good stuff ...she was handling her business up in heeerre, and I loved it.

Then, I got there. I arrived at that location where I did not anticipate that we would reach. It seemed worse than suicide, worse than homicide, worse than any drive by or gang bang shooting; that level of complete and total dominance known as reality.

"J.R., how long are you gonna be in that shower? My goodness! It seems like you been in there for hours. Can you please hurry up?"

"Yes dear! I am just about to get out" were the words

that I shouted back. SHUCKS! Reality had set back in, as Evelyn called me from the very best shower I had in days.

Oh Well, *it was good while it lasted*, were the thoughts that came to my mind.   I now had to resume my normal life, that of being a faithful and loyal husband to my wife. DANG! Talk about who shot J.R?

Chapter 5
Googoo Goga

I was in my home office alone very early on a Monday morning. It was about 4 a.m. and I could not sleep. I really had to have a clear mind in order to do the work required for the city's real estate commission report.

Two weeks had gone by and Loke's condition had gradually improved. However, since Loke's ex wife had come to town, my trips to the hospital had decreased. This was largely due to the ex wife and our clear dislike for one another.

I had managed to build about 128 power point charts for this special presentation of the city's real estate commission report. I wanted to scale down to about half that number on today and eventually 30 charts for the project's completion.

The telephone rang! I thought to myself, *it's Evelyn calling because she's the only one who knows I'm in the office this early.* She would often wake up early in the morning since her pregnancy. I answered the phone in a joking way, knowing that she was the one calling.

"The mighty J to the R."

The voice on the other end of the phone was very soft, pleasant, and comfortably confident.

"I am glad I caught you in this morning. Listen one moment J.R."

I quickly heard the sweet sound of a baby who was making the most peaceful sounds on the other end of the line. To be exact, I heard the voice of an infant, uttering sounds as though lying on his or her back and at perfect peace. I began to realize that the voice on the phone was not Evelyn. It was instead a nightmare from the past, resurrecting herself once more to torture me. The voice on the other end belonged to Doralee!

"I thought you might want to hear how our baby sounded. Also, you need to start paying me child support because it's your responsibility. Do you hear me J.R.?"

My stomach quickly turned, my head began to hurt, and my nerves started to race. My palms started getting sweaty and I started breathing real heavy as I listened to the voice on the other end of the line. Then, after hearing her speak her peace, I fired right back at her.

"Look, I have given you pay raises and I continue to employ you. What the hell else do you want now? I really don't appreciate you calling my home like this."

"J.R., I have a simple answer to your question. Pay me child support that is commensurate with your salary and then I expect you to be a responsible dad and come and visit your child. This concept is nothing new. Jesse figured it out and so did the former leader of the National Baptist Convention, so you need to figure it out too. They took care of their mistresses."

"Hold up Doralee! You are not my mistress. You are merely someone that I mistakenly slept with in my past, before I got married. Besides, regarding the names you mentioned, they both got in trouble and their mistresses squealed on them."

"Exactly J.R.! They squealed for a reason. You best handle your business or you will be squealed on too."

"Considering all that I have done for you Doralee, I really don't appreciate you threatening me like this." My voice got real loud and I was about to lose all my composure.

"I had our baby J.R. and you have done significantly

57

less than what I have done. Own up to your responsibility and be a real man and handle your business. You could learn a lot from both Jesse and that other preacher. At least they took care of their responsibilities."

"Look Doralee, I have paid you royally to keep this mess quiet and I will continue to do that, but you must leave me and my family alone." An angry voice shot back at me with much tenacity and determination.

"What about our family J.R.? You still seem to act as though you don't have a child with me, but you do J.R. and I won't raise this kid alone. Perhaps if Evelyn was made aware, I wonder if her pregnancy would encounter any difficulties from the mental stress of your infidelity. I'm warning you one last time J.R."

I really got upset as I was trying my best to keep my secret private, but Doralee seemed to demand more and more from me. Thus, I replied with absolute anger and defense.

"Doralee, you better stay away from my wife or else…" She interrupted me with louder words.

"Or else what J.R.? Or else what? You are in no position to be threatening me so I suggest you lower your tone. Now, I am giving you a short period of time to cooperate or your little secret will be public news." Click went the phone.

All I thought to myself was, *Dang!* I got Loke to be concerned with and I don't have time to be worried about this mess! I must find a way to slow her roll.

I remained in my office for a few more hours until morning had finally set in. I left my office after working on those power point charts. I was determined to find a way to stop Doralee in her tracks.

Later on that morning I went to my company office, and arrived around 8:30. I was still shook up over the conversation I had with Doralee. I could not believe that she was able to get the telephone number to my home office. As I recall, only Evelyn had that number. Then again, I seem to recall that Jewel and Loke had the number as well.

Anyway, I had no idea how Doralee got the number and not knowing how was driving me crazy. The mere thought that she could call my home was clearly driving me nuts, as she was way too close to reaching my wife.

I arrived at the office and Jewel was standing in the hallway. Evidently, she must have seen me pull up in my car. She followed me to my office when I walked in.

"J.R., can you please explain to me why Doralee Mayberry's salary is so much higher than the other regional managers? I really don't understand why you hired her at 150K and you are giving her quarterly pay raises. Is she doing extra work that I am not aware of J.R.? Hell, before long, she will be making more money than I am."

Oh my goodness! Is Jewel figuring out what is going on? That thought immediately entered my mind. I really had no answers to the very questions that Jewel posed so I kind of blew her off. Jewel had just concluded a budget review meeting with her staff and she noticed the payroll account of Doralee Mayberry evidently.

"Good morning to you too Jewel and I hope you are feeling fine on this lovely day."

She quickly realized that she had not spoken to me and responded by speaking.

"Oh! Good morning J.R. Please excuse my rudeness.

I'm just trying to comprehend these budgetary matters."

"No problem Jewel! Now, I got a very exhaustive meeting I need to prepare for in the next hour, so can we please discuss the matter regarding Doralee Mayberry's salary later?" Jewel quickly agreed and emphasized the fact that she was merely trying to finish up the budget review report.

"J.R., I just wanted to complete the budget review for your approval. That's all."

"I completely understand Jewel. Why don't we go to my office and discuss this in detail. I do have a minute or two before the meeting. Oh, and by the way, thank you so very much for your support of Loke's family. I understand his wife and kids were very pleased with your hospitality. I heard that exactly from the doctor himself."

"They are such nice people and Loke's son looks just like him," said Jewel. While Jewel and I were talking, we both went directly to my office.

"Honestly Jewel, I am trying to find a way to terminate the services of Doralee Mayberry. I just don't know how to accomplish the task under the swiftest and cleanest measures."

"J.R., I am so confused with the way in which you are handling Doralee Mayberry. First off, you had problems with the woman taking convalescent leave after being pregnant and giving birth to a child for crying out loud and now you want to fire her after she has returned back to work. Then, you give her these pay raises as though she has been promoted. I got to admit it is very confusing."

"Well Jewel, I don't like the way she took that pregnancy leave all of a sudden. I hired her not long ago and then she got pregnant and took all that time off." I was trying diligently to conceal my true demeanor regarding Doralee.

"J.R., I'm starting to wonder if you have become a male chauvinist pig. I clearly see no harm that she has done. She got pregnant, she had a baby, took convalescent maternity leave and now she is back and you want to fire her. She could sue your pants off if you would proceed under those conditions. Don't' even think about that. You would be the centerpiece story on CNN Headline News for firing a woman just because she got pregnant. The other side of the story which I don't understand is that you keep giving her these quarterly pay raises and then you talk about firing her."

Jewel stood up and walked over to the window in my office. She massaged the right side of her head and looked at me as though I had become a complete stranger. I just looked straight out into space while reflecting back on that one night Doralee and I spent together.

I felt like a complete idiot. I was in a total state of depression. Here's this woman who has obviously had my baby and was intent on making my life miserable with threatening phone calls. Jewel did not know the horrible act I had committed nor did anyone else know except Loke.

A part of me wanted to fire Doralee and pay her completely off. But then, the other part of me, my conscience was telling me that I should expose the truth and take care of this child, which was allegedly mine. I was really torn on the issue and the stress was beginning to affect every aspect of my life. Nevertheless, Jewel just stared at me and continued to talk.

"J.R., I'm starting to wonder what would happen to me

if I got pregnant. Would you want to fire me too?"

I was really beginning to see my ship sinking. The pre-marital events that had occurred began to take over my soul. I was more paranoid than I had ever been at any time in my entire life. And to add to this dilemma, I was also still gravely concerned about Loke's condition.

God! I hate being in this position. Lord, please help me get out of this and I promise I will never do anything like this ever again. This is like being in prison. Although I am physically free, I am all locked up within, with my worries and trouble.

Doralee got pregnant from our little escapade and gave birth to a baby girl about nine months later. I had been in silent torture since she started taking time off the job during the late stages of her pregnancy. I tried to justify firing her, but how do you do that when my feisty female partner, Jewel, makes certain that all my actions are above reproach. Jewel was not aware of my indiscretion and I was fighting a great temptation to tell her.

"J.R., are you even listening to me?"

Jewel had the most intense look on her face with both hands on her hips as though she was really getting ready to tell me off.

"Of course I am listening to you Jewel."

I folded my arms as though I was disgusted. She moved closer to my desk as I sat their leaning back in my chair.

"J.R., is there something that you need to tell me? You know you have been acting real strange towards me since I started dating Corey. I need to know right now. Do you have a problem with me dating him? If you don't, then what is your frigging problem?"

Now Jewel really caught me off guard with the Corey comment. Actually, I had been acting weird around Jewel since I found out that Doralee was pregnant. Doralee informed Jewel after she flew into Atlanta to do an offsite visit. She merely spared Jewel the details.

I must admit, the Corey avenue as a distracter was a good option for me to take as the Doralee option was clearly causing my stomach to turn and my head to hurt.

My current and number one stressor was Loke's condition. But riding a really close second was the fact that, as a result of a stupid one-night stand, I had gotten Doralee pregnant, and she had given birth to my child.

Now, what Jewel did not know was that Doralee had been threatening to tell my wife. If I did not grant her the company perks that we didn't even have, she would tell my wife without reservation.

Well, now I guess she has added child support to the equation, but she will not get both. I'm serious! She had been literally getting over on me and I could not seem to find the best way to bring her actions to a screeching halt. So now my only recourse was to fire her on the basis of? Well, that's the problem; I didn't have a legitimate basis because her work had not been outstanding, but it had consistently been at least average.

Nevertheless, I had to throw a curve ball to Jewel because I was not yet ready to tell her about my bottomless pit of torture with Doralee. I know that my time was ticking fast, but for me, now was not the time. Thus, I had to ride the Corey wave that she introduced.

"Jewel, don't you think that your getting involved with Corey was just a little premature? I mean, you just broke up with your fiancé a little over a year, and now here you are involved with another man. I just thought you would have taken more time to heal the wounds before entering into another committed relationship. Could it be that you're moving too fast?"

Darn, I was a fine one to address moving fast, considering how quickly Evelyn and I married, but the words rushed from my mouth.

"You know J.R., I figured that my dating Corey was your problem. I dated Corey for sometime and that has been well over a year. Also, my dating has not hindered my work ethic by any stretch of the imagination. Besides, Corey only flies down from NY on the weekends every now and then."

I stood up from behind my desk as to act as though I really cared.

"You see Jewel. That's my point exactly. Why would you stop dating a man who lived in NY, only to start a new relationship with another man who lived in NY? You would think that distance was a factor as to why your last relationship failed."

Oops, I may have gone too far. Darn, I was just trying to cover up my issues. Jewel's eyes started watering and she quickly walked away from my desk towards the door. I went to the door as fast as I could and I grabbed Jewel.

"I'm sorry. I did not mean that Jewel. Please forgive me!" She pushed me away and walked back towards the window as she was wiping the tears from her eyes. I felt like dirt. I went over and hugged her from behind.

"Look here Jewel, I am so sorry. I support whoever you choose to date. I'm serious! My problems have nothing to do with you. Let's wrap up and talk another time."

I noticed that Jewel had not pushed me away from her like she would normally do. I felt like crying on her shoulder as I thought about how Doralee tricked me.

I also noticed that I quickly became stimulated from the very touch of my pelvic area obtaining contact with Jewel's very nice backyard. The erection was so instantaneous that I did not even notice it at first. All of a sudden, there was a knocking on my office door which was closed. I quickly went and opened the door.

"Mr. Carter, Mayor Richardson's secretary is on the line and she would like to know if you're available now for the Mayor?"

Jewel quickly departed the office and, Agnes, my new secretary inquired, "Ma'am, are you okay?" Then she looked at me and said, "You know if I didn't know any better, I would think you two were love birds?" Then she smiled and walked out of the office.

Agnes was another piece of work. She was Evelyn's replacement, an older Caucasian lady who was a stickler for time constraints and businesslike in all her endeavors. She was also very nosy, very talkative, and very grandmother like. She was very talented, but once again, she was as nosy as they came. Nevertheless, I was forewarned by Julie. I could handle the nosy attribute as long as she did her job, but Jewel on occasion took issue with her inquiring mind. Anyway, I quickly picked up the phone and spoke with the Mayor, knowing that Jewel and I would get together and talk at a later time.

Chapter 6
Same Dance, Different Song

I woke up again in the middle of the night and gravitated towards my home office to work on those real estate commission charts. My conversation with the Mayor went real well and I was highly motivated. Yet, I was still plagued with worrying about Loke first and Doralee next. Another week had gone by and Loke was getting stronger by the minute. Then, at about 1 a.m. my phone rang.

"J.R."

"What's up my nigga?" said the voice on the other line.

"Thank the Lord! Man, I am so glad to hear your voice. How the heck are you? I'll be on my way out to see you."

"You better hurry up because I think the nurse is about to lock it down in here."

"Not until I get a chance to see you man! I'm on my way, as soon as I can put on some reasonable attire."

I was so excited to hear Loke's voice. I quickly got dressed and told my security guard where I was headed, in case Evelyn woke up early looking for me. I was so excited to hear Loke's voice that I did not know what to do. He sounded real good and strong too. As I was driving, I began to thank God for answering my prayers. I was just too excited and I felt that nothing could hold me back now.

I arrived at the hospital within 35 minutes, and after clearing it with the receptionist, practically kissing her butt, I rushed straight into Loke's room. There he was sitting up and looking up at me like he did not have a care in the world.

"Man, you really scared me. I was worried crazy about you."

I placed my hand on Loke's shoulders as to embrace him while being very gingerly.

"How ya living my brotha?" Loke said with a smile.

"Life is getting better man! You are the man of the past month. I am so glad to see you talking again. How are you feeling?"

"Honestly! Like I wanna knock that nurse way into next week. Did you see the backyard on that stallion?"

"You are crazy boy!" *But that's my boy* was the thought in my mind. I stood over him smiling and just glad to see that he was back. The nurse returned to the room.

"Mr. King, we need to bathe you in a few moments so Mr. Carter, you will need to step out."

Loke looked at the nurse and quickly replied like a little kid.

"Bathe me? Hey nurse, can't I just take a shower or something?"

Loke seemed very uncomfortable about the nurse bathing him. The nurse stopped and stared with her hands on her hips, and mighty big hips they were.

"Can you move yourself to where you can reach the shower? We have been bathing you rather frequently, but of course you were not consciously aware."

"Really? Yawl been bathing me? Well, I think I can handle the task now nurse, since I am aware of all my faculties."

"I say we, as in my nursing staff, because I have been on vacation and travel for quite sometime so I have never bathed you before. Since you can move to shower yourself, we can plan on that instead, and that way I will not have to bathe you then," she immediately explained.

Loke quickly looked at me and then looked back at the

nurse as she was bending over in front of him. Loke all of sudden seemed to notice her nice round bottom.

"Oh, ahm, on second thought nurse, all of a sudden, I'm feeling like I can't even move. Please bathe me real soon, so I can feel clean around visitors."

Loke seemed so sincere and acted like his condition had gotten worse all of a sudden. The nurse turned around and expressed that she would go and prepare the water. As soon as she walked out, I had nothing but words for Loke.

"You ain't no good boy!" He started laughing, but then realized he had some chest pain. I immediately drew near him.

"Loke, you got to be careful man. Take it easy. You are not healthy yet." He slightly moved in the bed and just stared at me.

"I'm okay man." Then he looked down and back up at me again and smiled.

"Can you believe this community house is gonna bathe me man?" Community house was the code word Loke used to describe a heavily endowed, fat woman. He was really feeling fat women of late and he personally thought that celebrities like Monique and Tocarra had influenced him to crave the overweight lovers. Anyway, back to our conversation.

"Yeah! Especially after you pretended to be so weak as to not be able to move. Besides, that's her job man."

He started to laugh again, but instead he had a smiling grimace as he realized he could not laugh like he had wanted to.

"Hey man, don't hate the playa, hate the game," said Loke.

"Loke, I'll be back after the nurse finishes her torrid job."

He looked at me smiling as though he had something on his mind.

"I'll be alright man. It's all good in the hood my brother." He started smiling like he was about to get paid.

The nurse came back in the room with a nice pan and warm water and told me I had to leave the room. I left the room and went out front as I waited for Loke to finish being bathed. I thought to myself, *my boy is back. He will have to get used to the chest pain for awhile, but at least he is back.*

When I arrived at the hospital front corridor, I jumped up for joy as though I was doing a slam dunk, but I accidentally hit a coffee table and fell as I came down. A medical assistant in the area rushed over and grabbed me.

"Sir, are you okay?" I was just laughing as loudly as I could as I was both embarrassed, but simply overcome with shear happiness that my boy was back. I sat up and looked at the nurse.

"Ma'am, I am definitely okay. I am probably the happiest man in the world at this present moment. My boy is back."

She helped me up and quickly told me to be careful while snickering under her breath.

While I was waiting upfront in the reception area and just glowing in my current state of happiness, Loke was getting bathed by the nurse. He was responding real well to the water.

"Now Mr. King, I need you to let me move your body okay. You just lay still and let me do the work."

"I sure will nurse. By the way, what is your name?"

"You can call me Holly."

"Okay, how are you Holly?"

"I'm doing fine Mr. King."

"I know that's right. You can call me Loke rather than Mr. King. You got a real nice body baby. You make a sick man wanna get well real fast."

She slightly chuckled. Now Holly was thick, as in Monique fat. She was a fine, well endowed, dark brown tanned looking sister with the weight in all the right places. I mean, she was much thicker than Loke was used to hitting on. She was about 5'4" and weighed about 170 pounds. Most of the weight seemed to be in her chest and buttocks' area.

"Mr. King, is this water too cool for you?"

"Not at all Holly, I like the way you are cleaning me too."

Holly gave Loke a total pan bath where she literally cleaned every part of his body. She noticed that when he turned over from his stomach to his back that there was a change in his body.

Loke had gotten excited from the nurse cleaning his body. His rod was really stiff and was pointing upward when he rolled back over.

"Wow! Looks like there has been an accident," said Holly.

"Oh, I'm sorry Holly. Looks like accidents occur when you least expect them. What can I say?"

Loke's johnson was boldly standing out and Holly somehow could not resist staring at that massive appearance. The more she stared, the more she seemed to fall in some sort of a hypnotized state. She observed the firmness, the upward, curve-like protrusion, the muscular organ with thick veins that stood out around his johnson.

"Let me make sure I clean this real well because sometimes it can be overlooked," said the nurse.

"I agree with you Holly. I am used to being cleaned real thoroughly."

Just after Loke completed the sentence, Holly grasped his rod in her hands.

"Wow! It is so thick, so big, and so juicy. That's a jackhammer if ever I seen one. My nurses have cleaned you on three other occasions and they have never spoken of such massive size."

Holly was leaning over towards Loke's johnson. She moved her long blonde hair from the left to the right side of her shoulder so Loke could see her complete left facial while he laid to her left. She seemed to be so magnetically pulled towards Loke's johnson.

"I have never seen such an endowed man before in my life," said Holly.

"Me neither," said Loke.

"I mean, I never had a woman like you before in my life." He lied.

"Wow! I guess there is some truth to the myth, huh?" Holly said that as she used her hand to go up and down the shaft of Loke's Johnson.

"Yeah, there is some truth to the myth, I guess," said Loke.

Holly bent over and tasted around the surface of Loke's Johnson, placing her tongue in the trenches surrounding the top, touching the plunging veins.

Then, she tasted all the way down his shaft towards his circular motors. Then, she tried to just engulf all of him in her mouth, but it wouldn't fit, as his johnson hit the back of her throat. She turned her head to the side and placed as much of his johnson that she could take in, on the left side of her jaw. Then, she patted her outer jaw lightly with her hand on the side of where she stuffed his johnson, while looking into Loke's eyes.

Then she maneuvered back up and down, sucking as gently as she could the meat that stuffed her mouth. She carried on forever it seemed just going up and down. Loke was letting her have her thrill and seemed to totally enjoy it as he started sweating in the face. She started pull sucking like she was trying to untangle meat from a neck bone.

She was pulling her head up and sucking loud as though she had a big lollipop in her mouth. Loke started breathing heavy and then all of a sudden, his body moved like a fish treading water for a moment and his johnson erupted like a volcano dispensing fiery lava.

The residual substance was gradually trickling down her lips and she just kept on sucking, kept on plunging her head up and down as Loke was lying back in his most tense mode, coming off that sudden release. She kept on going like she had not noticed that he had come, totally drying him out.

Then, about five minutes later and before you knew it, his Johnson was firm stiff all over again. Then, she increased the speed of her apple bobbing, going faster and faster as though she was rushing another early climax. Next, Holly quickly went to her purse, grabbed a raincoat and placed it on Loke's Johnson. She was surprised to notice that the raincoat barely covered up his upper one third surface, as it fitted so tightly on Loke.

"Wow! Don't you have a larger size? That one is suffocating all the life out of me."

"I don't have another size. I'm sorry. I will be extra careful and make this one work."

Then, she put her hands up her skirt and removed her pink panties and then she placed herself across the lower end of his bed, with her back to his face. She painfully and slowly inserted his protected Johnson inside her. Her arms suspended most of her weight in the air and then she humped up and down like she was out of control. Loke just let her have her way.

"Yes....Yes...OHHHHH.....this is so amazing," were the sounds that Holly made and then she quickly grabbed a pillow and screamed as loud as she could into the pillow, as her body collapsed as she came to a high peak climax. Loke laid there and thought to himself, *"Wow, that's the best bath I ever had. She must have come in record time."*

Chapter 7
Painful Words Spring Forth

The Texas High School State Championship Game this year was located in Dallas, Texas, which coincidently happened to be the home of the Lincoln High School Sharks. The sharks were undefeated and they showcased the likes of one of the most popular McDonald's All Americans.

The team's superstar, who rose out of nowhere much like Ricky had done on last year, was Jeremy Tull. This six foot six inch shooting guard was slated to go to Georgetown University.

Highly touted as the top recruit within Georgetown University's history, next to Allen Iversen, Jeremy possessed the speed and quickness well beyond the skills of any normal high school basketball superstar.

The difference between the two appeared to be their age. Ricky was only 15 and Jeremy was 18 years old. Two of the nation's greatest high school basketball players would seemingly collide like meteors in the middle of the sky.

Lake View Academy High School was no longer viewed as merely a college prep high school. The school was now a basketball powerhouse in the state of Texas, with much of the credit going to my stepson, Ricky, and Coach Lawson for the team's emergence.

Now the tone of this game would be dictated by the way in which Jeremy Tull basically ignored Ricky at the outset of the game. Ricky approached Jeremy as though he was all excited and ready to play.

"Good game partna," said Ricky and extended his hand. Jeremy basically ignored Ricky's hand.

"I ain't yo partna and I don't shake the hands of underclassmen, so get out my face junior."

Ricky was astonished, but he was pretty much accustomed to being ignored at the outset of a game because of his youth. The conclusion of most of those games always yielded a different outcome. Today, however would appear to be somewhat different, as Ricky and his team struggled on the offensive and defensive ends of the court.

The game was so bad for them that the score towards the end of the second quarter was not even close. Ricky couldn't find the basket as the Sharks' defense clamped down on him like no defense ever has before. After a brief timeout, Ricky went over to Coach Lawson seemingly frustrated and depressed.

"Coach, let me guard that guy. I know I'm not hitting, but I think I can stop him."

"Ricky, guarding him will wear you down and we need your full energy in the next half."

Ricky proceeded to try and convince the coach, but the horn sounded and the next four minutes of basketball would be compelling at best.

Jeremy Tull basically took over the game. This reality was so apparent that Ricky just started guarding him anyway. On the first defense of Jeremy, Ricky tried to keep him from posting up down low. That endeavor alone turned out to be a huge mistake.

"You bout to get-cho feelings hurt chomp! You overrated punk," said Jeremy to Ricky.

Jeremy got the ball while he was boxing Ricky up, down low near the basket. Jeremy dribbled the ball back into Ricky, faked going right and then spun around to the left side for a wind mill slam dunk. All Ricky could do was helplessly watch as he got shook inside his britches. The crowd roared and Ricky clearly had a distressed look on his face. For the first time ever watching Ricky play, I felt sorry for him.

On the very next play, Ricky caught the ball just past the half court line and he threw an errant pass to his teammate, but out of nowhere came these long arms and a flash of speed. Jeremy picked the ball off in midair and went coast to coast, finishing with a Tommy Hawk slam dunk. Ricky chased after him but it seemed as though he was running in slow motion, compared to Jeremy's blazing speed.

"Thanks for the gift, punk," said Jeremy to Ricky as he returned back down court. Ricky was clearly getting humiliated and an outsider looking in would think that he was on the verge of being intimidated by Tull's play.

"You ain't pro material! You just a pretty boy with no skills. I bet your mom is so embarrassed! I own Texas basketball and you a fake. I wish I played you every game. Ricky who? You NBA wannabee."

Those words were all statements that Jeremy said to Ricky at sometime or another, throughout the course of the game. Before he scored on him, most of the time he either shot the three ball or dunked on him like Ricky was nobody special.

At the beginning of the third period, Jeremy walked over to Ricky before the game resumed with a daring stare in his eyes.

"You know ya mama bout to have my baby, don't ya?"

Ricky pushed him and all the referee saw was a push and Ricky was quickly assessed a technical foul. Coach

Lawson signaled Ricky over to the bench.

"Son, I told you not to start jawing with this kid. Just play basketball."

"But Coach, he keeps on talking about my mom."

"Ricky, he keeps talking about your mom because he knows it bothers you. Just focus on the game son. I can't use you on the bench now."

Ricky took a deep breath and walked back onto the court, while Coach Lawson proceeded to talk with the referee.

"Now ref, you know that kid has been taunting and cursing the whole game. He needs to be put in check too."

"Coach I'm letting these kids play ball. Talking is a part of the game. If your top player can't handle that, he's in trouble."

The coach proceeded to engage further in conversation, but the referee blew the whistle to signify resumption of game play.

"I'ma kick yo butt after we send yawl back to Houston," whispered Jeremy into Ricky's ear.

On the next play, Jeremy was fouled by Ricky and he went to the free throw line and hit all his free throw shots. He was guarded tightly by Ricky, but he still made a poster child out of him, just dunking freely on him. It became so bad that Coach Lawson finally took Ricky out of the game.

"Coach, what are you doing?" Ricky said as he ran over to his coach.

"Ricky, sit down son! I can't have you going out like this." Ricky angrily sat down on the bench. He was upset, scared, and worried too. When the next whistle blew for someone to shoot a free throw as the result of a foul, Jeremy trickled over near the bench and said words to

Ricky that further quenched his spirit.

"Ricky, I saw your real dad downtown on the corner begging for pennies to support his drug habit. Maybe your future NBA dollars can serve some purpose."

Jeremy chuckled. The referee warned Jeremy to stay away from the bench. Ricky sat there with a blatant look of torture.

Those last words hit home. His mind went back to when his dad would beat his mom, went back to how they lived in infested drug projects in Dallas.

All of a sudden, he reflected back on the words of what his mom told him back after his dad beat her to the tune of two black eyes and a bruised shoulder bone. While in the back of a rescue squad where she was believed to be on her death bed, she told Ricky words that would prove to be his anchor for life.

"Son, I don't care how you choose to remember this, but please do. Don't you ever forget this day. Stay hungry to be the best you can be so you will never have to live in these conditions. Ricky, never, never, never let anyone stop you from achieving your goals. Never! I want you to someday build a foundation and not become a victim to drugs. Let your dad serve as your reminder."

Ricky recalled his mom saying those words to him. Although she could barely speak as she faded into unconsciousness in that ambulance, her words were vibrating in Ricky's ear right now as though he was reliving that horrible experience all over again.

Ricky became so mesmerized with those words that he seemed to be totally nonexistent in the Dallas gymnasium. A rage out of nowhere came over Ricky. He started thinking how he felt when his mom was so helpless and he could not do anything to make her feel better.

His focus clearly shifted from the game to that horrible experience he had the day that his dad beat his mom. His dad was clearly strung out on drugs, but Ricky felt so much guilt inside because he was not there to protect his mom.

He had been hard headed that day and went outside to play basketball and he returned to the sound of the ambulance and was quickly informed by his next door neighbor that his mom was in it.

Suddenly, the transformation of Ricky's mind was taking place. The Rocky music was playing in his head and Ricky was ready to excel, ready to seize the moment, ready to seal the coffin to returning back to the hood. He all of a sudden felt a new form of hunger rumbling through his body. He felt a dire need to get back in that game and beat off the demons of his past; the very demons that forced his mom to suffer as she did on that horrible day. Ricky suddenly looked down at the coach to get his attention. *Ricky, don't you ever return to the hood. Stay away from drugs and never, ever fail when the opportunity to stay clear of that lifestyle presents itself.* Ricky kept hearing his mom's voice over and over again in his ear. All of a sudden, this was not about the state championship; this was not about Jeremy Tull; this was not about a basketball ego. However, for Ricky, it was about seizing the moment to close the door to ever returning to the hood. It was about avenging the harm that his mom endured from his dad. It was about tasting that hunger to be great like never before.

"Coach, I'm ready," said Ricky.

Coach Lawson came and kneeled before Ricky on the bench.

"Ricky, this one is over son. This is just one game."

"Coach, you taught us that it's never over until it's over. Please just let me get in the game. I promise I'll play right."

"Son, it's not even about that. We had a good season and you will get to finish the season healthy and ready for the McDonald's All American game."

"Coach, I just need to get in the game right now. I really could care less about playing any other time than right now."

The coach could not overlook that fire in Ricky's eyes that he had not seen in quite awhile. It was that look of hunger, desire, leadership....that borne to rein look that matched Ricky's talents.

"Son, we are down by 18 with only six minutes left."

Ricky interrupted the coach as though the score meant nothing to him.

"Coach, this game ain't over. Please! Just let me in the game."

The coach felt the electric intensity of Ricky's words as though the kid placed hope back into the coach's current perspective on the game. Then, he quickly signaled Ricky to go into the game, but before he let him go from his arms he had a message for him.

"Son, let me remind you that you are the best high school kid in the game today. Don't let anyone ever take that crown away from you. Now, you go out there and take what's already yours."

The coach clinched the collar area of Ricky's jersey, like he was about to beat him down, and then he spoke words to Ricky that had him snorting like a bull to get in the game.

"I want to see the hunger in your game that I saw when I first met you." He slapped Ricky on his hips as he rushed into the game after the scoring booth sounded the entry buzzer.

Less than one minute in the game, Ricky picked off a pass and raced down the court for a switch blade slam dunk at the other end of the court.

The next ensuing play, he stole the ball from Jeremy Tull and pulled up for a three pointer, hitting clearly nothing but net. Ricky kept thinking about his dad beating his mom and his rage to dominate the remainder of the game made him clearly unstoppable. On defense, he shut Jeremy Tull down, blocking his shot six times in the quarter, while playing and not saying a mumbling word.

Jeremy even noticed a difference in Ricky. Although he was not aware, he had made a serious mistake of reminding Ricky of his, not so distant, past. That reminder had all of a sudden become Ricky's primary source of motivation. When Jeremy looked into Ricky's eyes, all he saw was the fiery, unwavering look of those belonging to a ferocious tiger. It's almost like Ricky was another person in the game. Then, the dunk that brought down the house.

Ricky stole the ball from his opponent as they were trying to make a fast break and then he went full speed down the court all to notice Jeremy was daring him to come down low. Ricky hesitated as though he was going to shoot a three ball, and he committed Jeremy to come out to guard him and then he went full speed all of a sudden up in the air and over the taller, higher jumping Jeremy Tull. It was the true poster dunk of the game as Ricky was peering down at Jeremy as he ascended with his arms outstretched and looking down at Tull.

Total silence was brought to the home court crowd and Ricky's whole bench jumped up and yelled out, "and one" as Jeremy fouled Ricky and he became upset over the call. That dunk totally took Jeremy mentally out of the remainder of the game.

Ricky, however, missed the free throw, but he came flying out of nowhere to capture the ball in midair and ram it down the face of the rim. That dunk would be replayed on Sports center as the top highlight of the season. Jeremy did nothing the remainder of the game, but commit turnovers.

At the sound of the game ending buzzer, Ricky had once again taken his team to another state championship victory, as his team roared back to win by three points.

Ricky ran over to Jeremy as though he was programmed to do so without distraction and with total humility.

"I was just kind of wondering if you would shake my hand now." Ricky extended his hand. Jeremy reluctantly shook Ricky's hand while looking down to the floor in dejection and disgust. Ricky started to run away from Jeremy, but quickly turned around and spoke in a very serious tone with a teardrop formed in his eye.

"Oh yeah, Jeremy! Say hello to my real dad for me." Then afterwards, he was quickly clobbered by teammates, fans, and reporters.

Chapter 8
Chilling on my Home Front

Oscar, get out of here right now. Go to the front of the house Oscar. I'm serious now. If you don't move this very instant, you will be sleeping outside tonight. You can act like you don't understand me, but I know that you do understand English."

I was standing over our family dog, trying to get that mutt to obey my orders. He just came into our bedroom and hopped up on the bed and started looking at me like I was crazy. Oscar was a very pretty black Golden Retriever who seemed to obey everyone in the house except me and I never could figure that out. It's as though the dog would tune me out whenever I spoke to him.

"Oscar, if you don't start listening and obeying my orders, you will not be in this house for long. Do you hear me? Do you know that in Korea you could be somebody's dinner? That's right buddy. They actually eat dogs over there and call it some nice fancy entrée. You just keep on messing with me and see if I don't make the arrangements."

Dang! That dog made me feel so powerless. I really was not feeling this dog right now. I have done nothing to the mutt, but he always ignored me like I did not exist. I was just about to find something to knock him upside his big head with, when Evelyn walked into the room.

"Hey there boy! Come give mommy some love." The dog got all happy and wagged his tail back and forth like he was so happy to see Evelyn. I stood there like I was so helpless as I saw the dog jumping for joy all over her. Evelyn seemed so happy to see the dog and all of a sudden it seemed as if this mutt was getting more loving than I could get. Then, out of the blue, Ricky walked into the room.

"Ricky, I thought you said that daggone dog was trained. I can't get this mutt to do anything I tell him to do. I thought Golden Retrievers were a lot smarter than that."

Ricky looked at me with that tiresome look over his face while holding his gym bag over his shoulder. He had just gotten home from the basketball game.

"They are smart J.R. Come here Oscar. Let's go boy." As soon as Ricky called the dog, he jumped down from the bed and followed Ricky. Ricky looked at me with a smart smirk on his face, as he left the room. Then, my cell phone rang.

"J.R.," I said as I answered the phone.

"Hello, may I speak to Chronic."

"Excuse me! May you speak to whom?"

"May I speak to Chronic?"

"Chronic? There's no one by that name here. I'm sorry, but you've got the wrong number." Evelyn quickly intervened.

"J.R., the phone call is for Ricky." I looked at Evelyn like she slapped me.

"What?"

"The phone call is for Ricky. They call him Chronic." I looked at Evelyn and then looked back at my phone.

"Why would someone be calling Ricky on my phone?"

"J.R., that is not the first time that someone has called Ricky on your phone, especially after he has played a game."

I looked at Evelyn again and then I called Ricky for him to come and get the phone.

"Honey, you just never noticed it. Ricky sometimes

gave your number out because he knew that when I would take his phone, I would turn it off and he would miss all his phone calls."

Ricky came running into the room as Evelyn was explaining to me what I clearly had not noticed.

"Sir, you called?" I handed Ricky my cell phone while asking him a question.

"What's up with this chronic name?"

"Oh, that's just what they call me at school." Then Ricky spoke on the phone.

"Hello." Ricky started walking out the room.

"J.R., you are really behind. Do you know that Ricky has been nagging me about changing his name to Ricky Carter as opposed to Ricky Lyles?" I responded immediately as that was the first time I had heard about Ricky wanting to change his name.

"But Evelyn, his name is out there as the most popular high school athlete in the country. He can't just change his name like that." Evelyn just laid on the bed and nodded her head.

"I know that J.R.! I've talked to him about the name change, but he still wants me to do it. He feels that his name should change too since mine changed. Honey, he just wants to have our last name."

"I tell you what. I'll talk to the boy. I'm not so impressed with that chronic name, but I can understand him feeling left out with his given name. He must understand that as a future celebrity, you can't just change names like that at a whim."

"I know J.R., Ricky is a kid and he really could care less about all that celebrity stuff."

"Evelyn, that's what I'm talking about. He has to begin

to start wearing the role. You were not at the game today, but that boy started out playing unlike he normally played; then all of a sudden towards the end of the game, he just took over."

I was standing over the bed talking to Evelyn as she was positioning her pregnant body on the bed. I helped her sit up more comfortably as she maneuvered the pillows on the bed.

"Honey, I know what you're saying, but you must realize this stuff is all new to Ricky. He is still a kid. I am really upset that he starts practicing for that McDonald's All American game in a couple of days. Jesus Christ, the boy just won a state championship. I ain't so crazy that he got to fly out to Atlanta, Georgia so soon."

I sat next to Evelyn on the bed and hugged her in my arms. My left hand was around her back and my right hand was rubbing her stomach. It was truly a Kodak moment for me and my boo.

"Evelyn, that's the life of a superstar. That's why they get paid the big bucks. They've got to be ready to fly out from state to state and city to city, sometimes with little notification. It's the life of a professional athlete. You must get used to that baby."

"I don't care J.R. Whether I get used to it or not, I still ain't got to like it. My boy is just a boy and I don't like how all this attention is shaping his growth and maturity. Sometimes I think he needs to give basketball a break before it somehow breaks him."

"Sweetheart, the boy is too young for that right now." I was having a deep conversation with Evelyn when Teralyn walked in the bedroom. She was clad in bare apparel as usual; white head band around her head with her hair in a pony tail, half size blue top with a deep V neck showcasing her cleavage from above. Her dark black daisy duke shorts seemed painted on, while both cheeks were hanging out the shorts

"E, you ready to go walkin?"

"Already T! I thought we were going later on in the evening?"

"Chile puhlease! I tried dat wit-chu the day befoe yesterday and you cried dat-chu was too sleepy. C'mon let's get it ova wit while da weather is so nice out."

"Okay T, give me about 20 minutes and I'll be ready."

"Huh? Chile, I'll meet-chu in 10 minutes in da kitchen. Dat way we'll leave out da back doe."

"Whateva! Are we talking this time or are you wearing your walkman?" Evelyn said to Teralyn.

"We can talk E, but make sure da baby gonn cooperate dis time. As soon as you start complaining bout how I don't know what it's like to be knocked up, I'm playin my music."

Teralyn placed both her hands on her hips as she made that last comment. I must admit that I could not believe Teralyn just walked around the house half naked like she did. I can't lie. Baby girl had it going on.

"Now T, I know you wearing more clothes than that. You're going to get sick wearing those kind of clothes in this kind of weather. Another thing, please don't bring that hardcore, how to be a hoe type music that you love to listen too. I can't stand that mess."

"E, you leave my Mia X CD alone. I'll see you in 10 minutes in da kitchen." Teralyn walked off quickly, but it seemed as if her butt cheeks left in slow motion. I mean, it just seemed like it took a long time for her butt cheeks to turn that corner. Afterwards, Evelyn quickly hit me with another shocker.

"J.R., I really don't care too much for that housemaid. She is always on the phone whispering like she got something to hide."

"Baby, come on now! Rosie is just doing her job. She has been working hard for me for some time. I think you're just easily irritated from being pregnant baby." I kissed Evelyn on the cheeks at the conclusion of those words. However, she pushed me away.

"J.R., I get so sick and tired of yawl telling me that I am the way I am because I'm pregnant. Stop blaming everything on the baby. I'm telling you one more time, I don't like that maid. She acts too darn suspicious around me and I'm not feeling her. I'm giving her two weeks and if she doesn't act right J.R., she will be fired."

Evelyn looked so funny sitting on the bed with her big stomach boosted up towards the ceiling. She just bopped her head while talking about the maid, causing her stomach to shake up and down. I grinned a little, all to be interrupted by Evelyn's serious facial.

"J.R., what the hell is so funny? I'm starting to feel like you are not taking me serious. I don't appreciate you laughing at me. That's why you ain't getting none."

OOPs! She really hit a nerve with those words. Matter of fact, she kind of pissed me off by bragging about the fact that she wasn't giving me any.

"Evelyn, I was not laughing at you baby. You just looked funny bouncing your head back and forth like that on the bed with your stomach facing skyward like that." I rubbed her stomach and she grabbed my hand and pinched me real hard.

"Ouch," was my loud scream as I pulled my hand back.

"Get your hands off me. I'm trying to tell you something on a serious tip and you busy making fun of somebody." Evelyn started to leave from the bed as I tried to talk to her.

"Baby, I'm not trying to make fun." I started laughing again uncontrollably as Evelyn was leaving and I couldn't even complete my sentence. Evelyn turned around towards me after getting out of the bed and started pointing her finger at me while talking.

"I don't appreciate you making fun of me J.R. Get your butt out my bedroom right now. You can forget about sleeping in here tonight too." I snapped into hysteria.

"Ahh! Come on now Evelyn. This is ridiculous." I started panting like a child as Evelyn continued to drop some hard words.

"Now, I'm giving Rosie one week to straighten up and if she still acts weird like she has been doing, she will be fired." SLAM! Evelyn went into our bathroom and loudly shut the door. I was pissed! I knew one thing. I sure won't be getting any for quite awhile. Wow! Talk about going into a real drought in the bedroom! Going cold turkey was absolutely no joke.

Chapter 9
What-cho name is?

Loke, what's going on playa?" I had just arrived at the hospital to pick Loke up as the doctor said he was cleared to return home. I had his Escalade all juiced up, knowing he would rather I pick him up in his new truck as opposed to my own vehicle.

"It's all good man! It feels good to finally get out of that hospital."

"So what do you think man? Is your baby looking good or what?" I expressed to Loke with my arms widespread to showcase his clean truck.

"Man, I was just about to say that the ride is so clean I was not certain as to who it belonged to. You did a good job."

"Hey man, you know I didn't do it. Congrats to my staff. They wanted to make sure your ride was tight."

"J.R., I definitely need to thank them man. What a nice gesture?" Loke leaned over, shook my hand, gave me a nice hug, and spoke to me in a very sincere tone.

"J.R., thanks for being there for me man. You really don't know what it meant to me to know that you had my back every step of the way."

"Hey! No sweat man! That's what I do for my boy! Heck, you think I was about to let you die and leave me out here all alone. Man, you must be crazy." I started laughing and Loke joined me.

"Hey man! On a serious tip, I owe you."

"You don't owe me anything man. We both need to thank God because that's who we owe. I'm sure you would have looked out for me had I been in your shoes."

I looked at Loke as I began to drive off from the

hospital. I realized that he and I had not discussed what really happened. I really did not want to be nosy, but this was just too important for me not to ask.

"Loke, what actually happened man?"

"Man, you know what happened. I took that white thickalicious nurse and turned her inside out. That's right! I brought some black thunder to her…" I quickly interrupted Loke.

"Loke, I'm not talking about the hospital escapade, but I'm talking about the shooting incident in the driveway of your dentist office."

Loke quickly looked away from me with a very straight face. You would think I had said something to offend him. He just looked straight ahead and would not even look back at me.

"J.R., I really don't feel like discussing the incident at this time."

"Loke, it's as good a time as any. I want to know what changes need to be made since this event." Loke still refused to look me straight into my eyes and his response really had me wondering.

"J.R., once again, I don't want to discuss that right now. It was very difficult for me discussing that night with the authorities and I am not ready to talk about it right now. Please respect my privacy."

Loke was looking down and away from me as he registered those words into my ears. I thought to myself, *why the heck does he act like he got something to hide? My goodness, he was the victim and not the perpetrator so why is he acting so suspicious about something? I guess I should respect his privacy….what? His privacy? After I just went through what I went through. He must be under the influence of those drugs or something.*

"Well Loke, I do apologize for upsetting you with the questions. I was just wondering what precautions needed to be taken and I guess I thought two heads were better than one in addressing the issue. I guess I was wrong."

"J.R., just respect my privacy for now." Then, all of a sudden, Loke quickly changed the subject on me.

"By the way, how is married life?"

"Hey man! You know. It's all that and a bag of chips. I love this lifestyle my brotha. Evelyn is due to have the baby anytime now and Ricky is a great kid." Loke looked at me and quickly interrupted.

"You in a living hell, aren't you J.R.? You can't fool me. I can tell your words are not even real. You even sound like you got on both ankle and hand cuffs my brotha. You see, you forgot that you are talking to a brother who's already been there and can recognize the signs."

"Naw, man! Actually it's all good. I am loving the life, the expectations of a happy husband, and the fatherhood all together." Loke quickly interrupted.

"J.R., save that for some fool that has never been married okay. You must think you're talking to some clueless hillbilly. That county seat must have gone to your head because you are definitely giving me the official commercial advertisement for marriage."

Dang! Was it that obvious? I really did not want to share with Loke how I really felt. Truthfully, the marriage lockdown was actually getting tougher than I could have ever imagined. I mean, Evelyn wasn't giving up jack, I'm turning down women like I'm gay or something, and Teralyn is walking around tempting a brotha to no end. I still could not share that with Loke. I was not totally happy, but I was pleased in a number of ways. The good part is that I still love my wife, my stepson and my baby to be. To me, that's all that really mattered.

"Loke, I don't understand what you're saying. I am totally happy in my marriage and I am so glad I got married." Loke continued to stare at me and then he continued to further question me.

"J.R., what's the latest with that crazy Italian woman in ATL?"

"Loke, I'm trying to handle the situation by firing her. She has really gotten out of control. I have increased her salary and she still threatened me by demanding more money and now she's screaming child support." Loke had a shocked look on his face as he responded to my words.

"Child support? What? There must be a baby in order for her to be talking child support?"

"Loke, I did not have a chance to tell you. One morning while in my office at home, Doralee called me and placed the baby on the phone. I don't even know how she got my home office number." Loke turned all the way around in the passenger side of his truck. His frown indicated his displeasure with the words he heard.

"J.R., stop playing man!"

"Loke, I'm serious as a heart attack." Oops! Wrong choice of words by me.

"I mean, I'm dead serious Loke." Oops! Wrong choice of words again.

"Loke, I mean…" He quickly interrupted me.

"Come on J.R.! Kill that crap! I don't have a heart problem and death is not an issue with me. Now finish the story. You mean to tell me that she actually gave birth to a child? Man! This mess is really out of control. How you gonna handle this? I mean, you got a baby now with the other woman. Whoa!"

"Loke, I don't know how I'm gonna deal with this man. I guess I got to own up to my responsibility and take care of the child. I mean I can't be putting a child through all this drama."

"Man I feel ya! I hate the drama my kids had to go through with my ex wife's crazy antics. I would not put that drama on any kid."

"Loke, you know what my biggest fear is?"

"Most definitely! You worried that Evelyn is gonna leave you and take half and that's a very legitimate concern from my view. I think we need to figure something out."

"Loke, I been trying to figure something out since I heard the news that I had a child. But with you in the hospital and me having to deal with this as well, I don't mind telling you it's been a real challenge." Loke once again looked away from me as though he had something to hide.

"J.R., you don't have to worry about me. I'm here to stay. We need to figure out a way to prevent unnecessary trouble from affecting your marriage." As Loke was talking, I drove through the gate to my house.

"Loke, I need to run in the house real quickly and check on an important fax from the Mayor's office. You are welcome to come in or wait out here until I come back. I'll drop you off at your house in a few minutes. Okay?"

"No sweat J.R. I'll just sit right here and wait on you. You got a way to get back from my house after you drop me off or were you just gonna take my truck?"

"My Lex is parked at your house. I'm straight. I'll be back in 5 minutes."

I rushed into the house and went into my office to check on my fax. To my surprise, Rosie, the house maid was in my office. I could have been mistakened, but I thought she was reading my paperwork that had come through on the fax machine. I thought it was sort of weird, but she was probably cleaning up the machine or something.

While I was in the house, Loke sat in the truck admiring my house. He looked over to the right side of my house and saw Teralyn returning from walking the dog, Oscar. As soon as he saw her, he immediately did a double take and got out the truck. He seemed to warp speed into a fast world of infatuation. Teralyn was standing in the front courtyard area. She quickly let Oscar into the house.

As she saw Loke approaching, she quickly shaped her hair with her hands. Loke briskly walked over to where she was standing.

"Excuse me, Miss! Don't mind me asking, but where in the world did you come from? Evelyn, is that you? It can't be because you are supposed to be pregnant."

"What-cho name is?"

"Excuse me?" Loke did not quite understand Teralyn's southern drawl.

"Oh, you dat sick guy." Teralyn was looking as fine as ever. She wore a dark blue spandex warm up suit. The outfit was a one piece that covered her whole body, while also showcasing her nice curves. She also wore a sweat jacket.

"Oh! I'm sorry. You seem to have already met me, but

I don't recall ever meeting you. My name is Latrell Oliver King, and people call me Loke."

Loke extended his hand to shake Teralyn's hand, but Teralyn just stood there staring at him with one hand on her hip and the other hand holding the towel. Then she intensely wiped the sweat from her face and other body parts.

"Don't even sweat yoself pretty boy. I ain't met-chu. I jest heard about-chu and I knew you were in da hospital. Looks like you doing fine nigh dough."

"Yes Ma'am! I am doing fine, but nowhere near as fine as you are. I would love to take you out on a date. You are some kind of fine baby gurl."

"Whateva nigga! I bet-chu say dat to all da women round here. Let me warn you scraight up. I'm out-cho league nigga so don't even bark my way."

Teralyn started to leave and Loke just laughed at what she said before responding with sincere words.

"Oh! Okay, I got your, I'm out-cho league comment. I realize you may be in another league, but before too long, you will learn that I am in a league of my own. You can best believe that."

Teralyn just kept on walking and did not look back. I returned from inside my house and saw Loke standing there with a grin on his face.

"Loke, I'm ready when you are." I saw him staring Teralyn down until she disappeared off to the other side of my house. Loke came walking swiftly over to me.

"J.R., who in the hell was that fine mutha f…?"

"Loke, don't even go there my brotha. That's my sister in law, Evelyn's twin sister."

"Twin sister? I never knew Evelyn had a twin sister.

Why am I just finding that out?"

"Hey man, brace yourself. Up until a few days ago, I didn't even know she existed. The next thing I know, she showed up here at the house. I don't exactly know why, but Evelyn has never discussed any members of her family other than her son with me."

"Wow man! That woman is fine! I think I'm in love J.R."

"Loke, get in the truck man. You done really tipped over to the crazy side."

"What are you talking about man? I'm serious. I would like to get to know her." I turned to look at Loke as he got into the truck. I pointed my right forefinger at him.

"Look here man! Promise me this one thing."

"What's that?"

"Loke, you must promise me that you will stay away from Teralyn."

"Is that her name Teralyn? Why in the world would I make a promise like that?" He was starting to make me angry. I leaned over inside his truck.

"Loke, you will make a promise like that because I am asking you to. Besides, she is a splitting image of Evelyn. How can you be attracted to someone that looks exactly like my wife? That would be disrespectful to me." Loke stared at me with his mouth cocked half way open and his forehead wrinkled from the frown on his face.

"J.R., you are kidding, right?"

"Naw man! I'm being real. You can't be into Teralyn because it's like cheating on me with my wife. The woman looks exactly like Evelyn."

"Look dude! You are just a bit twisted in your rationale. I cannot help that she looks like your wife. I'm interested in her and not your wife. Your words make no logic whatsoever."

"No Loke! My words make all the logic in the world. Teralyn looks exactly like Evelyn. I mean they are twins for crying out loud. I feel like she is too close to home, as in my wife."

"Well J.R., you keep on feeling that way, but I don't share your feelings. I have not seen a woman that fine in over 15 years. She seems to be a special woman and I deserve the right to get to know her."

I was getting real pissed with Loke. He was really starting to get on my last nerve. I started driving away from the house making sharp turns around the bin from my house.

"Loke, if you go there, our friendship will be seriously damaged. I'm very sincere about this matter. If you want to lose my friendship, you just go ahead and see her. However, keep in mind that your feelings will be hurt dealing with Teralyn. She is straight up street hood. Trust me when I tell you that a relationship with her would be like mixing oil and water."

"J.R., you let me worry about all that." I got real angry and stopped the truck in the middle of the road and I shouted at him.

"Man, can you, for once in your life, meet a woman you don't feel like you have to screw? Can you at least think about our friendship and honor my daggone feelings? You screwed Debbie right up under my eyes and could care less about my feelings. Then, you snuck around to be with her so Gina did not know. I am so sick and tired of your disloyalty to me." Loke threw his hands up in the air, before shouting back at me.

"Oh, you want to talk about disloyalty? I'll talk to you about disloyalty." Loke opened the door and got out the truck and I followed as well.

"At least I did not try and hook you up with a woman that I was already screwing and hid that very fact from you."

"What? I have no clue as to what you are talking about? I have not tried to hook you up with anybody. You just feasted on Debbie like she was yours."

"J.R., I am not referring to Debbie. Now, you look me in my eyes and tell me you never had sex with Julie?" Oh No! How in the world did he know that? Dang! I'm busted. I wanted to keep that a secret, but I was, once again, busted. I had to come clean with him.

"Loke, that was well before you and Julie met, okay. I did not sleep with her after you two developed interest for one another."

"J.R., could you have at least given me the courtesy of knowing that you were already sleeping with her, prior to introducing me to her? I would have never introduced you to a potential marriage partner without at least telling you I had screwed her in the past." I walked away from Loke as he was getting right up on me and pointing his forefinger into my chest.

"Loke, I don't quite agree. I personally feel that my past with Julie was strictly between the two of us. I really do wonder how you found out about that."

"Don't worry about that J.R., just take me home man." Loke started holding his chest as though he was experiencing some pain and he began to get back into the truck.

"Are you okay Loke?"

"I'm fine J.R. Just take me home man."

"Yo man! I apologize. I did not write the script on the Julie incident. You should not be arguing and raising your voice like that anyway." He opened the car door again and got back out the truck.

"Look here dude! Will you please stop trying to treat me like I'm about to croak? I'm serious J.R. I've had enough of your overwhelming concern to where it's making me really sick, okay. Now once and for all, I am fine." As soon as Loke said that, he caught his chest again as though he was experiencing some serious pain.

Then, out of the blue, my security guard Walker drove up seemingly out of nowhere and asked if everything was okay. I assured him that all was well.

"Mr. Carter, I was just checking because we have been calling your cell for the past 20 minutes to inform you that Miss Evelyn's water had broken."

"What? Oh my God! I gotta roll."

"J.R., you take Walker's car. That way he can take me home so you can go to the hospital right away and be with Evelyn." Loke quickly interjected.

"Excellent idea Loke! We will finish our discussion at a later time."

I rushed off towards the hospital where Evelyn had been taken. All the words that Loke and I exchanged really became second nature now. I was overwhelmed with thoughts of my wife about to give birth to our firstborn. I was nervous, excited, and yet happy at the anticipation of our baby finally arriving.

Chapter 10
Jamie Randella

The McDonald's All American high school basketball game was held this year in Atlanta, Georgia. Ricky led all players in scoring and earned the MVP trophy for the game. Nevertheless, he could not lead the West to repeat the championship as they folded to the East by a close margin of two points. While all family members were previously occupied with Evelyn in labor at a hospital in Houston, Ricky and Hudson, one of my new security guards, attended the game in Atlanta.

Ricky was presented the MVP trophy and interviewed on television. An interesting development occurred which would serve to transform his mental state beyond expectations. First off, one of his competitors came over to greet him.

"Chronic, good game man. You sure earned that trophy. You were clearly unstoppable," said one of the opposing ballplayers who had a scholarship to play with the Duke Blue Devils.

"Thanks Damon and I hope you the best at Duke. Watch out for them tar heels because if I were to go to college, that's where I would be going," said Ricky as they shook hands and hugged each other. Then, Damon ran off.

"Chronic, thanks for carrying the team man. We almost won that game because of you."

"Hey thanks man! That really means a lot coming from you big guy," Ricky said.

"I wanted to also apologize for my words to you during that state championship game. If I knew then what I know now, I would have shut my mouth up and given you much more respect," said Jeremy Tull as he started laughing and held out his hand to give Ricky dap. Ricky responded in kind. Then, Ricky expressed his thoughts.

"You know Jeremy, my coach said I should have thanked you because your words took me where I needed to go to rediscover my game. I owe you for that."

"Yeah I know, right? That's one time I really do regret running my big mouth. Let me get out your way Chronic. You got a long line waiting to greet you." Jeremy finally walked off.

"Excuse me Ricky, how are you doing? You played a very good game tonight. Your sister will be proud to know that her big brother is a very good basketball player."

Ricky looked at what appeared to him to be another fan who had found enjoyment in his game. All he noticed was that this fan was holding an infant child. Ricky just smiled and said, "Thank you Ma'am."

The lady came closer to Ricky and she looked up in his face and held out the infant child for Ricky.

"Ricky, this is your sister. She is named after J.R. Her name is Jamie Randella."

Ricky was totally perplexed. He looked at the woman and looked down at the baby.

"What are you talking about Ma'am? Did my mom have the baby already? What are you doing with the baby?"

The woman looked at Ricky with a proud smile and responded with glee.

"Actually, this is my baby that J.R. and I conceived just before he got married to your mom." Ricky's excited and curious face went from a smile to a very somber look.

"Ma'am, that's not true. J.R. does not have another

child. I'm his stepson and he has no other children."

"Ricky, I'm sorry that you were not aware, but you may want to confirm this fact with J.R. This is your baby sister. Now, aren't you excited?"

She smiled and leaned closer to Ricky. Ricky stood there in a daze as the coach called him over for an interview. He heard no voice, but instead he was feeling hurt and pain on the inside. Doralee quickly alerted Ricky to the fact that his coach was calling him.

"Ricky, your coach is calling you. Now Ricky, I don't think your mom is yet aware of our newborn baby so if I were you I would not bother to upset a pregnant mom, but you can definitely talk to J.R. about this."

Ricky stared at her like she was a ghost. His coach called him again! He suddenly snapped out of his thoughts and ran over to his coach and joined the television interview. He was stunned beyond words and rather inattentive during the remaining session of the interview, but he nevertheless went through the motions.

After the interviews and small talk, Ricky went to the locker room and could not wait to get an explanation from anybody about the child believed to be mine. He was hurt and disappointed, and the flight back to Houston was more of torture for him than anything. During the flight, he replayed the conversation with Doralee over and over in his mind.

Then, upon arrival to the airport, Ricky was met by Jewel and informed of news that took him by surprise.

"Hey there handsome! Congratulations on winning that big fine trophy!"

"Thanks Jewel! Where is J.R.?"

"Let me hold that nice trophy for you as I give you the

exciting news." Jewel took the trophy that Ricky carried in his hand.

"Oh! I forgot to tell you that Mr. Hudson extended his stay in Atlanta. He told me that he had already informed you guys. He took me to the airport and saw me off."

"Thanks Ricky! Hudson shared that before he left. Now, are you ready for the good news?"

"What's the good news?"

"Your mom's water broke and she had to be rushed off to the hospital. So, J.R. and Teralyn accompanied her."

"Really? So she's about to have the baby then?"

"Well, let's just say she is about to go into labor and hopefully you will be the proud brother to your baby sister real soon. Aren't you excited?"

"Well, yes Ma'am! I think I really need to talk with J.R. though." Ricky and Jewel had been walking towards the baggage claim area to get his suitcase.

"That's fine sweetheart! J.R. is at the hospital and we will be joining them soon to cheer your mom on."

Jewel grabbed Ricky's cheeks, noticed he had a very sad looking persona. Jewel, who sensed all hurt in the family like a hunting dog sensed deer. She held Ricky's hand and stopped him in the middle of the airport.

"Ricky, what is wrong baby? You seem so different."

Ricky's eyes started collecting tears, which began to trickle down his face.

"Jewel, I did not know that J.R. had another baby." Jewel pulled Ricky closer to her.

"Another baby? Ricky what are you talking about? The only other baby J.R. has is you, and you sure are a long ways from being a baby. What are you talking about?"

Ricky started sniffing, his nose became real stuffy, and the tears were flowing. Jewel got out some handkerchiefs from her purse and started wiping his tears.

"Ricky, come let's sit down over here for a moment. What is wrong baby? Now, tell me what are you talking about? Where did you get this information from?"

Ricky sat down next to Jewel and then he shared with her his hurtful experience regarding Jamie Randella.

"Well, after the game tonight, this woman came up to me with a baby in her arms and told me that J.R. was the father. She showed me the baby and told me the baby was named after J.R. and that her name was Jamie Randella."

Ricky began to cry louder like a little baby. Jewel embraced him and wiped his tears away.

"It's okay baby. You can best believe that I will get to the bottom of this. What was her name Ricky? Did she tell you her name?" Ricky took a deep breath.

"Yes Ma'am. Her name was Miss Dora somebody."

"Dora who Ricky? Can you remember her last name? Think back to when it happened." Ricky paused for a moment and thought back.

"I think her name was Miss Dora Mayberry."
Jewel immediately leaped in her seat. She went right into deep sea level thinking.

"Ricky, is her name Dora or Doralee Mayberry?" Jewel inquired.

"That's it. Her name was Doralee Mayberry and the baby she had was less than a year old. She said that she got pregnant by J.R. right before he married mom."

Jewel's eyes got extremely wide as she heard that name confirmed. Suddenly everything began to become much clearer to her. She continued to embrace Ricky, rub his head, and wipe the tears from his eyes.

While they were sitting down, a group of people had gathered right across from them who recognized Ricky and they saw him crying. Nevertheless, this one guy who asked was everything okay, asked for an autograph after Jewel said everything was fine.

"I'm sorry Sir, now is not the time for an autograph. Please understand okay, thank you."

The guy walked off and repeated Jewel's words to the small group behind him that had formed and they disbanded right away. Jewel embraced Ricky like he was her son and sat there wrapped up around him, just letting him vent his feelings. From a distance, the picture looked rather awkward. From a closer view, it was obvious that a woman was consoling a young kid.

"Ricky, what else did this lady tell you?"

"Well, that she and J.R. had this baby girl and my mom would not know anything about it, but J.R. would. She also told me that it would not be good to mention this to my mom because she was pregnant and it might hurt her. She showed me the baby and told me Jamie Randella was my baby sister."

Jewel became immediately furious with both myself and Doralee. She thought to herself, *there are a number of ways to handle this situation and for Doralee to impose this type of stress on this child was totally heartless and unfair. I can't believe that J.R. No wonder he was paying her all that darn money. He's having a serious love affair with this woman. Am I stupid or what? And I thought I knew everything about him and his associates, family, and friends. I feel so stupid, so ignorant, so taken advantage of. These men out here are nothing but lousy dogs. Oh well, I will take care of Ricky. And next up, J.R. and Doralee will feel my wrath. I won't be going out like this. Oh hell naw! Those idiots done messed with the wrong woman! Having a love affair at my clueless expense, oh hell to the naw! All I got to say is some real dirt is about to go down now!*

"Did you look at the baby Ricky?" Jewel reengaged despite her depressing thoughts.

"Yes Ma'am! For a moment I looked."

Ricky had stopped crying and he seemed to be doing better, having talked it out.

"Okay baby, you okay now?"

"Yes Ma'am! I just didn't know J.R. had another baby."

"Sweetie, learn a lesson from that experience. We don't know all of the truth yet, but you can best believe that Auntie Jewel will fix all of this, okay."

"Okay Ma'am!"

"Now, I need you to make me one promise."

"What is that?"

"Your mom is going through a major hurdle right now with pregnancy and labor. We don't want to say anything to her to upset that process because her condition at this time is very crucial. I promise I will get to the bottom of this and I will handle it from here okay?"

Ricky just stared at the floor like he was in a daze.

"Ricky, do you understand?"

"Yes Ma'am? I don't want my mom to be hurt while trying to have a baby."

"Exactly! She does not deserve to be hurt and we definitely won't bring that on her, okay?"

"Okay Ma'am. I don't feel right talking to J.R. either about it."

"Good Ricky! Let grown folks handle grown folks' business and then I will have J.R. talk to you. I'll talk to him first and have him explain everything to you. Fair enough?

"Yes Ma'am! That's fair enough."

"Okay hun, let's go get your bag and then we will get out of this airport."

Jewel stood up and kissed Ricky on the cheeks and hugged him once again.

"Also, we need to celebrate your winning the MVP trophy and make certain you treat it like it really is, a very big deal."

Ricky seemed to have gotten better as time was passing by. Both he and Jewel started walking towards the baggage claim area.

"Ricky, do you feel like signing autographs now because the crowd is still following us?" Ricky smiled.

"Sure Ma'am, I don't mind now. I'm okay." Ricky signed several autographs before he and Jewel proceeded to claim his luggage from the baggage claim section of the airport. After they got his luggage, they left the airport and headed to the hospital.

Chapter 11
Baby to Be Drama

What's up champ?" I said to Ricky as he and Jewel entered the waiting room area of the hospital.

"Hi J.R., where's mom," said Ricky.

"Evelyn is *A* okay Ricky. They are preparing her for the delivery room. Aren't you excited? You are about to have a baby sister."

Ricky smiled, but really wanted to confront me about my baby daughter that I had been keeping a secret. I gave Jewel a hug and she smiled as she greeted me.

"Jewel, I get to go in the delivery room to witness everything. Right now, Teralyn is in there helping them prepare Evelyn, and before long, we will be in the delivery room. Can you believe it Jewel? I'm about to have my first natural born child."

Jewel looked at me with half a smile on her face as her brain was working overtime during this exchange. She was mentally pre-occupied with the following thoughts: *Yeah, I wonder if this is the second time your butt's been in the delivery room. I cannot believe he can stand there and tell me that bold face lie. The more I think about it, the more I am inclined to resign from this job. I cannot be a part of such major hypocrisy. J.R. knows he should be ashamed of himself. I think I'll prepare my resignation letter tomorrow. I am not about to continue to support this cheating liar. I mean, how long does he think he can continue hiding his other child while still screwing Doralee? I will definitely have a major surprise for his butt when this delivery is all over with.*

"Jewel, did you hear what I said?" Jewel's mind seemed to be wondering off into space.

"UH Huh! I heard everything you said J.R. You are definitely a very fortunate man too."

Jewel was merely feeding me words to pass the time away. I could not tell that she was clearly upset and pissed off at me. While I was so excited and continuing to talk with Jewel, the doctor came and grabbed me.

"Mr. Carter, could I speak with you for a second?" I turned around to the sound of Dr. Jones and quickly headed his way beyond some double doors.

"Are we ready to do this Dr. Jones? I can have my scrubs on in a minute."

"Mr. Carter, there is a problem that we need to discuss." I stopped dead in my tracks while looking directly at the doctor.

"Sure Dr. Jones, what's the problem? Let's address it right now."

"Well, we do have a concern. We have not been able to detect the child's heartbeat for quite sometime now." I stared at him like he just told me some minor details of a very serious process.

"Okay doctor, so what? I mean, you got to get around all that stuff in a woman's stomach, you know what I mean, like water and food and all that stuff. I mean the baby can be playing peak-a-boo I see you or something doctor. Am I wrong?"

I was just joking and even started laughing at my words, but the doctor did not share my humor. The doctor had a very serious look on his face and he was not laughing at all.

"Mr. Carter, we have not been able to detect a heartbeat for over two hours. All indications are that the baby has lost the heartbeat and could have possibly aborted." I got downright scared and just stared at the doctor.

"Come on doctor! Don't babies do that regularly? I mean, hasn't the baby been kicking my wife's stomach and everything?   What are you saying in so many words? What's the bottom line here?"

"Mr. Carter, I'm saying that I think the baby has self aborted and we need to remove the fetus to preclude any further danger to your wife. We can do that a couple of ways, but I need your approval."

"Dr. Jones, have you told my wife that yet?"

"Mr. Carter we have not yet discussed the subject with Mrs. Carter, but we do need to have the conversation right away. We need to manually initiate fetus abort procedures and remove the child." Oh no! Why does my head hurt so hard?

"Dr. Jones, are you sure?"

"I'm about as sure as I can be, but not totally certain. Either way, as we initiate by Cesarean incision, we will be sensitive to the fetus as we attempt to retrieve. If for some reason the baby is still alive, we will be able to safely remove her from the birth canal area."

I did not believe what I was hearing. How come Evelyn just could not have a normal baby like everybody else? Now Lord, here we go again!

"Well Dr. Jones, it's not like I have any idea about this whatsoever. I just want to make certain we're making the right decision, that's all."

"Mr. Carter, let's go in and discuss everything with Mrs. Carter? You will need to be present because in cases like this, pregnant women can be very defensive." I did not give much thought to anticipating Evelyn's reaction, but I was certain that she would yield to what was right.

The doctor and I went into the room and Teralyn was giving Evelyn ice as we walked in. Evelyn quickly looked up.

"J.R., what's taking so long? What's wrong?"

Evelyn's eyes opened up with anticipation. I looked up at Evelyn and I held her hands prior to explaining the problem to her. Before I proceeded, I hinted to Teralyn to give us some privacy. She looked at me and quickly left the room.

"Evelyn, the doctor seems to feel that the baby has aborted." Evelyn had an immediate frown on her face and responded accordingly.

"What J.R.? The baby has done what? You need to speak English okay."

"Baby, the doctor believes that the baby has been lost." Evelyn quickly turned her head up towards me.

"Lost? J.R., lost where? The baby is inside of me. She is not lost. It's their job to help me deliver the baby. What the hell are you talking about?" Evelyn got real loud.

"Evelyn, the baby is believed to be dead." Evelyn immediately started shouting.

"Dead? What baby J.R.? Yawl betta get the hell up out of here. My baby is not dead. I can feel her breathing inside me." The doctor immediately intervened.

"Mrs. Carter, we have not been able to detect a heartbeat for well over two hours. All indications imply that the baby is no longer alive." Evelyn became unglued.

"J.R., did you bring him in here to tell me that. If so, both yawl can get the hell up outta here because I'm having this baby and she is alive." I tried to rub Evelyn's back and console her.

"But Evelyn, the doctor knows best sweetheart. We need to focus on your health right now. We can overcome this baby. Trust me." She pushed my hands off and started shouting and swinging her arms.

"J.R., you and that quack better get outta here right now. I'm so disappointed in you. You supposed to believe in God for everything, but you too busy listening to that quack. Get yo nonbelieving butt outta my room and you can take that duck Dr. wit-cha." Evelyn was not buying into the doctor's theory. She scared me very much as it was the angriest I had ever seen her.

"Evelyn baby, we need to do the right thing now. The doctor is really concerned about your well being and this may be the only way to ensure your safety.

"J.R., I want you and that fake ass Dr. outta my room right now. You are a disappointment to me in every sense of the word. Get out right now. I'm getting sick just looking at-cha."

"Evelyn, would you please just…" She interrupted me while pounding her fist to the bed.

"J.R., get yo butt outta here now and take that doctor wit-cha and please send my sister back in here with the nurse."

I quickly moved as though Evelyn had a gun with the trigger pulled. The doctor and I went outside and Teralyn quickly rushed inside. I was both confused and nervous. I went out in the hallway and reached for my cell phone. I needed to talk to my momma. I could not believe that Evelyn would not listen to the doctor. Hopefully, my mom could help me through this troubled time. I quickly dialed the digits to my mom and dad's house.

"What it is?" That was the sound of the familiar voice

on the other side of the phone. Cousin Mike answered the phone at my mom's house like the task was clearly a paid position. Yeah Right! The boy was probably on the other line.

"Yo Mike, I need to speak to mom right away. This is an emergency." He slowly responded like he was all mellowed out.

"J, what it be like cuz? I was just thinking bout cha."

"Mike, I really don't have a lot of time to talk right now so could you please get mom on the phone?"

"Slow yo roll playa! What seems to be da problem? Nigh you know Auntie Em gonna ask me befoe she come to the phone."

Now see, Mike was just trying to do what he does best; get all up in other people's business so he can sound like the news reporter after I get off the phone. He was really trying my patience!

"Mike, this is serious man! Get off the phone now and get my mom on the daggone phone. I'm not playing man!"

"Hold on J.R. By the way, when you coming back to Ocala? Can you bring me a pair of dem new Jordans? I'll pay you for it and you know I'm good for it." I shouted at Mike as loud as I could.

"Mike, get off the damn phone now!"

"But J.R., you need to..." I quickly interrupted with a louder tone.

"Mike, get my mom now or I will come there myself to evict you from her house. Do you hear me?" He immediately scattered and the next voice I heard was my mom.

"J.R., this better be urgent boy. Ya dad was in rare form, doing what he does both less and best and you interrupted us."

Man, it seems like every time I call and dad is home, mom and dad be knocking boots. It ain't that much loving in the world.

"Mom, I'm at the hospital with Evelyn and she is about to have the baby, but the doctor said the baby was dead. Evelyn won't listen to us. She still believes the baby is alive. I have no idea what to do mom. The world from my view is really looking bad right now." Mom took a deep breath and then shared her perspective.

"J.R., is there another doctor in the hospital that can give a second opinion? Then again, there might not be time for that. I tend to think that the mother knows best in these situations. This is a common occurrence with some hospitals to misdiagnose these symptoms." I responded to mom in sheer frustration.

"Mom, I really don't have time to care about the problems with other hospitals. I got to address the situation that I am in right now."

"Step back boy! I don't need you giving me advice because I didn't call you. You called me. If you too proud to listen to me, I'll gladly hang up so I can go get my bi-monthly servicing."

"Mom, what should I do? Evelyn won't cooperate."

"Son, let time take it's course. If the baby is alive, it will make it's presence known eventually. If not, then a second opinion from another doctor is what you need to consider. Give me a call when you find out."

As I was talking to mom, the doctor came and grabbed me and informed me that my wife was headed to the delivery room.

"Hey mom, I got to run. Looks like it's time to move

Evelyn into the delivery room."

"Good! Cause yo dad can't always get it up and he is in rare form right now. Let me know how everything turns out." Gees! Like I care to hear that kind of detailed information about my dad.

"Okay mom! I'll call you as soon as I know something. Bye bye." I got off the phone and the doctor came over to speak with me.

"J.R., it appears that the baby is still alive and kicking and her head had made it's way towards the birth canal. We are moving quickly to the delivery room because all of a sudden the baby is rapidly positioning for delivery."

"Okay Doctor Jones! I'll get my scrubs on in a minute and come straight to the delivery room."

I found the closest room and immediately changed. I was so glad to hear those words from the doctor. Wow! It's really happening. I'm about to be a real dad.

Chapter 12
Dominance Nicole

I ran out of the delivery room shouting like a man possessed. Evelyn had finally given birth to our daughter and we agreed on the name Dominance Nicole. She weighed eight pounds, nine ounces. I rushed out to the waiting room area and alerted Ricky, Jewel, Julie, Teralyn, Walker, and Loke, who had just arrived at the hospital.

"Somebody sound the trumpet! Somebody call the cops because my baby girl has been born. Dominance Nicole has finally arrived at 9:57 pm."

There was a sparing cheer and a clap or two as everyone seemed so happy for me. I started hugging everyone and kissing them on the cheeks. Loke had the pink bubble gum cigars that he handed me and I started passing them out.

"J.R., how is mom doing? When can we see her?" Ricky asked.

"You will be able to see her in a few minutes Ricky. She's fine."

"J.R., did you take a picture of the baby after delivery?" Julie asked.

"Awhrah....honestly Julie, I fainted as the baby's head had gradually surfaced from Evelyn. I was awakened by the doctor and they were already cutting the umbilical chord and gently making certain that the baby was alive. She bellowed out with a cry from heaven."

"You really fainted J.R.? You such a wuss," said Teralyn.

"Yeah, whatever girl! You need to be careful how you talk to me from now on because I am now the proud father of a baby girl."

I had my baby girl, mack swagger on, as I was too proud to be distracted. The nurse came and carried them to see the baby. I was so at ease and my thoughts were flowing like I had just won the lottery. Loke came up close to me and slightly distracted me.

"J.R., I really do think I'm feeling your sister-in-law. Whenever I am around her, I lose sight of everyone else with exception of her."

"Loke, please spare me the details on that man. Can I at least enjoy this cigar and the arrival of my newborn baby girl for now?" I pretended like I was blowing smoke from my mouth as I had that bubble gum cigar in my hand.

"J.R., you should be on top of the world. I recall when my first child was born. I was so happy and you could not tell me I was not the proudest man in the world. Matter of fact, one reason why I will never get back with my ex is not because she cheated on me but she took my kids away from me. I will always resent her for that." Loke became very serious while talking about his kids.

"How so Loke? I mean, couldn't you have gotten your kids?"

"J.R., you will learn that you can do that but over the years they had bonded more with their mom than with me, so I would not force them through such a drastic mental change. In situations like mine, I had to do what was best for my kids. I just miss them tremendously and they are growing up real fast." Loke was getting more and more saddened so I tried to lure the conversation back to the focus of my newborn.

"So you know how I feel Loke! I am a father of a beautiful baby girl. Lord, I want to thank you for sparing my wife and baby girl. Dominance Nicole is in the howoussse!   Loke, we must celebrate my brother.   I'm ready to do some serious dancing."

Chapter 13
Jewel on Fire

Mr. Carter, aren't you gonna take some baby convalescent leave? That is what men and women do nowadays, not just the women anymore." My secretary peeped her head in my office and asked me that question, which soon became a prelude to my laughter.

"Agnes, are you serious? That's for those weak guys. I don't need to take any convalescent leave. It's not like I did anything because my wife did all the work."

"Well Mr. Carter, I will assure you that times are changing now. Do you wake up at night to tend to the baby or does Mrs. Carter solely handle that responsibility?" Agnes was really starting to get nosy, and I really didn't feel like answering those personal questions.

"Actually Agnes, my wife prefers those honors. I mean, I can do the job, but she would not have it any other way." What I really refused to tell her was that hired help would eventually take over that job, but not until Evelyn was ready to give up the reigns.

"Don't you help out with her taking care of the baby or are you just one of those dads that tend to the baby during normal daytime hours?"

Here she goes again. Now Agnes was about to get on my last nerve with these questions. I was trying to focus on another presentation I had to present to the Mayor at next week's city council meeting. Three days had gone by since Evelyn delivered the baby. I had been out of the office for two of those days; now I was ready to get back to work. Just as I was getting ready to tell Agnes to give me some privacy, Jewel stepped into my office.

"I'm sorry Agnes and J.R., am I disturbing you two?" I

noticed that Jewel had a folder in her hand and as she entered the room, she acted unusually formal.

"Well actually Ma'am, Mr. Carter and I were having a discussion about the importance of both couples taking convalescent leave from work, after childbirth." Jewel looked at Agnes and then she stared at me, prior to commenting.

"J.R., you should take more time off so you can bond with Dominance Nicole during her first couple of weeks," Jewel said.

"Ma'am, I was just telling Mr. Carter that he should take some time off so he can mutually bond with his wife and child. Anyway, that's my two cents for the day." Agnes walked out of my office and left Jewel and I alone.

"J.R., we really do need to talk. I got an important announcement that I can no longer contain." I immediately pulled myself from my computer and gave Jewel my undivided attention.

"Jewel, thanks for interrupting me and Agnes. She was really starting to irritate me with that convalescent leave baby stuff. Now you have my complete attention. What's up? Is it anything urgent or extremely important? Is everything okay?"

Jewel quickly placed a letter down in front of me, without saying a word. I began reading the letter. Then, I stopped reading and looked up at Jewel in total disbelief, and then went back to reading the letter.

"Jewel, what in the world is this? Please tell me that this is some kind of joke." Jewel stood straight up, placed her hands on her hips and began to speak.

"J.R., you always told me that if I ever decided to leave this company, I should give you my one month notice; this is what I am now doing. I can no longer work for you. I'm terribly sorry, but I can't live a lie." I stood up from behind my desk with a shockingly surprised look on my face.

"What lie are you talking about Jewel? I am very confused at this point. Please tell me what you are talking about."

"I'm talking about you and Doralee, J.R. You should be ashamed of yourself. I trusted you like you were the royal knight in shining armor, but boy was I wrong."

I was simply devastated at the news coming out of Jewel's mouth. I felt literally defenseless. Although I wondered how Jewel found out, I was too weak physically to even play innocent. I looked down at the floor and began to talk to Jewel in a very evasive state.

"Jewel, please have a seat and close the door. We must talk about the entire incident. How did you find out?"

I looked aimlessly out into space as though I was in another world, just prior to returning to my seat. Jewel closed the door and came and sat in the closest chair to my desk.

"I just want you to know that I have always held you in such high esteem...more than any man I ever knew. But you know what, you all are nothing but liars, cheaters, and dogs." Tears started flooding her eyes and all I could do was remain totally quiet.

"The nerve of you two! You had to go and involve a kid, and bring him into your foolish affair." I lifted my head up with a puzzled look on my face.

"Jewel, I have no idea what you are talking about now. Other than the child she gave birth to, there was no other kid involved."

"Oh! You don't know huh? You mean your lover didn't

tell you what she was doing prior to her doing it? She didn't consult you about how she involved Ricky?" I gave the sternest look toward Jewel and I was getting really emotional.

"Jewel, I don't know anything about Ricky being involved, and Doralee is not my lover. I made a mistake with her one time and I have been regretting that mistake ever since. Now, what is this about Ricky?"

Jewel jumped up from the chair after I mentioned Ricky's name the second time and charged my desk while pointing her left forefinger at me as to deliver a threat.

"J.R., don't lie to me anymore! I want nothing from you, but the God forsaken truth, do you hear me? I cannot take another lie! You and Doralee have been seeing each other for quite sometime now and that's why you have been giving her pay raises. You are the father of her child and I bet you are still f-----g her, aren't you? Tell me the truth J.R. or I am done with this conversation and you will never see me again." I stood up from my desk with my hands out to Jewel as to plead for mercy.

"Jewel, I slept with Doralee just one time which was just prior to my wedding. I have not been seeing her at all. Instead, I have been trying to keep her quiet because she demands that I be a part of her life and apparently my other daughter's life. Please tell me what Ricky has to do with all of this. I am so very curious."

"J.R., I'm gonna tell you one more time not to lie to me." She pointed her left forefinger at me again as though she was threatening me two times over.

"Jewel, I have not lied about anything."

"J.R., you are telling me you slept with Mrs. Mayberry one time and that was prior to the wedding?"

"Yes! Do you remember that trip I made to Atlanta to interview possible candidates? I accidentally slept with her then."

"J.R., please don't you dare insult me with words like accidentally sleeping with someone. You did what you wanted to do. I knew you were acting funny when you came back from that trip. I even asked you if everything was okay and you said that you were just tired and thinking too much about who to hire. How in the hell does someone accidentally sleep with someone J.R.? That just doesn't make any sense whatsoever."

"I know Jewel, but it was clearly a mistake, an accident, an act that I had no intention of committing." I walked away from behind my desk and put my right hand on my forehead as I continued talking.

"Doralee came to my hotel room and said she had cooked dinner for me and I let her in. She insisted that I taste her special wine and eat some of her food. I went into the bathroom to wash my hands and when I came out, it happened."

"What happened J.R.?"

"I looked up and there she was nearly butt naked. I tried to get her to leave, but she wouldn't."

"What do you mean when you say you tried to get her to leave? Did you threaten her with the authorities?"

"No."

"Did you use force J.R. and demand that she leave? I mean you are much bigger than she is."

"No."

"Then how did you try to get her to leave? J.R., you better not lie to me or I'm outta here."

"I don't know Jewel. I told her to leave, but I did

eventually give in to her. I sort of lost my head and she went buck wild on me." Jewel stood directly behind me and she was listening with the intensity of a judge.

"J.R., you screwed her without using any protection?"

"Yes! I'm trying to tell you Jewel. It happened so fast and before I knew it, I was caught up in the moment."

"So now you have two daughters? One named Dominance Nicole and one named Jamie Randella? Did you name that girl after yourself J.R.?"

"No Jewel! I didn't even know I had a girl by Doralee until she called me one day out the clear blue sky. I was working in my office at home and she called and told me about the baby."

"J.R., you mean to tell me you got this woman calling you at your house? Are you out of your ever loving mind?" I turned around to face Jewel and I pleaded with her.

"Jewel, I did not give Doralee my number to my home office. I have no idea how she got that number."

"Why did you bring Ricky into this triangle?"

"Please tell me what you are talking about. How is Ricky involved with this? I did not involve him."

Jewel slowly walked away from me and then quickly swirled around with a very straight face.

"Doralee confronted Ricky with his so called baby sister at the conclusion of the McDonald's All American high school game. She showed Ricky the baby and all. Were you not aware of that?"

"Jewel, how could I have been aware of that? I had no idea that Doralee had done something else so foolish." I turned around and walked to the sofa adjacent to my desk and just stood there.

"She is really out of control and I am so sick of her. I

can't believe she would stoop to such a dirty level. My goodness! How is Ricky handling this?"

"Ricky is fine now. I asked him to keep this between us until I had a chance to talk this over with you and get to the bottom of the entire ordeal. He was truly devastated at the news, but mostly hurt that you had cheated on his mom."

The more we talked, the more depressed I became. I wished so badly that this was one of my dreams and I'd wake up from it and find that none of this ever really happened. First up, I experienced Doralee's blackmail attempts and then her pregnancy. Then, Loke gets shot. Not long after that, my wife experiences potentially losing our baby, which really scared the dickens out of me. Now, this debacle involving Doralee and Ricky will definitely hurt my relations with Ricky.

"I need to talk to Ricky and explain everything."

"J.R., you need to do a lot more than that and a lot sooner than that. You need to first take care of Doralee accordingly. Then you need to somehow figure out a way to tell Evelyn the truth. I cannot continue to have this boy blocked from talking to his mom about your other daughter. It's not fair to him nor is it fair to anyone else. You got decisions to make." Jewel turned to walk out the door.

"Jewel! Is that it? You just gonna walk out on me now after I have poured out my heart to you? I need you Jewel. I need you now, more than ever in my life. Please! Don't do this to me." Jewel quickly turned around.

"J.R., I'm not doing anything to you. You did all this to yourself. I can't believe you would risk your lovely bride for some trick in the night like Doralee. I can't believe you would put all your goods out for the snatching like that."

Jewel walked over and picked up her letter of resignation and tore it into shreds and then placed it in the garbage container. Her actions produced an astonished look on my face.

"Jewel, I made a serious mistake the night I slept with Doralee. I have not been unfaithful to Evelyn since that time. I'm serious! Scouts Honor!"

"J.R., don't throw that boys scout code at me like it means anything to me. Sidney used the same ploy. You have the chance to come clean now and tell me all I need to know to preclude any more hiccups. Who else is there?"

"Jewel, I promise you, there is no one else. I'm serious! Well, I mean...technically there is no one else." She started to walk towards the door again and I immediately followed.

"Jewel, I have been faithful to Evelyn since our marriage. However, since she has been pregnant, she does not want to have sexual intercourse. So, I kind of take long showers while I think about Miss Brownstone every now and then."

"J.R., please be serious! I really don't care to hear about who you are thinking about when you are relieving yourself in the showers okay. The actual act of infidelity is another thing. Now, as long as Miss Brownstone does not become reality, infidelity is not an issue. Therefore, we need to focus on that. Who the hell is Miss Brownstone anyway?"

"Jewel, she is just someone on the mayor's executive staff. We don't even know each other like that and trust me, we never will."

"Well J.R., if that is the case, why are you thinking

about her in the showers? Never mind J.R., we got bigger fish to fry anyway. You men are a trip!"

"Jewel, what do you think Evelyn will do once she finds out about Doralee?" Jewel looked at me and answered my question without batting an eye.

"If she hears about it appropriately from you, then recovery should be in sight. If not, she would probably be inclined to divorce you and take half." Her candid words hit me like a Barry Bonds' baseball bat hitting a ball over the fence for a home run.

"Jewel, are you serious? I mean, come on...I only slept with her for one night and that was prior to us ever getting married."

"J.R., you asked me and I gave you an honest answer, okay. You should have thought about all the consequences before you jumped in bed with that devilish woman." I looked down to the floor again as I processed in my mind the fate that awaited me when Evelyn would find out about my indiscretion.

"Wow! Jewel, what am I gonna do? I mean... sounds like I'm screwed."

"Well J.R., you are screwed, but we can't focus on that right now."

"What do you mean Jewel? What else will I be able to think about for the next 24 plus hours? I am screwed like a mug." Jewel got up, got a note pad and pen as we sat around my conference table and tried to come up with a plan to deal with all this drama in my life.

"Okay J.R., first things first. I will have Sidney's investigation team check out Doralee and see what we can find out." I immediately responded in disagreement.

"Jewel, please don't go messing around with that

woman. I don't want to give her any other reasons to try and screw me again."

"J.R., you need to sit your ass down, shut the hell up, and listen to me. You have lost the leadership role on resolving this case." I responded to her every call and sat down as I was told.

"Now, as I said before, I will have Sidney's investigation team check out Doralee. We will find out everything we can about her. Once that is done, I will advise you further."

"Well Jewel, what about Ricky? Can this investigation be determined real soon so I will know what to eventually say to Ricky and Evelyn?" Jewel stood up from the chair and leaned across the table just prior to sharing her words.

"J.R., you need to talk to both Ricky and Evelyn right away and make your confession known so they want hear worse information from anyone else."

I thought seriously about Jewel's words and I must admit, she was giving me good counsel. I still couldn't stop thinking about the fact that Evelyn might leave me for screwing Doralee.

"Well Jewel, what time frame are we looking at for Sidney's investigation team?" As soon as I said the word Sidney, I realized that Sidney was back in Jewel's life. I honestly had not given much thought about whether or not they were an item until that minute. I mean, I assumed he was relocating to make serious attempts to recover their relationship, but I was very reluctant to draw to any further conclusions.

"J.R., I need to attend a meeting, so please keep quiet about this investigation. I would not even mention this to Loke if I were you."

"Okay Jewel, my lips are sealed."

"You really don't need to be talking to Doralee either J.R. Try your best to avoid her at all costs, even if it means hanging up on her. I don't want her to have any hints that we are coming after her."

"I got you Jewel. Hey, thanks for being there for me once again. I can't imagine what I would ever do if you were not here for me." Jewel gathered her belongings and headed out my office.

"I got to run. I'll speak with you later."

Jewel rapidly left the office. Gosh, I went from feeling like being at the pit of hell to tasting some nice cool water. I'm glad that Jewel now knows the truth.

My very next hurdle, but not at this instant, would be trying to figure out a way to tell Evelyn, and pray that she does not leave me. I guess getting a fine woman can be one major accomplishment, but keeping her is definitely another, more phenomenal task. Lord help my life.

Chapter 14
Daddy Drama

While heading back home I was listening to Tupac's song called *Mama Raised A Hellraiser* when my cell phone suddenly rang.

"Hello, this is J.R."

"Son, can you turn down that noise." Snap! That was my dad. I immediately turned down the music, but not before he had a chance to hear the thumping, loud curse words of Tupac.

"Hey dad! How's it going?"

"Okay…ahhrah….did you wire the money yet?"

"I'm sorry dad. I totally forgot, but I will take care of it in about 30 minutes. Is that okay?"

"Yeah! I guess it will have to be okay. Can you increase the amount by another 5k? You know I'll pay you back real soon."

I hated when my dad would say he would pay me back because he has never paid me back. Nevertheless, I would still send him money. I really don't know what he does with all this money I have been sending him. I'm starting to feel slightly used, but I did not want to challenge dad just yet.

"Okay dad….hello…hello…" I lost the signal while talking to my dad so I checked my last incoming call for his number and hit the dial button.

"Hehehehe….hello" There was a woman laughing on the other line and I quickly looked at my cell phone to see if I had dialed the wrong number. The number was the correct number which was my dad's cell phone number.

"Give me that phone! I told you about answering my phone. You do it one more time and you better get to packing." I heard my dad speaking to someone and I could tell that he was trying to cover up the phone, but he was clearly blocking the wrong end of the phone.

"Oh yeah right! That's not what you said when you were busy packing my p----." My dad quickly interrupted the female voice in the background with a loud whisper.

"You better hush your mouth now. I told you I'm talking to my son. Shut your trap or I'll kick your ass out of here. I mean it." I clearly heard dad whispering to some woman. I always wondered whether or not my dad was cheating on my mom. I sure hope this was not the case.

"J.R., are you there?"

"I'm here dad. Who was that?"

"Who? Well, ahhrah...I was just having a discussion with the hotel maid. I told her I needed business taken care of or I would take my business elsewhere." I thought to myself, *why in the world does my dad have to make me out to be so stupid? Like I couldn't hear everything he said to that woman.*

"Are you still in Tennessee?" I asked.

"What...ahhrah...ahhrah....yeah! I'm still here...right here in Memphis, that's right." Dad was lying and I could tell.

"You been there for quite awhile huh dad?"

"What? Look here boy, you ask way too many questions okay. You know how the trucking industry is. Sometimes you can be on the road for days. Hurry up and wire me that money son. I want to surprise your mom with a real nice gift."

Dad sounded a little tipsy. I keep loaning or I should say giving money to my dad in exorbitant amounts. He always claimed that he was buying my mom some gift.

The problem is that she never got the gifts for some reason.

"Dad, I asked mom about that nice Cardigan sweater I bought for her when I was on Rodeo Drive in California. Do you remember? It's the one that you told me to get her that was actually a size eight, but mom wears more like a size 18."

"Look here boy! What's your point? What are you trying to say? You know I don't pay much attention to what size your mom wears. I need to go so you need to hurry up." I could tell my dad was getting very angry at the questions I was posing.

"I'm not trying to say anything dad, except that I just hope all this money is for mom, and not another woman." Ouch! I can't believe I had the audacity to say that to my dad.

"What did you say boy? You know you got some nerve talking to me like that. Now see, that's why you were the result of a one night stand. Your mom and I did not plan on having you, and now I think we should have had that abortion. I really don't appreciate you making these accusations of me."

"Dad, I'm just trying to make a point. I have asked mom about several gifts that you said you gave her but she always acts as though she has no idea what I am talking about."

"And what the hell has that got to do with the price of tea in China? You done pissed me off boy...all up in grown folks' business. You think because you making a little money that you all that. Your mom was so right about you. That money done went to yo head and it's blocking out your common sense."

"Dad I'm just saying that I'm not gonna keep giving you money so you can support other women at the expense of my mom. I don't mean to be disrespectful but I'm just making a point."

"Forget you boy! You ain't my God. That's why yo momma said you had to pay some project hoe with a child to marry you because you are a loser. Em was right about you all the time. I tried to give you the benefit of the doubt, but naw, she was right all the time."

Wow, those words hurt! I knew my mom did not approve of me marrying Evelyn, but I thought by now she was over that fact. When you think about how she responded to me when Evelyn was in labor, I guess she was still holding a grudge. Then out of the blue, the female voice once again surged out of nowhere.

"Henry, come on to bed baby. Leave the boy alone." All of a sudden I heard a loud slap as though a hand hit a face.

"B----h! I done told you to let me talk to my damn boy." I heard her crying from the words and the slap. I could not take it and I started to hang up the phone.

I told dad that I was going to let him go, and I was hanging up so he could take care of his business at hand.

"I ain't finished talking to you boy!" Then he shouted as though he was talking to his female companion again.

"Shut up b-----h! I ain't telling you no damn mo." I heard the female weeping in the background. I had to get off the phone as my dad was really being abusive to another woman, much like he had been to my mom until she hit him upside the head with a frying pan one day.

"Dad, I really need to go."

"Boy, you ain't going nowhere til I finish. Now, when

you gonna send me the money?" The female voice crying in the background was bothering my concentration and it was apparent that she and my dad were intoxicated.

"Dad, I got to go. I'm sorry but I'll talk with you later."

"Oh no you ain't boy! You gonna talk to me right now dammit."

"Bye dad!"

"Boy, if you hang up this phone on me you will be a fatherless son, do you hear me?"

"Henry, I can't believe you called me a b----h. I thought you loved me." The female sound lunged forth again.

"Jamie, Jamie, can you hear me boy?"

"I hear you dad but I can't deal with this anymore. You are cheating on my mom. I can't take this."

"You better shut the f---k up. You don't know what I'm doing and you better not repeat this to nobody. I knew I should have signed them damn abortion papers but no, I had to be too stupid. I better get that damn money today, do you hear me boy?"

"Henry, please don't hit me no more! Please don't call me a b----h no more Henry. Henry, please talk to me now." The female voice was getting louder and louder and I really could not take it anymore.

"Jamie, I want you to go straight to the bank right now." I hung up the phone. My dad called again but I did not answer so he left an ugly voice message.

I was so depressed as I replayed all actions in my mind that occurred today. I really did not feel like going home so I just deviated from my drive and went straight to Loke's house. I thought about the abortion that my dad had mentioned. I can't believe I was a mere mistake and a one night stand in which he and mom contemplated abortion. I also thought about him cheating on my mom which really added to my anger.

I sure hope Ricky don't think that about me in the same manner. I really got to rectify that situation. I can't believe my dad was cheating on my mom. I don't want to send him any money because I have no idea what my dad is doing with all this money. My heart was definitely troubled and I wanted to bounce some of these feelings off my boy Loke.

Thus, rather than taking all the stress I was feeling home, I elected to go straight over to Loke's place. I will say this about Loke; he does give me good counsel when I'm in my most stressful state. I guess that's a major reason why he is my boy and I'll do just about anything for him.

Chapter 15
Loke, My Brother's Keeper?

You betta not come nigga, you betta not come! Get all up in dere and bring it harder." Swish, swish, swish was the sound as Loke was back to his regular form tearing up some honey's backside. At least he thought he was hitting it hard as she was in a doggy style position.

"Oh! Oh! Good snatch baby! Good damn snatch! Oh! Oh," were the seductive sounds that Loke uttered.

"Man! It seems like it's been so long for me baby. Dang, this stuff is some kind of good."

"Don't-chu come on me. I need-ju to hit it harder. Come on and break me off now. Come on now, bring it harder."

"I'm hitting it as hard as I....oh....oh.... OHHHHHHH!! AWW," uttered Loke as he came.

"Damn yo soul, you came. Get off me." The woman pushed Loke away from her.

"Is dat all you got? Dang, dat was a waste of my time." Loke quickly began to explain, as he was slightly out of breath.

"Oh see....ya...you don't understand. My health condition has made me come prematurely because I'm normally the last one to come."

"Yeah right! So what happened to you jest nigh? You so full of yoeself dat it makes no sense."

In the midst of their conversation, I rang the doorbell, expecting Loke to answer the door while seeing his cars parked in his garage. I had no clue as to where Loke was located in his house. However, Loke on the other hand, looked quickly outside the tinted window of his Escalade and saw my car.

"Damn!"

"What-chu damn about?" Said the woman.

"That's J.R. at my door. I recognize his car."

"So! What's wrong wit dat?"

"Ahm, it's a long story, but he doesn't want me seeing you."

"Ont see why not, Puhlease! What's wrong wit-chu seeing me? He's a married man so why should he care?"

"Well, he seems to think it's taboo for me to be interested in you because you are Evelyn's twin sister." Loke began to get dressed as he was talking.

"So what-chu got to say bout all dat? Hi u feel?"

Teralyn was getting dressed too as she spoke. Loke spotted me from the corner mirror on his garage top. That mirror enabled him to see the front of his house.

"Dang, he is still looking around for me and still ringing my doorbell. I guess having both car garage doors up with both my vehicles parked does give the indication that I'm home."

"Ont know why you trippin. I told yo ass to close the garage doe, but naw you wanted to be bold. Ain't studding J.R. and I could care less bout what he thanks," said Teralyn as she was about to get out of the truck.

I was still ringing the doorbell and then I finally got smart and decided to call Loke on his cell phone. No sooner than I rang his cell did I hear the distinct sound of his phone ringing. He responded to the phone ringing in his truck.

"Oh shoot! My phone is way up in the front, underneath the driver's seat," said Loke to Teralyn.

"Ont know why you stressin about dis. If you don't answer, you jest don't answer," said Teralyn.

I looked off to the side of the house where Loke's garage was and where I parked. I walked to where I heard the distinct sound of his phone which led me towards his garage. There, I saw the foggy windows of his truck as I heard Loke's phone ringing loud and clear. When I realized that Loke was indisposed, I proceeded towards my car. I did continue to let his phone ring however.

"Hello," Loke finally answered his phone.

"Hey man, I apologize. I see you busy so let me talk with you later on."

"Sure J.R.! You know how it is. I'll give you the details later. I had to break my truck in. You know how it is." Then Loke said some words that made no sense to me.

"Hey! Where are you going? Don't do that! What are you doing?"

"What's that Loke? I was just gonna hang….." I could not complete the sentence as I saw why Loke was in the background pleading, as sweet walking Teralyn got out the truck and walked towards me. I thought to myself *that hard headed son of a gun. I told him not to mess with Teralyn and here he is screwing her in his new truck parked inside his garage, during broad daylight. Loke will never seem to learn.* Teralyn walked towards me like she was Miss Baddass.

"Well Loke, I guess we need to talk." I hung up my cell phone as Teralyn approached me right away.

"Ont appreciate-chu bad mouthing me." While Teralyn was talking to me, Loke was composing his clothes appropriately as he came running behind Teralyn. He did not notice, but his shirt had gotten caught inside his zipper as the shirt tail was sticking out.

"Teralyn, I have not bad mouthed you and I don't know

what you are talking about. I do wonder what you are doing over here at Loke's house though."

Loke closed in on our conversation. He was sweating and breathing heavy indicating that he was really out of shape.

"Hey J.R., what's going on man? I was just showing Teralyn the inside of my new Escalade."

Can you believe he was trying to cover up the truth? It was obvious from the fogged-up windows in his truck that something fishy was going on inside.

"Yeah Loke, I'm sure you were." I stood there with a sarcastic look on my face, indicating the displeasure of finding him in that position with my wife's sister, Teralyn.

Teralyn was just staring at me with her fine self, constantly reminding me of Evelyn. She just stood there with her hands on her hips.

"Hey man, I just wanted to stop by and check on you. I think I better get home and see whose helping my wife take care of the baby. It's obvious the person she flew here to handle that responsibility is not there to do the job." Teralyn walked up on me like she was ready to fight.

"Ain't nobody studding you J.R.? I do a good job and dat's why you can go to work like you do. You need to leave me alone." I looked at Teralyn and Loke quickly intervened.

"Hey man, you got time to come in and have a few hooks? I got some of those nonalcoholic natural drinks from the islands. You know, the ones that you love."

Loke knew he hit one of my weaknesses with those island drinks. I don't know who his source for those drinks were, but he definitely had the hookup when it came to obtaining those drinks. Teralyn looked at Loke as though she was disappointed that he invited me inside.

"Loke, thanks for the invite man, but I do need to get on home and handle my business." Teralyn walked past me and went into Loke's house. Loke had the look of guilt in his eyes.

"Hey J.R., we really do need to talk about Teralyn when you slow down man." I was walking to my Lex and Loke trailed me. I turned around quickly in disgust.

"Loke, there is nothing for us to talk about. I told you to stay clear of Teralyn and you are already screwing her in your truck. I guess you two have already christened the whole house as well, huh?" Loke threw his hands up in the air like he was really pissed. Then, he pointed his right finger at me as he began to talk.

"Man, you really don't understand. I am seriously falling for Teralyn. I can't keep her off my mind since the first day I saw her at your house." I pushed Loke away from me.

"I'm sure you are Loke! You said the same about Jewel and Julie too for that matter. You are always in love at first, and then you revert back to your normal ways. I asked you nicely to stay away from my wife's twin and look at you now."

"J.R., what the hell do you want from me man? I am just as human as you are. No one could talk you out of marrying Evelyn so, you of all people, know what it's like when you meet that proverbial Miss Right." I looked at Loke like he was clearly losing his mind and my anger begin to really set in.

"Loke, how many times I got to hear this from you. At first you said that Jewel was the one, then you swore it was Julie, and now my wife's twin is the one. You are so full of it Loke. All you care about is satisfying your own desires. You don't care anything about Teralyn. I know you too well man."

"J.R., you are really starting to piss me the f--k off. You don't know what I see in Teralyn so kill the foolishness dude."

"I know what you see Loke. You see some new coochie to satisfy your lustful appetite, for what Loke? Will she be on the one month program or the two month program? How long will she last?"

"That's it J.R. Get the hell off my lawn right now. You don't have any respect for my feelings." I went to my car, opened the door, and was getting ready to leave.

All of a sudden, Teralyn came out Loke's house with her garment bag. She turned to Loke and gave him a quick smooch on the lips.

"Hey baby, where you going?" Loke said.

"I'll call you later. I'll jest catch a ride wit J.R. on back to da house."

Loke looked at her as though she was leaving him for good with no intention to return. Teralyn continued on as she attempted to open the passenger door to my car. I just watched her.

"Can you please open da doe?"

"You sure you want to ride home with me?"

"Not really, but I might as well. Nigh, open da damn doe."

"Excuse me! You watch your tone Teralyn. If you think you are going to get into my ride with that attitude, you got another thang coming. Now, as I see it, you are the one in need, not me. I suggest you come correct!"

Teralyn stood there and folded her arms and just

stared at me with a nasty smirk on her face. Since I seemingly silenced her for the moment, I quickly snapped the unlock switch on my door, letting her get into the car.

Loke just stared and then he turned around and walked back toward his house. Then, all of a sudden, he stopped and ran over to the driver side of my car and insulted me.

"Make sure you realize that she is your wife's twin and not your wife. You hear me?" I rolled my eyes at him and then I countered.

"I don't have a problem knowing what's mine and what's not. You had that problem from the first night we met, remember?"

I quickly drove off while leaving Loke standing there. He kicked his foot into the air like he was clearly upset. As I was driving away from Loke's house, Teralyn initiated conversation with me.

"What da hell waz yawl talkin bout?"

"Nothing that I care to discuss with you," was my disgusted reply.

"Ont know why you tryin to pretend like you don't want Loke gettin to know me. If I didn't know any betta, I'd think you waz interested in me yoself." Teralyn stared at me as I was driving to my house.

"Not interested in you in that way! You are my wife's twin sister and I would never cheat on her." I didn't even bat my eyes nor look her way as I spoke.

"Nigga you don't gots to lie to me. I know da deal."

I quickly looked at her, wondering if she knew about Doralee. I know her and Ricky were very close, so I thought for a moment that he might have told her.

"I know bout-cho little secret. So don't be playin me

like I'm some bimbo lost in da dark."

I had to pretend like I was above her words to preclude showing her my card. I was not about to discuss any of my wrong doings with Teralyn.

"Teralyn, I have no idea what you are referring to and I would appreciate it if you did not bring this type of drama into my house. I am not trying to welcome controversy at all."

"J.R., as I see it, you need me. I know you ain't had none from E for quite sometime." She started to chuckle.

"I jest want-chu to know it's a well kept secret wit me."

"Well-kept secret? Is that what you're referring to?" I was really anxious to hear her reply.

"Dat's right big boy! I betcha yo friend Loke don't know dat you ain't got none since E been pregnant."

She started to laugh again, but honestly I almost felt like laughing because I was too worried that she knew more, and totally relieved that she did not. Gosh, *I have got to resolve this emotional time bomb real soon*, were the thoughts that permeated my mind.

As we pulled up to my house, Ricky was outside playing with Oscar. After he saw me pull up, he just kind of looked away from my car which was very difficult for me to bear. This bothered me because he had avoided me ever since he returned from the tournament in Atlanta.

Today, I was determined to speak with him, as I was not about to lose my step son. I remembered the good times when we used to go to war with each other while engaging in play station 2 into the wee hours o the morning and spend numerous hours competing on the basketball court. All of our male bonding had recently changed, and I had to find some way to restore those

144

times. Lord, it's time for me to get my step son back. I miss him way too much and I can't let this drama continue to keep us apart.

Chapter 16
Eyes Dripping Sweat

I called out Ricky's name as he was about to rush into the house. I had sorely missed the times we used to share. Now, I was compelled to reconnect with him. I rapidly approached my step son.

"Hey champ, what's going on man?"

I could tell that Ricky was not really interested in having a conversation with me, as he kind of looked away and displayed no excitement to see me.

"Hey J.R., where is Aunt Teralyn?"

Ricky did not see Teralyn get out of my car and run into the house. She wanted to take a shower since she had engaged in having sex with Loke and was probably conscious of her fragrance. At least that was my story, and I was sticking to it. Nevertheless, I gave Ricky the appropriate words regarding Teralyn.

"She rushed in the house to check on your mom and the baby. I don't think she realized that you were out here."

I thought maybe I would try and get Ricky to at least talk to me. I pushed him like the kids did at school when he would do something great on the basketball court.

"What's going down man? What have you been up to? You know I been nice to you lately because I have not had a chance to wear them hind parts out in play station 2. I bet you been practicing quite a bit."

I was determined to carry on with Ricky in conversation as though nothing had happened, even though I knew he was affected by Doralee's treacherous actions.

"I haven't practiced nor played in quite awhile J.R. I've

been too tired lately. After playing with my baby sister, I usually go right to bed."

I quickly changed the subject.

"Hey Ricky, let's go change into some basketball clothes so I can take you out on the court. You know I owe you a beating since you won your last trophy."

I pushed Ricky again and then grabbed him in my arms. He was still reluctant to say much, but he did agree to a game of basketball.

"J.R., I'll meet you in the gym in about 10 minutes to give you another beating."

He said that without any emotion and just went straight into the house. I went inside and as soon as I spoke with Evelyn and kissed her forehead, I played with my baby girl. Evelyn was in the bedroom watching taped recordings of old soap opera shows. She called that time of the day, her time. So, I really tried not to disturb her at all. I don't even think she noticed me much as I went in and out of our bedroom. Nevertheless, my little baby was laying in the bassinette and I played with her for a moment before hitting the basketball court.

"Hey gurl! How are you doing? Daddy is finally home so now you can kick and smile and make all the noise you like."

I kept rubbing my baby girl's cheeks and I melted when she looked up into my eyes and smiled. I got very excited and quickly shared with Evelyn my joy.

"Evelyn, she is actually smiling at me like she knows I am her father. It's amazing."

"J.R., she smiles at everybody honey. I hope you are not putting your hands in her face without washing them first. You know babies can pick up germs very easily so please go and wash your hands before you play with her like that. I can't believe I have to tell you that everyday. I can understand having to tell Ricky because he is a kid, but you are a grown man."

I thought to myself, *here we go again. I guess I should expect another lecture from Evelyn. She acted like I was gonna poison my baby or something. Sometimes she really got on my last nerve. What she needed to be doing was out there walking with her sister Teralyn so she could lose all that weight she gained. Instead, she is in here barking up at me like I got a problem, with her chubby self.*

"J.R., you ready?" Ricky walked into our bedroom.

"Ricky, I told you about barging into my room without knocking. Go back right now and knock on the door like you should. You are so hard headed."

"But mom, J.R. said..," Evelyn quickly interrupted Ricky.

"Boy, did you hear what I said? I'm not gonna tell you no more now."

I winked at Ricky and told him I would be right out. Then I quickly changed into some shorts, a tee shirt, and my Jordan basketball shoes before I went to my gym.

I noticed when I arrived that Teralyn was in there with Ricky and they were just shooting around with the basketballs in the gym. Ricky was trying to demonstrate to Teralyn how to shoot free throws.

"Ricky, you are wasting your time with Teralyn. She can't even dream about hitting a basket, okay." We both started laughing.

"Bump you J.R.! I bet I can beat-chu in a game of basketball cause you don't look dat good at all." Ricky looked at Teralyn and nodded his head.

"Ricky, you better tell her something before she gets her feelings hurt." Ricky quickly interjected his slant on the conversation.

"Aunt T, you can't beat J.R. right now, but I'll beat him for you. You welcome to stay and watch if you like."

"Oh I'ma do jest dat. I would love to see him get tow up cause he talk too much Ricky."

Ricky started laughing and I did too, and then we started playing a game. Before we totally engaged, I had to talk my last bit of junk to Teralyn.

"Yeah T, you stick to helping pregnant women and babies and leave the men alone. Consider yourself forewarned. Ahahahahaha!"

I went right into instant laughter and it really felt good being able to pick on Teralyn.

"Ricky, kick his as...ahh...Oops...Ricky kick his butt for me, okay."

"Okay, Aunt T," said Ricky.

The game started with us just kind of playing around at first and we did not even play seriously, but then something happened. All I know was that I scored twice on Ricky and I, of course, knew that I could not beat Ricky. Towering now at about 6 foot 5 and weighing about 194 pounds, Ricky was still as quick as any kid in the game. Thus, I kind of figured that Ricky had no intentions of playing me seriously as I posed no threat to really beating him, as his skills had soared way past mine.

Nevertheless, he had a cheerleader in Teralyn and a very competitive challenger in me, if not but only in my mind.

"Kick his butt Ricky! Don't let him have any room to brag at all," shouted Teralyn as she sat in the bleacher seats. Then, her cell phone rang and she walked out of the gymnasium.

"Ricky, looks like your cheerleader has gone," I said to him just chiding while pointing Teralyn's way. He laughed at the comment. I did notice that his game became very loose as though he was going to let me win. I started talking junk, thinking he would spot me to a certain score, all to beat me ragged. I drove to the hoop and easily went by Ricky for a lay-up and out of nowhere he crammed down on me with a hard foul. He knocked me to the floor and my body felt as though it was hit by a freight train. I looked up at Ricky as I laid in pain on the floor.

"Yo man! What in the world are they teaching you all these days? That was well beyond a hard foul Ricky. I don't know if I can even get up."

I laid on the court for a minute and noticed that I did not hear Ricky's voice. I turned around and he was standing there with tears running down his cheeks.

"Come on Ricky! It's not that serious okay. I'll be fine." Ricky just continued to stare at me.

"It is that serious J.R. You don't like my mom anymore?" He started breathing real heavy and even started crying.

"Ricky, what on earth are you talking about?" I rolled over and realized my back was somewhat out, but I was able to at least position myself to sit up.

"You cheated on my mom! Why?"

I was shell shocked and speechless as I looked up from the floor position at this mountain of a kid. The sight was not so pretty as he was crying like a baby. Nevertheless, I knew I had to have this conversation with Ricky but I really did not know when to engage. Thus, I guess now was as good a time as any.

"Ricky, first of all, it happened before we were married. I had been drinking and I just really made a big mistake."

He just continued to stare at me as I spoke, but he did not even bat an eye.

"My real dad used to cheat on my mom and he would beat her too. I still hate him for that. I thought that you could be trusted though. I thought you were different."

His eyes were ever so piercing as I was feeling the intensity of his stare. Although he was a kid at heart, I knew Ricky had the strength of a bear. I was speechless. I had to fight for the right words because I did not want to lose this kid. He meant way too much to me.

"Ricky, you don't know how sorry I am for being so stupid. The mere fact that I can't make this go away eats at me day and night. All I can say is that I am sorry. I will never cheat on your mom again and I love her very much. I also know that I must tell her and I will do that real soon."

He continued to stare at me as though he was trying to believe me.   The tears kept coming down his face. I had to ask him one more question just for my own sanity.

"Ricky, who else have you spoken to about this other than Jewel?" He quickly replied without even blinking his eyes.

"I have not told anyone. Jewel told me to keep quiet and I have not said anything. I don't want to hurt my mom but you need to know that she means the world to me. She wouldn't cheat on you."

"Son, I know she wouldn't. I would not normally cheat on anybody. Now, since we have been married, I have never cheated on your mom. That happened before we got married."

"But J.R., is there really a difference? My math teacher would always say that a person is gonna do what a person is gonna do, regardless of circumstances. He said the heart of a man dictated his actions."

I thought to myself, *dang*! How the hell am I supposed to respond to that? The words alone ripped through my heart like a hollow point bullet. Nevertheless, I had to recapture my stepson.

"Ricky, your math teacher is totally correct. All I can say is that it will never happen again and I need you to trust me on that. I got to find a way to tell your mom and pray that she forgives me so that I can stop feeling so paranoid."

Ricky came down to me on the floor and for some reason he just hugged me as tears continued to trickle down his face. I wiped the tears from his eyes.

"I love you son. I apologize for hurting you and your mom. I promise I will right this wrong."

Tears took over my eyes and I fought crying, but then it happened.

"I, I...am...so sorry."

Tears fell down like water from the Niagara Falls as I broke down completely. I continued to talk although it was very difficult.

"I wish I could replay that night over again so badly." Then I paused and got silent and began to cry like a man cried. Though the tears fell down uncontrollably, no sound was made, while a straight, non eye blinking facial expression only is displayed. Ricky then started wiping tears from my eyes and before you knew it, we were both having the most genuine father/son moment. We just breathed one another's air and held each other for an

Alabama minute. Then, I saw Teralyn entering back into the gym.

"Hey man, your aunt is coming so act like you are helping me up so she won't ask too many questions. Let's wipe the tears from our eyes like we are wiping sweat off our brow from competing in basketball."

Ricky just smiled, but then complied. He got up first and then he helped me up.

"Why ain't I surprised? Dat's what-cho ole butt gets. Tryin to play ball like you all dat."

I had to respond back to Teralyn to hide the special moment that Ricky and I shared. It was truly a moment overdue for both of us.

"Naw....see....you missed my shot. I just kind of hurt my back which is an old injury from playing back in the day."

Oh my goodness! My back was really hurting badly and I really did need Ricky to help me balance and walk.

"Yeah right J.R.! I can't wait to tell E dat she done married a man with a weak back, nahnahnahnahnah!"

Ricky obviously felt sorry for me and chimed in while he was helping me walk.

"But Aunt T, J.R. won the game. He actually beat me."

I knew Ricky was being nice. I had to maintain my junk talking image with Teralyn.

"Yeah...ahm, that's right Ricky...tell her the deal...I, ahm, I won the game....yeah, that's right."

I sounded off, knowing that Ricky really didn't even compete with me. That's some maturity I am seeing in him. Why should he waste his skills beating up on someone who literally no longer brought him any competition?

"Whateva! Dat little bit I saw, Ricky won't even playin but he was jest letting you do stuff."

We exited the gym and went into the long hallway of my house. As soon as we walked through the door, I saw Rosie, the maid, walking down the hallway. I noticed that she just looked around and saw us and just started walking briskly ahead for some reason.

"Teralyn, all I got to say is that once I get my back healthy again, I can take you out on the court and snatch yo dreams away anytime. You will respect my game before you leave here."

Ricky and I chuckled together as he continued to help me walk. Teralyn was just walking slightly ahead of us and still talking noise. As soon as we entered the central area of the house, Teralyn was quick to tell Evelyn what happened as Evelyn looked on with shock.

"E, you need to come get yo broke back ass husband." Evelyn quickly corrected Teralyn.

"T, don't you see Ricky right there? I told you about cursing around my son."

Teralyn quickly looked at the fingernails of her left hand while placing her right hand on her hips, and smacking her lips.

"Chile Puhlease! Ricky done heard more den dat, Okay! You need to chill!"

Evelyn was staring at me with greater intensity as Ricky continued to help me to my bedroom.

"Okay, don't tell me! J.R., you tried to make some miraculous move on the court and got hurt again?" Ricky quickly tried to explain.

"Mom, it was my fault. I fouled him too hard and hurt his back."

I looked at Evelyn with an expression of pain on my face.

"Ricky, I hear what you are saying, but I have told J.R. time and time again that he needs to stop playing ball with you young boys. For that matter, he needs to quit playing against you. One day it's the knees and the next day it's the back. That's okay! He will listen to me one day."

I just looked at Ricky with one of those see what I got to put up with looks and we both just smiled. Teralyn's phone rang out loudly.

"Hey Loke, what-chu doin?"

Just the sound of his name, knowing that they were hooking up, seemed to make my back hurt a little harder. She sped off towards the other part of the house. Ricky helped me lay down on my bed and Evelyn trailed behind us.

"I'll run you some bath water J.R. so you can soak in the tub," said Evelyn.

"Thanks baby! You took the words right out of my mouth. Please put some Epsom salt and baking soda in the water, along with my bubble bath soap."

Evelyn ran the water and Ricky helped me take off my socks and sneakers and then Evelyn returned back into the bedroom.

"J.R., did you talk to Ricky about his name?"

I knew that I had complained to Evelyn about people calling Ricky the name Chronic, but knowing what he and I shared, I was not about to mess with him at all. He was my current hero. I also knew that Ricky's former name was changed and I had balked about it before, but not anymore.

"What about Ricky's name? I knew you had his name

changed to Ricky Carter from Ricky Lyles and I don't have any problem with that."

"No baby, I'm talking about that name Chronic."

"Mom, that's just what people call me. They don't mean any reference at all to marijuana."

Evelyn quickly darted her eyes at Ricky.

"Ricky, once again, you are in the room, but this is an A and B conversation. Be quiet sweetie and C your way out of our conversation, and let J.R. and I talk."

"Evelyn, it's just kid talk baby. When I was a superstar ballplayer, they used to call me a nickname too. Those kids are innocent and harmless. They don't mean bad by it."

Evelyn looked at me as though she was completely surprised at my reply. I did kind of switch up on my perspective without telling her.

"J.R., what nickname did they call you back in the day?" Ricky inquired.

"Hold up now son! You say back in the day like it was a century ago. Anyway, they used to call me Broken Ankles because whenever someone guarded me, I would shake them so badly to where it was equivalent to them breaking their ankles on the court."

We all started laughing but Evelyn, like normal, was persistent about her inquiry.

"Okay J.R., so you have no problem with Ricky being called Chronic?"

"None whatsoever baby! As long as he knows not to mess with any funny cigarettes or cigarettes at all, I don't have any problem with it."

"J.R., I don't smoke nor do I intend to ever do that. Some guys at school do, but Jewel told me that smoking and alcohol does not mix with the professional athlete's profile." Evelyn quickly commented.

"Ricky, are you telling us that this was the first time that you have ever heard anything regarding alcohol and cigarettes?" Ricky looked at Evelyn as though she took him totally off guard. Evelyn did not give him a chance to respond.

"Never mind boy! I have spoken to you on numerous occasions about this same subject. Now, speaking of Jewel, J.R. where has she been?"

Evelyn hinted to Ricky to leave the room by staring at him and pointing at the door.

"Ricky, give J.R. and I some privacy. Did you clean your room up?"

"Mom, I thought that was why we had a maid."

"Boy, I have told Rosie to stay out of your room because I want you to handle your own responsibilities. You are too spoiled."

"Mom, when I come home everyday from practice, my room is already cleaned." Evelyn shifted her attention back to me.

"J.R., we need to talk. I have major issues with that maid. Go ahead Ricky and give us some privacy. Stay away from your sister's room because she's been sound asleep now for quite awhile, so don't you go in there playing with her. I'm serious Ricky."

Ricky quickly left the room as I proceeded to climb into the bath tub.

"J.R., I am so sick and tired of Rosie. She walks around this house like she got something to hide. Sometimes she is whispering on that phone and she stares at me all the time like she's about to steal something."

I quickly came to the defense of Rosie. But I really wanted to hear what Evelyn had to say about Jewel as she had mentioned her name and then got distracted.

"Evelyn baby, a maid is just being a maid. Rosie is just trying to handle the responsibility of maintaining the house baby. I don't know why you hate on her so much, but you do what you feel you must do. What were you getting ready to say about Jewel?"

"Oh no J.R., before I get to Jewel, I got a bone to pick with you." I became immediately concerned.

"What's up Evelyn?"

"Why are you hooking my sister up with Loke? I realize he is sick and everything, but J.R., you know Loke has a reputation."

"Evelyn, I did not hook Teralyn up with Loke. They met one day when she returned from walking Oscar, all clad in skimpy attire and all." Evelyn quickly interrupted me.

"J.R., don't even try it. I told you not to complain to me about my sister before I had her flown in here. Don't even try and turn this around."

"I'm not trying to turn anything around Evelyn. You didn't tell me that your sister dressed everyday like she's at a strip club. Also, you told me not to complain about your aunt."

"J.R., don't even try to change the subject. I don't know if I feel comfortable with her messing with Loke. I don't want him using my sister."

"Evelyn, I perfectly understand, but Loke acts like she got him all open and everything."

"J.R., who is Loke not open for?"

"I understand Evelyn. I just want you to know I had

nothing to do with them hooking up. I am not the one. The night that you had Dominance Nicole was when the two of them did their collaborating. Loke knows that I do not approve."

Evelyn looked with an offended facial expression.

"Why don't you approve J.R.?"

Darn! I really did not want to go down this road. I had to respond to that question from another angle. I just found it hard for me to tell Evelyn that Loke seeing her twin sister was too uncomfortable for me.

"I just don't think they are a fit for one another Evelyn, that's all."

"J.R., what are you trying to say? Are you trying to say that Loke is too good for my sister?"

Oh Lord! Here we go again. I got to find a way to change this subject.

"Baby, why would I think that? I just don't want any drama to develop with that relationship that would make it's way to our house. That's all I'm saying. It's all good. Now Evelyn, what were you gonna ask me about Jewel?"

Evelyn paused with a lengthy stare up towards the ceiling as though her mind shifted to another subject.

"Oh! I just noticed that Jewel does not stay at the house anymore and I just wondered why."

"Well, I think she has been real busy lately and I also think that she was sensitive to the bond that you and Teralyn have and did not want to be a distraction."

"J.R., Jewel is no distraction. I really enjoyed her presence and company here at the house. It really feels strange that she no longer stays here. You know my sister thinks the two of you are screwing each other?"

Those words made me jerk my back as I was lying in

the tub and Evelyn was sitting on a stool next to the bath tub.

"Somehow Evelyn, that does not surprise me. Teralyn does not know our chemistry and any outsider would assume such."

"Well, that's why I think Jewel should continue to come to the house like usual. I mean, even Ricky asked me why Jewel no longer stayed at the house."

"Evelyn, I recommend that you talk to Jewel about that. I must also inform you that her ex-boyfriend is also in town. Now, whether or not they are spending time together, I don't know. I do know that she has employed his professional services however."

"But J.R., I thought Jewel was seeing Corey?"

"Now see Evelyn, don't get me to lying. That's why yawl need to talk. I believe she is seeing Corey, but I think she has begun to view him differently; something about how she always found long strands of blonde hair at his New York apartment whenever she went to visit."

"Really J.R.? So Corey is cheating on Jewel too?"

"Evelyn, I really don't know about all that now. I'm just telling you what she told me. Now please don't repeat this to Jewel. Most of the time, I just act like I'm not even listening to her when she talks about Corey. I don't know what's going on. Please get it from the horse's mouth."

"MMM! I sure hope he's not cheating because that poor woman has tolerated cheating men for a long time. I would be very surprised if she got back with her ex-boyfriend after he did all that mess to her. I tell you what, if you ever cheated on me honey, it would clearly be the end of our relationship. Ricky's no good dad cheated on me once and I kicked him to the curb so fast that he became addicted to drugs. I don't play that mess."

My goodness! This conversation had truly taken a turn for the worse. I was actually planning on telling Evelyn about Doralee, but her words just persuaded me otherwise. Dang!

"Evelyn, so Jewel's ex-boyfriend took her through a lot of mess?'

"Show nuff! Didn't she tell you? As much time as you all spend together I figured she would have told you everything."

"Not necessarily honey! Jewel has not told me any detail about her ex. She gives me bottom line messages minus the details."

"Oh well, my bad! You didn't hear anything from me."

"Naw Evelyn, I want to know what happened."

"J.R., if Jewel did not tell you, I won't tell you. Besides, she told me a lot of stuff in confidence. Now, not to change the subject, but my sister has expressed interest in possibly working in this area."

I started coughing at the sound of those words, and created such a wave in the tub that some of the water overflowed onto the floor.

"Really baby? What does she plan on doing?"

"Well J.R.," she immediately came closer to me and started rubbing my chest.

"That's where you come in."

"Evelyn, what do you mean?"

"Baby, can't you find a nice job for her somewhere in your company? She would really be a great asset."

"Evelyn, I don't know about that honey. I have to really check and see what is available."

Evelyn made this loud teeth sucking sound as she sat

161

straight up on the stool.

"Check and see what's available? J.R., didn't you tell me that you were gonna create a job for your Cousin Mike? If so, why can't you create a job for Teralyn? I mean, she is my sister, J.R., and we all know that your Cousin Mike does have issues."

"Evelyn, I understand honey. I'm just saying I need to give it some thought. The only reason why I was creating a job for Cousin Mike was so he could stop leeching off my mom. I'm trying to help my family out as much as I can."

"Baby I don't have no problem with that as long as you realize that my family is your family too so you need to help out both sides."

"Okay baby, I feel you. I'm just saying I want to make the right move, that's all." She rubbed my chest again.

"I knew you would see it my way baby. Think about it while I think about trying to fit into my new Victoria Secrets' outfit."

Oh shoot! Somebody hold me down. Then again, there was no need to because my back was already doing the job.

"Evelyn, how you gonna do that now, knowing that my back ain't acting right?"

"J.R., your back might not be acting right, but as long as all other parts of your body work, it will be all good. You feel me?"

I looked up towards the ceiling of my bathroom and I thought about how Michael Baisden would respond on his radio talk show when he would hear words that brought him joy. He would jubilantly utter out from the excitement of some news or information, "That's my GURLL."

Chapter 17
The Thickness Missed

Who in the hell is J.R.? And how many frigging times are you gonna keep mistakenly calling me by his name? I mean, come on Veronica, it ain't funny no more."

Veronica was somewhat busted! She had tried to move on from my world since I informed her over a year ago that I was getting married and would not see her again.

"I'm sorry Scoont. You just remind me so much of J.R."

However, she immediately thought to herself, *okay, I lied to him again. He is nothing like J.R. I can't believe this is the third guy I have been with since J.R. and he is just as tow up as the first two. I mean, nobody brought it in bed like J.R. did. I thought by now that I would be over him and I darn sure have tried, but it just seems that as time lingers on, I am still battling feelings of love for that man. Sexually, I missed his thickness, his richness, his get up and go quickness. I also missed his companionship. I missed his unique way of laughing, how he smiled with that little boy-like charm. I missed the passion he showed when he made love to me. He would make it clearly his first and foremost interest to please me. I would see the magnetism and attraction in his eyes. I mean, I know he is currently married and all, but I love him just like he was mine and it still feels as though I just made love to him on yesterday. Oh well, back to my bed of hell.*

"Veronica! Veronica!"

While Veronica was thinking about me, her current lover was calling her name. Then, all of a sudden, she snapped out of it.

"I'm sorry once again Scoont. I really do have a lot of stress going on and I have been distracted with my personal issues. Perhaps this just wasn't a good idea. I really do feel like I led you on."

Scoont leaned over and placed his arms around Veronica, knowing this was just too good for him.

"Veronica, what are you saying baby? I understand if you have been distracted with problems, but I sure ain't trying to lose you baby. I tell you what; I'll just look over you calling me J.R. for now. Is that okay baby? I'm definitely not trying to lose out on this stuff." Veronica felt so defeated in her thinking alone.

Just as I thought! He too will settle for me calling him whatever name that comes out of my mouth. I cannot continue to date these losers. I have been trying my best to move on, but J.R. is someone I just cannot seem to recover from. I really cannot continue to go on this way.

"Well Scoont, perhaps we should slow down and just get to know each other for real. We did kind of jump in the hay rather fast."

"Veronica, we dated for four months before we even kissed or did anything. That was a first for me. I think we just got to get used to each other's body."

"Oh really? Is that what it is?"

Veronica was not so convinced, but Scoont continued to drop his rap.

"That's right baby. Now, making love to you is almost like being in heaven baby. I love your body and I feel so emancipated being inside of you."

Veronica listened to her current lover, but deep in her mind she was still not feeling Scoont. *He can talk all the sweet words he likes, but he really just doesn't do it for me.*

I think about how J.R. would hit all my erotic zones. Making love to him left me so sore that I could barely walk the next day and that was a feeling that I totally enjoyed. I mean J.R. had me floating. He knew how to excite every inch of my body and now I feel like a drug addict in need of a fix, but what can I do? He is married and gone. I would even pay to get him to put his hands on me, if only for 30 minutes. God! That would be so nice.

"Scoont, I got to go because I have so much work to do."

Veronica, all of a sudden, had to leave Scoont. She could no longer bear going through the motions.

"But Veronica, I thought you were off today. Why do you have to leave so soon? By the way, when do I get a chance to come to your house?"

Veronica was anxious to leave Scoont's condo after coming to the conclusion that she was seriously settling for companionship mediocrity.

"I am off Scoont, but I need to leave now. I'll give you a call later, okay?"

Veronica was lying straight out of her mouth as she had no intentions whatsoever of calling Scoont again. She even clearly ignored his question about visiting her house.

"You promise boo? I'll be waiting on your call. Veronica, I really do believe I am falling in love with you baby. I love the way you make me feel."

Veronica listened to his words, but deep down inside her thoughts were fading away from him. *The exact feelings that he has for me is what I am feeling for one man and one man alone, that damn J to the R. I have got to find a way to get J.R. to at least meet me one more time. I still got his phone number and as soon as I get out of this condo, I will be ringing his phone and hopefully he will answer and comply with my wishes. Please J.R.! Don't fail me now.*

"Scoont, do you love the way I make you feel or is it really the sex you are referring to? I think you are just p… whipped."

"Naw baby! I am seriously falling in love with you. I been feeling this way for about a month now and the feeling gets stronger and stronger. I was hoping we could move in with each other one day."

"Scoont, I'm sorry baby, but I don't do the shack attack."

"But baby, we could live together and really get to know one another on an economical basis. It's a great idea."

"Scoont, once again, it is against my religion and I won't be doing that any time soon. There is no need for us to even talk about living together anymore. Let me get out of here so I can take care of some business."

Veronica got up out of the bed and began to get dressed and Scoont came from her backside and started to grind on her, but she gently moved away and convinced him that she really needed to leave.

"Okay baby! I apologize for being greedy. I sure can't wait to get back on you again. I love you baby."

Veronica got dressed and got her bag and headed for the door.

"I'll call you later. You take care okay." She kissed him on the cheeks and left.

As soon as Veronica got in her car and started to drive off, she called J.R. on her cell phone.

"J.R." Her insides melted at the sound of those

pronounced two syllables. It had been such a long time since she had spoken with him. She had to admit, at first she was angry at him for the way in which he just stopped seeing her, stopped wanting her, and stopped craving for her. Normally Veronica would be the one that conquered her man, but J.R. disrupted that trend.

"Hey Mr. J to the R! How have you been doing all this time?"

I got excited as I heard her voice.

"Roni, what's going on girl? This is definitely a surprise."

Veronica began smiling and found herself getting extremely excited.

"Wow! You still remember my voice. I am so glad that you did not change your phone number after all this time. How is marriage life treating you?"

Veronica was anxious to know, but her thoughts wanted to hear the worst possible scenario about my marriage. *Please tell me it sucks. Please tell me you made a mistake and it's on the rocks. Please give me just a ray of hope J.R., please!*

"It's all good Roni. We just had a baby girl named Dominance Nicole. Can you believe that? The J to the R is a biological dad now."

I started laughing, but noticed I was laughing alone. There was silence on the phone.

"Roni, are you there?" Veronica's heart was truly shattered as she listened to the words that truly made her realize that it was probably too late to get back with me.

"I'm here J.R. I am so happy for you and your wife." *Please let me at least sound convincing although I was being very untruthful,* was Veronica's most dominant thought.

"What is her name again J.R.? It has been quite awhile since we last talked." Veronica continued to think to herself about me. *I wish J.R. and I could have had a baby together. It was probably not a good idea for me to even contact him because I was starting to feel overwhelmed by him again. Why did he and I have to part? Was she all that for him to just slice me off the menu? Hell, as much as I hate being number two, I would have easily been his woman on the side. Matter of fact, I would still even assume that role if the offer presented itself. I wish it would.*

"Her name is Evelyn, Roni. It has been a long time since we last spoke and I am glad to hear from you. This is such a surprise. How have you been doing and what have you been up to?"

"J.R., I have been enjoying life to the fullest. I am really loving the single life and I can't believe that it took me so long to experience happiness like this. I only answer to me and that is the way I think I will keep it for quite sometime."

Veronica wanted to impress me as being very happy and free, but her true feelings were imbedded within her true thoughts. *That's another lie! I could not afford to let J.R. know how much I really missed and wanted him. Gosh, what else could I say to him? I craved him body and soul!*

"That's great to hear Roni. Are you still enjoying that house?"

"J.R., the house is my fortress, my palace, my lodge of protection. I loved that house from day one and I still love it tremendously."

"Wow Roni! I don't know how you can handle a house like that by yourself."

"Oh J.R., my mom and my sister live with me now. The house is big enough for all of us and we definitely take advantage of the space to get away from each other from time to time. They love the house as much as I do."

"Hey Roni, how are your folks doing by the way?"

"They are both doing real well J.R. My mom often asks about you. You know you made a very lasting impression upon her. She jokes with me all the time about how stupid I was to let you go."

Veronica felt stupid making the last comment. *Gosh! I did not mean to tell him all of that detail. I wish I could have those words back.*

"Really Roni? Tell your mom and your sister Clarissa both I said hello. Hey, I got to run right now to a meeting, but do keep in touch Roni, okay?"

"J.R., I sure will. You know my mom and sister would love to see you. Perhaps one day you could stop by the house. What do you think?"

Veronica was plotting in her own way. She wanted to see me, but really did not feel comfortable broaching the subject.

"That sounds good Roni. Perhaps I could bring my baby by for you all to see. What do you think?"

"Ahm, sure J.R. That will be fine. We need to do that real soon. I am so anxious to see your little baby."

Veronica was lying up a storm as her true thoughts ripped through her brain. *What? Oh no, he cannot be serious. I am not about to let him bring the baby of his wife to my house. If that's what I got to do, to see J.R., I would really be going to the lowest form of desperation. I can't even think twice about that. Then again, maybe I just need to give that some consideration. In reality, I just wanted to see J.R. If this is what I got to do to see him, I might have to give heavy consideration to the idea.*

"Okay Roni, let me run now and do keep in touch my dear."

"Bye J.R."

Although Veronica was glad she was able to contact me, she still seemed disappointed within. She was not ready to get off the phone with me and she wanted to hear me say that I was missing her. The thoughts of a woman feeling somewhat scorned. *He didn't even seem like he missed me. You would think after all this time that he would at least have thought about the good times we had. Darn! I hate being a sucker for a challenge but I was not going out so easy. I will find a way to get J.R. back into my arms where he belongs, even though he doesn't seem to be interested right now. He could have at least told me that he missed me. Oh well! When he comes to visit and bring his little baby, I will be looking some kind of fine because I'm gonna be bringing all the goods.*

Chapter 18
Drama in My House

Evelyn woke up late on a Friday morning and decided to check out Ricky's room to see if he had cleaned it up. She had told him the night before to thoroughly clean his room before going to basketball camp this morning. As she headed to his room, she heard Rosie talking on the phone in Ricky's room. Not that Rosie's talking on the phone bothered Evelyn, but when she heard her name, and then my name mentioned, she elected to listen to the conversation. Rosie had her back to the door and had no idea that Evelyn was listening to her conversation.

"Doralee, you are making a serious mistake. It's enough that you have gotten as far as you have with Mr. Carter. I want to stop right now. I think it's time to cease the operation now. You do not need to send a letter here telling Mrs. Carter that Mr. Carter is the father of your baby. That will upset this home tremendously. Don't do it. You need to quit while you are ahead."

Evelyn heard those words and quickly went to her room to get her cordless phone. Due to her request awhile ago, she had Ricky's phone line tapped so that she could often monitor his telephone conversations. This was a feature that Evelyn had requested, to make certain Ricky was not getting mixed up with the wrong crowd that would detract him from his education. All Evelyn had to do was dial in a code on her phone and she would be listening to the line in Ricky's room. Therefore, she did just that while sitting in her bedroom. The following words were exchanged over that phone line.

Doralee: "Rosie, why are you reacting this way? Now that you got your American citizenship, I noticed that you have become very disloyal. I brought you from a long ways and I don't think that I am asking too much of J.R. I just want him to own up to his responsibilities and provide child support to his baby daughter. All you need to do is continue to spy and provide me information as to everything I need to know about J.R. and his family."

Rosie: "Doralee, the problem I have is that we have done well without disrupting this family. You have gotten enough money from him and we have done well, so now we should quit and leave him and his family alone."

Doralee: "Well Rosie, that is easy for you to say, but you did not screw J.R. like I did okay. Matter of fact, Valerie failed to handle that order as well and look at where she is right now. J.R. and I must have screwed four times in one night and he did not use any protection. I gave birth to our child and he should be man enough to provide child support. You see, the reason I have decided to write this letter to his wife is because J.R. keeps ignoring my phone calls.

Rosie: "Doralee, I think we have made enough money off this scandal and I want out. I don't agree with what you are doing and I am ready to quit. I have been spying on this family long enough. Now, I just want to be a loyal employee to Mr. Carter because he takes real good care of all of his employees."

Doralee: Rosie, I made you what you are. I was the one who enabled you to get a job with J.R. by illegally manipulating your immigrant citizenship paperwork. You should be loyal to me for the rest of your life. If not, I might find a way to have you shipped back to Mexico. Don't cross me Rosie because I mean business. You see what happened to Valerie. I don't honor disloyalty."

Evelyn listened to the conversation over the phone and she became immediately hurt, disgusted, and somewhat confused. Nevertheless, her first course of action was to fire Rosie. Then, she called Walker and directed him to escort her from the premises. Here is how it went down. She got off the phone in her bedroom. By that time, Rosie had terminated her conversation with Doralee. Her hanging up abruptly probably had something to do with the fact that she heard the sound of Dominance Nicole crying in her room.

Rosie quickly entered the baby's room and grabbed the baby as she was crying at the top of her lungs. Evelyn entered the room afterwards and grabbed her baby from Rosie.

"Rosie, you're fired! Get all your junk and get off my property right away. Walker will be in to escort you out within a matter of minutes."

Rosie looked at Evelyn and covered her mouth with her hands, and bent over as though someone had punched her in the stomach.

"Mrs. Carter, please give me another chance. Please tell me what I did wrong or what did I not do right."

Evelyn was about to leave the room, but she turned around quickly to respond to Rosie's request.

"Rosie, I have no words of explanation for you. You know exactly what you did. Spare me your ridiculous insult by questioning me. Get out of here right away. Don't you ever step foot on my property again. Just get out! Your services are no longer required."

Rosie just exploded by crying loudly. Evelyn was just getting started. With a crying baby, she called her sister, Teralyn, to assist her with the child. Teralyn was in the kitchen making herself some breakfast. As soon as she heard the baby crying, she ran and gathered the baby from Evelyn's arms.

"T, I need to take care of some business. Please take care of Dominance Nicole while I'm gone."

"E, what's going on gurl?"

"Just some business I need to tend to right away." Walker walked into the kitchen with a curious look on his face.

"Walker, Rosie is in the maid's quarters. Please see her off the property as soon as she can gather her things." He obliged and headed towards the maid's quarters.

"E, are you sure everything is okay? What is going on?" Teralyn followed Evelyn while also trying to silence the baby.

However, Evelyn was not about to share her personal business with Teralyn just yet.

"T, I fired the maid."

"Geddout! Fa real doe? What did she do E? I knew you never liked her anyway."

"No T, she got on my last nerve, that's all. I need to take a shower and take care of some business."

Evelyn proceeded to her bedroom to take a shower. Teralyn took the baby to her room to take care of her. Evelyn diverted from the shower path and went straight into her sauna. There, she sat in the sauna and replayed everything in her mind, while tears flooded her eyes.

She was deeply hurt. She felt betrayed, deceived, dejected, and a litany of other harsh feelings. *I cannot believe J.R. I thought he was the perfect husband ...faithful, loyal, and dedicated. I remember when we first met. I thought it was love at first sight. He blew me away*

by the mere concern that he had for my son alone. The truth of the matter is I really fell for him before he even declared his interest in me. Now, he has a baby by another woman named Doralee. Who in the world is Doralee and why would he ever do such a thing to me? I mean, if J.R. did not want me, he should not have led me on to believing that I was all that to him. I really don't understand why men cheat. I can't take this! I am married to a man who has cheated on me, fathered another child and has not even said a word to me about it. I mean, what should I do? How should I respond to these allegations, other than to just leave? I know many will think I am stupid for leaving a man as wealthy as J.R., but I don't think I will be able to handle his indiscretions. I can remain, but I just don't believe that I can trust him again. My heart is so heavy right now. I don't know if it's the embarrassment of this whole ordeal or the hurt derived from knowing my husband has cheated on me and, to add to this, is the father of this woman's baby. I wonder if Jewel knows anything about this. I really don't know how to approach her with this, but I've just got to find out if she knows.
Evelyn got on the speakerphone and called Jewel.

"Hello," sounded the voice on the other line

"Jewel, how are you? This is Evelyn."

"Hey girlfriend! You know I recognize your voice. How have you been doing? I have been thinking about you, but I also knew that the baby has kept you pretty much pre-occupied. How is Miss Dominance Nicole?"

"She is doing real well Jewel. My sister Teralyn has been a great help with the baby. How have you been doing?"

"Evelyn, I have been busy as ever. Your husband

does a great job keeping me busy. He is nonstop and his business mind is forever at work."

Evelyn's thoughts were so loud. *Yeah right! He sure is nonstop with his cheating ass. I can't believe he has done this to me. His screwing mind must be forever at work too.*

"Jewel, I need to talk to you."

"Okay girlfriend! Do you want to do lunch, dinner, or chew the fat at the house? We could always hit a night spot too if you like."

"Jewel, I don't know. I'm not feeling well."

"Well, we sure can't have that going on! Are you sick? What's going on girlfriend? Do you want to meet right away? How about sometime today? Just let me know and I will be right there."

"Well, why don't we meet at Damone's off Martin Luther King Ave for a late lunch? I can be there in about two hours."

"Alright Evelyn! I'll see you there."

"Jewel, please don't tell J.R. about this meeting."

"No problem Evelyn! What he doesn't know won't hurt him! You don't have to worry about that. I'll see you in a shake."

"Okay Jewel! Bye bye."

Evelyn got off the phone and proceeded with her shower. After getting dressed, she quickly checked with Walker to confirm that Rosie was escorted off the primacies, kissed her baby, told Teralyn she was going out for awhile, and had Walker dispatch a driver to take her to meet with Jewel. While riding along in the back of her Bentley, Evelyn started reflecting back on her relationship with J.R. She remembered being impressed with J.R.'s initial interest in Ricky's academic standings first, and his efforts to ensure he found exactly the right coach and team for him to play basketball. *J.R. was so caring and focused on making both of us happy, and he did just that! I just cannot believe he would cheat on me like this. I actually did love him the moment I saw him, or maybe it was after the first time I heard his voice on the phone. That really did do it for me. Now, I'm feeling like a woman who has been used and abused and cheated on. I really don't want to break up a home, but I don't know if I will ever be able to trust J.R. again. If I can't ever trust him again, then I really do need to move on.*

Evelyn had almost arrived at the restaurant. Jewel waited for her in the entrance of the restaurant. When she saw Evelyn being dropped off, Jewel waved at her. As she drew closer, they hugged each other and engaged in girlfriend conversation.

"You are looking good gurl. I can tell somebody been walking up a storm because all that baby fat has left that gorgeous body."

"Well, you would think so after Dominance Nicole keeps me up practically all hours of the night. I don't know why I elected to breast feed her."

"How is she doing? She was such a beautiful queen when I last saw her."

"Jewel, she is such a darling. J.R. got all excited the other day when she lit up to see him. He is so proud to have a baby girl."

"I can imagine he is. How is everyone else doing?" Jewel asked with much anxiety and excitement in her voice. Then, their conversation was suddenly interrupted by the hostess as they walked into the restaurant.

"Ladies, your table has been reserved and it's located in the corner just as you requested."

The hostess directed them to their seats. They both grabbed their chairs and patiently waited on the waitress to arrive to take their orders. Then the two of them continued their girl talk.

"Jewel, I had to fire the maid, Rosie. I overheard a conversation she was having with this woman named Doralee, revealing the fact that she had been spying on our household."

Jewel all of a sudden became uncomfortable and developed a very curious look on her face.

"Evelyn, are you serious?"

"Just as serious as I can be Jewel and that is just the beginning. J.R. apparently is the father of her child."

Evelyn started crying without even trying to hold back the tears. Jewel retrieved a handkerchief from her purse and started wiping Evelyn's face as tears continued to stream down.

"Evelyn, I am so sorry that you had to find out about J.R. and this woman this way. I know that he has been miserable trying to come up with a way to tell you about all this." Evelyn looked up at Jewel with a look of complete astonishment.

"Jewel, you knew about this?"

"Yes sweetheart I knew, but we are still investigating the details. I did not want to say anything to you while you were going through labor. Afterwards, I felt that it was J.R.'s rightful place to tell you."

"Jewel, that lying cheat has not said one word to me about this. I am so disappointed in him."

"Now Evelyn, in his defense, he did plan on telling you,

but I think he chickened out when you spoke of how you did not tolerate cheating."

Evelyn just stared at Jewel, feeling both worried and concerned as she did.

"Jewel, please tell me the truth."

"Of course I will girlfriend. What do you want to know?"

"Are you sleeping with J.R.?" Jewel lowered her head as though she was totally taken off guard.

"Evelyn, sweetheart, I realize you are hurt over news regarding J.R.'s infidelity, but trust me I would never do that! I am really a better person than that."

Jewel felt both insulted and offended. However, she understood how Evelyn may have felt this way, and she also knew that Evelyn was probably suspicious of any female close to her husband.

"Jewel, if you did, would you tell me?" Evelyn was still crying with more intensity. Jewel just stared like she was being confronted by a total stranger.

"Evelyn, if my closeness to J.R. has caused you to wonder about my loyalty to both you two, then I can fix that very quickly. I can assure you that J.R. and I have never even came remotely close to being that way with one another. We are now, and have always been, plutonic friends, and that's the truth. Evelyn, I'm really sorry if I've ever given you any cause for concern in those regards."

"Jewel, I'm sorry. I just feel so bad about this whole new revelation. What have I ever done to J.R. for him to cheat on me? Have I not been good enough to him?"

"Evelyn, don't even put yourself through that kind of trauma. Now, if there is any consolation whatsoever, I understand that the incident happened prior to your wedding."

"So Jewel, how did you know about this and how long have you known?" Evelyn was as distraught as ever.

"Evelyn, J.R. discussed his dilemma with me recently. I think he was practicing with me, in preparation for telling you. You really do need to talk with him about the details."

"How can you just tell me that? I want to know everything Jewel, from whomever I can get it from. I won't be able to carry on without knowing the truth. Okay Jewel, so J.R. had an affair before our marriage? How long had the affair been going on?"

"As I understand, it was just a one night stand."

"A one night stand Jewel? If so, why didn't J.R. use protection? Why would he be so irresponsible?"

"That's my question as well. I think you need to speak with J.R. and get all the answers. I do have an investigation team verifying that the alleged infant is J.R.'s child and that Doralee Mayberry was legitimate in her actions."

"Who in the hell is this Doralee Mayberry?" Evelyn seemed angrier now than hurt.

"Evelyn, she is the lady that J.R. hired to oversee the properties in Stockbridge, Georgia."

"Why in the hell would he hire that hoe? What was he thinking? Perhaps I need to go to Stockbridge and pay her ass a visit? Hell, I don't even know where Stockbridge is. I've never even heard of it before."

"Evelyn, I will take care of Doralee as soon as we conclude this investigation. I do encourage you to get the full details from J.R. however. He does owe you an explanation. The answers to all your questions are certainly long overdue." Jewel gave Evelyn a hug as she continued to wipe the tears from her face.

"Jewel, I don't know if I can even face J.R. right now. I got to decide whether or not I will remain with him."

Jewel jerked her face away from Evelyn as though Evelyn was a dog trying to bite her.

"Evelyn, you do realize that his indiscretion was only that one night and it was before you two got married."

"Jewel, I don't give a damn if it was two weeks before we got married or a month before. He cheated on me and if he did it one time, he will probably do it again."

"Evelyn, I can't address that issue, but I can assure you J.R. is very sorry for what he has done and for even being involved with Doralee. Trust me; he is suffering just as much, or even more than you are right now."

"Jewel, you don't know that. I've got to deal with his infidelity and this so-called child if I choose to remain with him." Jewel displayed that obvious look of disbelief as she continued to talk to Evelyn.

"Evelyn, don't do anything rash until you've had a chance to look at this from all sides. Please, don't leave him! Sweetheart, you are just experiencing the initial pain of knowing. This too shall pass." Jewel was still taken by the words disclosed by Evelyn.

"Jewel, I don't know if I can continue to remain J.R.'s wife if he in fact cheated on me. I'm sorry, but I have a very serious issue with infidelity." Jewel was at a total lost for words and Evelyn just stared at her with the most sincere look she could possibly display.

"Evelyn, I understand how you feel and I know what you are going through."

"Jewel, have you ever been married?"

"No Evelyn, I have not."

181

"Then you have no idea what I am going through okay. At some point and time you need to stop defending J.R.'s cheating ass and talk to me with more sensitivity."

Jewel just stared at Evelyn, as though she had spat in her face. *The nerve of this woman,* she thought to herself. *I cannot believe that she has the audacity to talk to me like this. I'm starting to wonder whether or not she really does think that J.R. and I are trading sweat with each other. I have got to brace myself because Evelyn seems to be having doubts as to the real reason she married J.R. Besides, I work my butt off for this family, and I really don't think I deserve these accusations or the insults. Therefore, I will take this conversation and package it where it belongs …I'll simply charge it to her head, and not to her heart.*

Chapter 19
Evelyn on the Run

In my mind, I had just left the deal of a century. I was walking outside of the Business Metropolis in Northwest Houston, feeling as proud as I could.

I had just procured a two story building that was a perfect structure and location for Evelyn's daycare business. Her dream of a lifetime was to own her own childcare facility. Therefore, I felt so good netting this sale in the midst of historical tycoons.

I grabbed my cell phone and started to call Evelyn and let her know of the good news. Then, after thinking about it for a few moments, I decided to surprise her with the keys to the building.

As I was approaching my Lex, there was this Mexican looking female leaning on my car. At first I thought the woman was one of the ladies that worked with me on the city's real estate council, but after I got closer, I realized that she was a total stranger.

"Mr. Carter, how are you doing?"

The lady walked towards me with much caution as she seemed very uncertain as to how I would respond.

"I'm doing fine. Do I know you?"

I was very skeptical myself and I started looking around to make certain there was no shady activity going on near me.

"Actually Mr. Carter, you don't know me, but my name is Valerie Dominguez. I left my name and number on your car sometime last year because I was trying to warn you about Doralee Mayberry."

Her words immediately captured my attention. She wore a black dress, red shoes, a red lace belt that matched the shoes, and her hair was flowing off her shoulder like a black smooth river with defined waves.

"Oh really! Ma'am, I don't think I care to have this conversation with you. I don't know you, and frankly, don't know if I can trust you or anyone else for that matter."

I proceeded to open my car door as I walked right past her. I thought to myself, *hell naw! I am not trying to expose myself for any further trouble with anyone that has anything to do with Doralee Mayberry.*

"Mr. Carter, you don't know me, but you do know Rosie. She was your maid for quite sometime before you fired her."

I hesitated and looked at Valerie as she was waving to someone. Out of an old, rough looking gray truck, Rosie emerged. I stared at her and then stared back at Valerie, while I thought to myself, *what in the world is going on up in here?*

"I did not fire Rosie. I don't even know what you're talking about." Rosie got closer and closer and as she did, I could see her tear stained eyes and the very shameful look on her face.

"Rosie, can you please explain to me what in the world is going on here?"

"Hi Mr. Carter." She immediately started crying and Valerie hugged her.

"I am so sorry. Please forgive me," uttered Rosie.

I continued to stare at her with a stunned look.

"Okay Rosie, I am so very much in the dark as to what you are talking about. Please explain to me what is going on because I am becoming more confused by the minute. Did my wife fire you?" I walked over to both Valerie and Rosie.

"Yes Sir! I'm so sorry Mr. Carter."

Rosie, what are you so sorry about? Did my wife fire you for disobeying her directions?"

"Yes, I mean, to some degree. I did something I am very ashamed of Mr. Carter and I hope and pray you will forgive me."

I began to sharpen my stare at Rosie. As I also looked around the parking lot, I spotted my new trailer security guard, Wilcox, observing my interaction from afar.

A security guard as my trailer was the result of my rapidly increased financial worth over the year. I had eventually yielded to Jewel's demand to have a security guard at my disposal at all times. In all actuality, I've never liked the idea of having someone follow me wherever I go but after a great deal of persuasion, I finally conceded to this arrangement. Wilcox was very clandestine. I'm absolutely sure that these ladies didn't have a clue that he was there watching my back, armed and ready to protect me with his life if need be. I stared at Wilcox and scratched my head to signal to him that I noticed his presence and that all was cool.

"Rosie, what did you do and what do you and Valerie have in common?"

"Mr. Carter, Doralee offered me a proposition that I am now ashamed to admit. She paid me to spy on you and your family. She fixed it where I got the job working for you and also fixed my immigration status so I would not have to return to Mexico."

Rosie looked down at the ground to hide the embarrassment on her face in relation to what she had done. She was afraid to meet my eyes head on. I just couldn't believe all of the things that were being shared.

Then, Valerie had more to add.

"Mr. Carter, Doralee tried to use me as well to manipulate you. She wanted me to attempt to seduce you so that I could gather information to bribe you. I refused because I did not want to be a part of that type of activity." I looked at both Rosie and Valerie as though I was in the midst of a nightmare.

"So, you mean to tell me that Doralee had targeted me for entrapment prior to me even meeting her? How did you all ever come in contact with me? I thought I met Doralee for the first time in Georgia, but now it seems like she had to know me from somewhere else. Where did you all first come across me?"

Suddenly, they both stared at each other! Valerie appeared to be the leader of the two.

"Really Mr. Carter, we would prefer not to disclose that information. We really don't want to say anymore because we don't want to get someone else in trouble."

"What? Somebody else in trouble? Ladies, I'm still trying to figure out why we are here? Rosie, why did Evelyn fire you? You have yet to tell me." I was really getting inpatient with these two women.

"I think Miss Evelyn fired me because she heard me talking to Doralee on the phone. I assumed so, because right after I heard the baby crying and I picked her up, Mrs. Carter walked into the room, took the baby out of my arms, and fired me."

"Hold up Rosie! You were talking to Doralee on the phone in my house? Does Evelyn know about Doralee? Were you in my office or somewhere else when you were talking to Doralee?"

"I was in Ricky's room."

"Oh shoot!" I was immediately concerned.

"Rosie, did Evelyn see you on the phone in Ricky's room?"

"Mr. Carter, I am really not for certain. I didn't notice her when I was talking on the phone to Doralee." Oh my goodness! The race of stress is on again! I could not get answers fast enough from Rosie.

"Rosie, what were you and Doralee talking about on the phone? Please answer me right away!"

"Mr. Carter, Doralee was demanding that I continue to spy on you and provide her information. I was trying to quit, but she was threatening me to continue." I could not wait any further without asking the next question.

"Rosie, does Evelyn know about what happened with me and Doralee?" I walked right up on her and insisted on an immediate response.

"Mr. Carter, I really don't know." I really got very emotional and upset.

"Rosie, you have to know. Then why did my wife fire you?"

"I think she fired me because she overheard my conversation with Doralee, but I can't be for certain." Oh Lord! My world just got shook again. I had to leave these two women right away and call Evelyn.

"Okay Rosie! I must admit I am so disappointed in you. I would have never thought that you would conspire against me. I trusted you like family Rosie. You have truly offended me." I was really upset with her. Valerie tried to intervene as Rosie was just standing there crying like a baby.

"Mr. Carter, she really meant no harm. She is really very loyal to you. She only did what she thought she had to do."

"Okay Valerie! Now, let me do what I think I have to do. Rosie, you need to understand that some people don't trust others because of devious acts such as what you have committed. If my wife was totally aware, she would really clean your clock. I got to go."

I got into my car as fast as I could and Valerie walked around and asked me another question.

"Mr. Carter, can we contact you later? We have a problem that we know you can help us with."

I knew the typical problem that the Hispanics had in this area and I knew exactly what they wanted. Although Rosie crossed me, she was still a kindhearted woman and I could never turn my back on her. Thus, I reached into my wallet and handed Valerie this business card.

"Look here! This is Carlos Panedras' business card. He is a special friend of mine. Give him a call and he will take care of you. I know what both of you are concerned about. Tell him J.R. sent you and he'll take care of you immediately. Just do me a favor and stay away from me and my family or the next time I see you, it won't be this pleasant."

I gave Valerie the business card and slid a few hundred dollars behind it because I knew they needed the money. As soon as they both saw the card and money, they both got real excited. Valerie was smiling with joy.

"Thank you Mr. Carter, Valerie said. I really do thank you so very much. I will call him right away." Rosie immediately approached the car with tears streaming down her face.

"Thank you for your generosity Mr. Carter. I will never forget you."

I waved at both of them and drove off. As soon as I got out of the parking lot, I called Evelyn on my cell phone to see what damage had been done. Her phone rang for awhile and I got her voice mail message. Instead of leaving a message, I hung up and called her at my house. Teralyn answered the phone.

"Yo butt is in deep pig slop! You are a cheating dog! E is through wit-chu and packing as we speak!"

Oh no! I immediately started speeding for home. I did try to get Teralyn to put Evelyn on the phone.

"Teralyn let me speak with Evelyn."

"She ain't talkin to you! She said you da last voice she wants to hear and she is tryin fast to leave befoe you get home. She don't want to see yo face no mo."

"Teralyn, stop playing now and put Evelyn on the phone, please!"

"Nigga I don't play like dat! E is packin as we speak. Call one of yo security boys if ya think I'm lyin. She is done wit-chu!"

"But Teralyn, things are not as they appear. That mess happened long ago. You got to talk to her for me. Come on now! At least have her wait until I get home. I'm serious!"

"I think she overreactin, but dat's just me. E can be crazy like dis dough. I'll try my best, but you should be ashamed of yoself. Who is da baby by anyway?"

DANG! Looks like Evelyn knows everything and the fear of losing her was all I could think about now.

"Teralyn, I got to call Walker and see what's going on. Please at least try and talk Evelyn into staying. My goodness, the house is big enough where I can just stay in another room for now. There is no need of making a big scene because once I talk with her, I'm confident she will understand."

"Good luck on dat man! You only saw a taste of E during her delivery. She can be a real vindictive b---h when you cross her, and I thank you already done dat. All dat elegance goes out da window when she feels like she been crossed. I pity you."

"Okay, call me back after you talk to her. I'm serious Teralyn! I will take care of you for that." I got off the phone with Teralyn and quickly called Walker.

"Hello, Walker are you there?"

"Yes Sir!"

"What's going on man?"

"Ahm! Sir, you need to hurry home to talk with the Mrs. She got me on a mission right now."

"Talk to me Walker! What kind of mission does she have you on?" There was silence on the phone. Walker was not responding.

"Walker, are you there?"

There was no answer. I began to wonder why Walker was not responding. I called him again and his phone just rang. He knew that as my chief security officer, he must be accessible to me at all times. I was really getting concerned. I dialed again, and again, and again. I also tried to call Ricky's cell phone. I got nothing but his voice mail. These were the most stressful minutes I've ever experienced, besides my wife's delivery night. I put the pedal to the medal and went speeding down the highway like crazy.

Less than five minutes on the highway, I got distracted by flashing blue lights.

"Dang! Dang! Dang!" I immediately stopped the car. I

realized I was speeding and had been pulled over. I hit the steering wheel with my fist and then proceeded to get out of the car. I actually got out of my car before the officer did. The officer jumped from his car, placed his hands on his gun and ordered me to get back inside my car.

"Excuse me Suh! I need you to return to your car and wait until you have been approached."

"But officer, I have an emergency..." He interrupted me right away.

"Did ya hear what I just said Suh? I need ya to return to ya car and close the door." He kept his hands near his holster where his gun was located. I immediately got back into my car. The officer took, for what seemed like forever, to approach my vehicle, but when he did I was quite surprised.

"Mr. Carter, ya need to slow it down some. Did ya realize you wuz going bout a hundred miles per hour. Ya got to slow it down Suh." I had already gotten my license and registration in hand to give to him and I extended it.

"I'm sorry officer, but I'm in a hurry and I got distracted." He cut me off again with his good old country boy swagger.

"Well don't let me hold ya up. Let's just consider this a warning and you go on bout ya business Suh, ya hear? I knowz about the great thangz ya doing in the city of Houston. You just need to slow it down some Suh, okay." Thank goodness! The cop was letting me off.

"Thank you officer! I will definitely slow it down."

I got back on the highway and called Walker again, but to no avail. I called my house again and this time Ricky answered the phone, and it was as though I heard him crying.

Before I had a chance to say anything to him, someone managed to grab the phone away from him and there went the dial tone. Somebody hung up on me. I knew I had to get home as fast as I could. I had to explain everything to Evelyn before this situation got completely out of hand. I tried to place myself in her position right now.

I wanted to know what she was feeling, thinking, and plotting. I wanted to know the right words to comfort her. My thoughts ran so deep that I forgot about calling my girl Jewel for help. Besides, just maybe she would be able to shed some light on my present dilemma.

Chapter 20
Slow Torture

The traffic on the Beltway North nearly came to a screeching halt as I was so anxious to get to my house and get to Evelyn before she jetted on a brother. While I was waiting in traffic, I called Jewel to see if I could solicit her support and advice.

"Hello," sounded Jewel on the phone.

"Jewel, you won't believe what's going on."

"Well J.R., I actually have an inkling of an idea."

"I don't think so Jewel. Word on the street has it that Evelyn is planning on leaving me over the Doralee incident."

"J.R., I met with Evelyn for lunch and we talked."

"Jewel, what exactly did she say to you? I mean, is she leaving me or not?"

"Well J.R., you should have told her about Doralee. I believe if you had done so, it would have softened some of the pain that she is now feeling." I was sensing somewhat of a cold reaction from Jewel. She seemed somewhat distant and not interested.

"Jewel, I tried to tell Evelyn, but I guess I didn't try hard enough. Did she say anything to you about leaving me and did she tell you how she found out about Doralee?"

"Yes, she did mention the possibility of leaving, but she did not share any details. She found out about Doralee by a phone call in Ricky's room where Rosie and evidently Doralee were engaged in conversation. She told me that she clicked in on the conversation and apparently all was revealed."

"You know Jewel I regretted ever getting that line in Ricky's room and I always felt like that was an invasion of

Ricky's privacy. Whoever thought that I would be the one that would suffer from that stupid phone line?"

"J.R., the fact of the matter is, what has happened has happened. You need to focus on the here and now."

"Jewel, I just find it very difficult to believe that Evelyn would be leaving me just like that, don't you?"

"Well J.R., I don't necessarily share your perspective. I mean, some women are very different when it comes to infidelity." As I was talking to Jewel, my phone rang and I quickly had Jewel hold on as I clicked over.

"Hello," this is J.R.

"Mr. Carter, this is Rosie."

"Rosie, I am really busy right now and I don't have time to talk. Did I not give you and Valerie the right number to call?"

"Mr. Carter, we got the right number and we have even been assigned jobs and assisted with a place to stay. I just wanted to share something with you that Valerie felt I should tell you."

"Rosie, go ahead, but you only got a few seconds, okay."

"Mr. Carter, I just wanted to make you aware that Mr. Lyles often would call the house when you were away and that Mrs. Carter would call him as well."

"Rosie, who is Mr. Lyles? What are you talking about?"

"Mr. Lyles, you know, Ricky's dad! I have often walked in on Mrs. Carter telling him that she..." I became very impatient with Rosie and rudely interrupted her.

"Rosie, Ricky's dad is a crack head okay. I'm certain they had to talk sometimes, although I rather doubt it. Now, do you have anything more constructive to tell me because I really do need to go?"

"I do apologize Mr. Carter. I just wanted you to know what I had heard. I will leave you now. Thanks once again." I quickly clicked back over to Jewel as I felt that Rosie was basically wasting my time.

"Jewel, are you still there?"

"I'm here J.R. You must be stuck in traffic."

"I am very much stuck in traffic Jewel. I'm trying to get home to stop Evelyn from leaving. What advice do you have for me Jewel? Please enlighten me."

"Well J.R., I think the best advice I can give you at this time is that you protect your assets. I don't mean to say I told you so, but that prenuptial agreement that I encouraged you to sign prior to your marriage would be very applicable now."

"So Jewel, how do I prevent Evelyn from leaving? I think we can work through our problems, but living apart will not solve anything."

"J.R., you need to get home and talk to her and express your sincere and most remorse apology. Then, explain to her how you two can work through all the trouble."

"Jewel, how is the investigation coming?"

"The investigation should be concluded within the next week J.R. We are on the brink of some very vital information, but it would not be worth sharing until we are for certain."

While I was talking to Jewel, I all of a sudden felt a need to make certain that Evelyn would not be gone by time I arrived at the house so I elected to call Loke and ask for his assistance. Immediately after I got off the phone with Jewel, I called Loke.

"Hello," responded Loke on the other line.

"Yo Loke, I need help right away man. I need you to go to my house and keep Evelyn from leaving." As I was talking to Loke, I thought I heard a female voice in the background. Then again, that would be so typical of him.

"J.R., I don't know about that man. I'm hearing that it is not looking good on the home front."

"Loke, what have you heard man and from whom?"

"Well man, you know who I get the 4-1-1 from. I heard that Evelyn is really upset with you and she is making plans as we speak to relocate. I can't believe it J.R. I mean, to me, you really did nothing wrong and I think Evelyn is overreacting and Teralyn thinks so as well."

"Loke, is Teralyn at your house now?" He better not tell me that he got another woman over there.

"How did you know man? Just so you know, Teralyn also believes that Evelyn is suffering much pain from her discovery of the information."

"Well Loke, once again, I need you to go and keep her from leaving until I get there. I am currently in congested traffic out of hell."

"J.R., I don't mean any harm man, but I really don't want to come between you and Evelyn. I will do what I can, but I can't make you any promises. Besides, you know Evelyn is not a big fan of me. Therefore, the possibility of her listening to me would be very minimal at best."

Okay, Loke was starting to piss me off, although he was probably sharing the truth. He could have kept those last words.

"Loke, I need you to do this for me man. I can't seem to get a hold of Walker or any of my security employees.

Matter of fact, even Wilcox who was trailing me is not answering his phone. Then again, he is probably stuck in traffic from trying to keep up with me. Did you hear me Loke? My trailer today was Wilcox and he probably got lost in traffic, but he still won't even answer his cell phone. I have no clue as to what is going on and no one is answering any phones Loke. I need your help."

"J.R., I did not want to share this with you because Teralyn told me not to, but I think Walker is going with Evelyn from best I can tell."

Okay, I don't understand at all what is going on, but I am suspicious as to why Walker was not answering my phone calls. I cannot believe this is happening.

"Loke, I am really finding that hard to believe, but I hear you. Please go to my house man and take over matters and let me know what is going on. I can't seem to gain much ground out here in traffic. I wish I had enough room where I could call in a chopper to pick me up and get me home. I am in the death slow ride home."

"J.R., you gonna be alright man. I always told you about not knowing Evelyn long enough to even be marrying her man, but as you recall you would not listen to me."

"Loke, come on man! I really don't need to have this type of conversation now okay. Please help handle my affairs as I cannot. Get Teralyn to help you keep Evelyn from leaving at least until I get there man, okay?"

"JR., I'll do as best I can man. Teralyn said that Evelyn made these moves as though she already had plans in motion."

"Well Loke, you know some things that Teralyn says should be taken with a grain of salt. It's not like she's an authority on anything." Loke started to laugh and quickly responded.

"Why you hating on my woman, man? You got to admit that she probably knows Evelyn more so than anyone as her identical twin sister. You need to improve your opinion of her as she will be around."

"Loke, she won't be around my place. When Evelyn leaves, she will be leaving my house too. I won't need her hanging around."

"Look J.R., let's just focus on your scenario at hand as there are so many unanswered questions."

Although Loke was accurate with his assessment, I did not sense his mutual perspective regarding Teralyn. This slow ride home really did birth a lot of thoughts within my head. *Okay, I did cheat on Evelyn, but it was in a very unpremeditated manner. For crying out loud, I got set up. The Hispanics vouch to that. I ran into a modern day fatal attraction and I messed up. Nevertheless, I don't think Evelyn should leave me over a premarital mistake, as I have been truly faithful to her ever since I said I do. Man, I cannot believe this is happening to me. I wish it was just one of those nightmares that I just had not awakened from yet. Well, what next after Evelyn? I tell you Lord, I won't be marrying another woman again. This is it. I just assumed be single for the rest of my life, but not live the type of lifestyle that Loke lives. I wonder how Julie will respond to my trauma. Let me play this over in my mind again. I am so much in love with my wife that I was going to give her the dream of her lifetime on my birthday, which is just a couple of days away. What will I say to mom? She will seem to be right. Man! Why does my head hurt so baaad?*

Chapter 21
Flipped Script

The highway traffic finally started moving more rapidly out on the beltway, and thus I had really started gaining ground on reaching home. Once I got off the highway, I found myself getting more nervous as I rapidly approached my house. I got really anxious as I got closer to my house.

I could not remember the entry code to the huge iron gate that protected my estate. I never had to remember the number because my security staff would normally know where I was and would automatically open the gate for me.

Therefore, I had to pull out my wallet and get the code. I processed the entry code and like clockwork the gate opened up for me. I quickly drove up to the house, and noticed that there was no one in sight. There were no lawn maintenance personnel, no carpenters, and no sign of security anywhere.

Although it was quite unusual for me, I tried to imagine what the heck was going on. I found myself entertaining thoughts in my mind. I knew that if Evelyn left, she would not have taken everyone with her. I also noticed that I did not see Loke's truck anywhere. I started to concede that I was too late. Where the hell was Loke and why didn't he come over as I asked him to? Could it be that he came here and it was too late, and he just returned to his house? If so, wouldn't he have called me to let me know the outcome?

I was perplexed and confused as I approached my estate. I opened the door to the car garage and parked my car. Evelyn's ride was nowhere in sight. Matter of fact, the only vehicles present were mine. I even noticed that the limousine was gone. I got out my car and I proceeded into my house. For some reason, it took me awhile to open the door. I went from the South end to the North end of my house, traveling via my nice corporate hallway. I stopped and opened the door towards the main entry way of the house.

Evidently, the door was locked and I had to push and push and then it finally opened.

"SURPRISE!" There was this huge crowd located inside the house. I was totally shocked at what happened next. All of a sudden, there was a huge roar from within. Everyone commenced to singing happy birthday to me.

"Happy birthday to you! Happy birthday to you! Happy birthday J.R., happy birthday to you." I stood there feeling like a clown. Guess who was the first person to come and greet me with the baby in her arms?

"Happy birthday J.R.!" She gave me my typical hug and kiss.

"Evelyn, this is certainly a surprise, but today is not my birthday. Do you know what's been going on in my mind for the past two hours?"

I stood there looking at Evelyn while also thinking about all the drama I just went through. Everybody was present at my house for what appeared to be a concocted surprise birthday party. Julie, Jewel, Loke, Teralyn and all my cast of friends were there. I was in total awe!

"J.R., do you know what's been going on in my mind for the past eight hours? We can talk later, but all your worry could have been prevented if you would have kept your instrument inside your pants. I realize it's not your birthday today, but there is no way we would have been able to do this on the day of your birthday. Besides, I don't even know if I will be here for your birthday."

"Evelyn, I owe you a serious apology. Please tell me you are not leaving me. I really need to talk to you alone; I need to tell you everything that has happened."

Evelyn just looked away from me as though she was really not interested in hearing what I had to say. Then, I did what I felt I had to do. I silenced the crowd and prepared to give my speech.

"Can I have your attention please? I have a very important announcement that I want to make at this time."

Everybody, with the exception of Julie, looked at me as though the news would be bad. Evelyn had a horrifying look on her face as she had no clue as to what would come next. I took out the keys to the new building I purchased and held them up in the air.

"I have here the keys that will unlock the dream of a lifetime for a certain person in this room." The crowd was overwhelmingly quiet; you could hear a needle drop in the room if one fell.

"I have in my hand the keys to Evelyn's Drive through Daycare Center located in Merrick Park. My lovely wife Evelyn will be the owner and she now gets to fulfill the dream of her lifetime by owning her own daycare center."

I immediately handed Evelyn the keys to the building. Evelyn almost fell to the floor as she was in such a state of surprise.

That's right! I flipped the script. When I saw the expression on Evelyn's face, I almost felt like screaming out *what's.... my.... name*? Instead of it just being a surprise birthday party for me, I made it a very big surprise for my boo. What?

"J.R., oh my goodness! I can't believe this. I thought you told me that Merrick Park was way too expensive for the daycare center."

"I did baby, but I just want you to know I'd do anything for my girl. Now, can this gift please help you forgive me for my mistake?" She immediately pulled away from me with a smile on her face.

"Well, this could be a start, but I can't make you any promises."

Then she showered me with kisses. I felt so good feeling her kisses all over my face because to me it meant that my girl would not be going anywhere other than, perhaps with me to the sheets. Then Julie tapped me on the back with the smile of a lottery winner.

"Happy Birthday J.R.! You should have seen the look on your face when you opened that door. We got you real good, didn't we? Congratulations on the Merrick Park acquisition. I'm proud of you," said Julie. I spoke to Julie in a very low tone.

"Thanks boss! You all really did surprise me. Who would have ever thought that I would come home to a surprise birthday party? I was expecting somewhat of a surprise, but certainly not this! Oh yeah, thanks for hooking me up with the Merrick Park acquisition. All roads run through you Ma'am." Julie listened to my every word and responded right away.

"J.R., I'm glad I can once again be of assistance. By the way, what type of surprise were you expecting?"

"Nothing special Julie! I just thought some work on the house would be completed today, but I guess not, especially with both carpenters in here celebrating at my surprise birthday party." I had to come up with words right away without divulging to Julie my personal trouble.

"Hey, by the way, Dominance Nicole is so beautiful.

You two have done a great job. I am so proud of you. I can't stay long, but I could not turn down the offer to surprise you."

"Thanks Julie for making time to come out. I will be calling you real soon to talk business with you, okay?"

Little did Julie know, life was not that pleasant with Evelyn and me. At least according to what I had been hearing, but with that new property acquisition, I really believed that I was firmly back in the house. Ricky affectionately and playfully pushed me from behind.

"J.R., we got you man. We got you good, didn't we?"

"Ricky, you most certainly did." Ricky was laughing uncontrollably. He got a real kick out of seeing me surprised. I put my arms over his shoulders as I got real serious with the following words.

"I know the National Basketball Association announced today the new age requirement for kids entering the NBA would be at least 18 or 19. Anyway, you just stay focused with your endeavors and time will permit you to make that move. Besides, now you get to do what you have always wanted to do, taste college basketball life." Ricky responded as though the landmark decision had not fazed him at all.

"I'm excited J.R. about being able to go to college. I get a chance to go play with UNC when I graduate from high school." Coach Lawson rushed over to join the conversation.

"J.R., you got to admit that we totally surprised you man and really had you going."

Coach Lawson was just smiling with the biggest grin on his face. I'm certain it had something to do with the fact that Ricky would now be remaining in high school. In addition, he would be playing ball for Coach Lawson a couple of more years.

"Charlie, I got to admit you all did surprise the heck out of me. What do you think of that decision the NBA made?"

"J.R., I think it's a great move. However, I must admit that it does hurt guys like Ricky." He placed his arms on Ricky's shoulders as he continued to talk.

"He is definitely ready for the challenge of the NBA, but I get to enjoy his skills longer here in high school and then before you know it, he will sweep college hoops. He only has to play for about a year and then he will be ready after that."

As Charlie was jabbering on, Loke came over with a very sly grin on his face. I looked at him quickly while I continued to listen to Charlie as I did not want to be rude. Loke gently punched me in my left side in a way of a greeting.

"Loke, you were wrong man."

I whispered to Loke as Charlie was still talking. He just continued to laugh and punch me on my side. Charlie spoke to Loke and then excused himself to join his wife on the other side of the room. Loke was anxious to joke with me about the surprise.

"J.R., how does it feel to be played so badly playa? I mean we got you so good that I was starting to believe all the information that was used to trick you."

"So Loke, was all the information used merely to fool me? I mean, were you joking with me on Evelyn's plan to leave me?" Loke immediately took the smile off his face for a more serious and stern look.

"Hey man, I'm not certain about all that. Teralyn did not seem to be joking about Evelyn's plans of leaving. I think you need to talk with Evelyn real soon."

"I know Loke, and I plan to talk with her right after these folks leave. However, I think that property acquisition took her by surprise." Loke pulled me closer to him and whispered in my ear.

"Man, the acquisition of that commercial property was major league huge. That move may have saved your marriage. I'm serious. Hey man, on a different note, is it me or has Julie always been that fine? That woman was show nuff representing up in here."

I immediately looked towards Julie as she was leaving and I did have to agree with Loke that Julie was looking more fit than she ever had looked before. She dressed so lady like and was as sharp as any model in the media. Nevertheless, this was my opportunity to pick on Loke regarding Teralyn.

"Well Loke, I'm sure you are not interested in Julie anymore since you met Teralyn."

"Yo man! I'm just saying that she looks as good as she ever has. I'm not trying to declare interest in her. She has already conveyed that I didn't do it for her and I'm cool with that. I was just paying her a compliment."

Not long after Loke made that comment, Teralyn walked over to both of us and addressed Loke.

"What-chu got a problem wit-cho eyes? I saw you lookin at dat white woman like you wuz undressing her. Look! I don't do disrespect!" Teralyn snapped her right hand while jerking her head at the same time.

"Don't-chu thank you gonn be cheatin on me like J.R. did Evelyn. If you do, you got anotha thang comin. Ain't no new building gonn make me forgive you either."

As soon as she finished with those insulting words,

she glared at me like she was trying to pick a fight. I could not believe Teralyn would go there like that, and thus, I had to respond.

"Teralyn, I really don't appreciate you bringing me in you all's business. Let whatever is going on between you two stay with you two. Don't get me involved with your insecurities."

I was quick to try and correct Teralyn of course, but she was not hearing it.

"Back-up off me J.R. wit-cho cheatin self. I don't even know if I want-chu hangin round my man. He don't need none of yo ideas."

Loke immediately started whispering in Teralyn's ear as to tell her to be quiet. I just stared at Teralyn with one of those looks that basically told her, she would need me one day. Then, she walked off and Loke hit me with a not so serious question.

"Yo man, why you hate on my woman?" I looked up at Loke as though he clearly offended me, but I knew he was really trying to be funny with a smirk on his face. I played along with his humor.

"Loke, what do you think man? I mean, for one thing, Teralyn drinks beer." I said in way of a joke, but slightly serious.

"J.R., what's your point?"

"Well Loke, the majority of the women I have dealt with in my past, drank wine, not beer. Any woman drinking beer over a long period of time will have a beer belly. Women should not drink beer because the barley is too much for their stomachs and they will develop what we often refer to as guts, and it looks similar to them being pregnant."

Loke looked at me like I was losing my mind before dissenting with my words.

"J.R., women have been drinking beer for years, well prior to Teralyn's time. You just need to stop the hating and realize that she will eventually become your major source for understanding Evelyn. I really don't see why you cannot seem to comprehend that fact."

"Loke, I refuse to kiss up to some high class hoochie extraordinaire."

"Come on J.R.! Don't talk about my woman like that okay." I kept on talking after Loke's comment.

"I would be in serious trouble if I relied on her to help me understand Evelyn anyway."

I continued to talk as though Loke had not interrupted me. Then within minutes, we stopped our talking as Jewel approached and spoke to both of us, and then she proceeded to talk.

"J.R., I got to give it to you, you really know how to pull off a great deal. Congrats on securing the building at Merrick Park. That is very impressive. I commend you highly. Now, how do you feel after being so deceived?"

"Jewel, for the most part I feel okay, but I still don't' feel totally secure with my relationship with Evelyn."

"J.R., you need to have a nice talk with Evelyn so the two of you can smooth out the wrinkles of your relationship."

Jewel and I continued to talk and eventually addressed old times. Meanwhile, my security guards came over and apologized for the part they played in the surprise, trying to explain their disappearance and their not answering their cell phones when I was calling them.

I felt very excited about my marriage now, especially

according to how Evelyn responded to me purchasing her daycare center building. She no longer had to wait to have her lifelong dream fulfilled. As Loke said, I practically salvaged my marriage as Evelyn will never again show any signs of leaving me. Okay yawl, leave me alone. Call me whatever you choose to. Sometimes, a brother has to do what a brother has to do. What?

Chapter 22
Holla If You Hear Me

The stage was set for Evelyn and I to talk about my indiscretion. Yet I found it more difficult than ever to talk about the details of the incident. However, prior to our talk, I met with the new house attendant who would be Rosie's replacement; his name was Bentley. He was a tall dark African American male who stood about six feet five inches tall. He had a native English accent and was very proper. He had some very profound physical characteristics, and walked as though he might be gay. I was impressed with how fast Evelyn had wasted no time and basically found a man that seemed highly qualified but very feminine. I'm almost certain that she had already discovered this guy well prior to firing Rosie.

Anyway, another thing that impressed me about him was the manner in which he dressed; he wore a stylish black tuxedo. I wasted no time sharing with him some of Evelyn's pet peeves, and some things that I needed him to work on that would help me surprise Evelyn.

Finally, the last visitors were exiting our house. After their departure, I quickly approached Evelyn and asked her if it was a good time for us to have our talk. Evelyn was looking for her pocketbook in the living room of our house.

"J.R., let's talk and walk okay because I want you to show me my new building for that child care center. I am so excited about that."

Wow, I was beginning to really understand just how big that building was to my marriage, even though I just nonchalantly purchased it on today.

"Sounds good baby! I will get my carrying case from the office."

Somehow or another, Ricky must have heard us talking because he came out of the blue and jumped into our conversation.

"Hey, can I go with yawl to see the child care center?"

I quickly said yes, but Evelyn quickly said no and we both said it at the same time. Then Evelyn looked at me as though I was out of line. If I could just get Ricky to go then I knew that Evelyn and I would not be discussing my past around Ricky. However, I could not ignore her serious stare. Evelyn explained to Ricky why he could not come.

"Ricky, there will be plenty of times for you to check out the daycare center. This evening, J.R. and I really need to have a serious talk."

"Mom, can't I be a part of the serious talk? I mean I am the big brother here." Ricky pumped his chest and started laughing.

"What did I tell you boy? No, you ain't going, okay. Go play some basketball or something and don't even try pouting in my face because it will not work." Ricky shrugged it off and started walking to his room.

"Yes Ma'am! I hear ya." Ricky seemed so dejected.

"Hey son, we will do something together tomorrow, okay? By the way, when do you leave for that Duke Basketball camp?"

"I leave on Friday. On Thursday, Mr. Loke and Aunt T are gonna take me along with them to this new theme park in Dallas." Evelyn quickly responded.

"Ricky, I didn't tell you that you could go to no theme park with T and Loke." Ricky walked back in the room swaying his head as though he was upset.

"Mom, Aunt T said she would talk with you about it."

"I don't care what T said, I ain't told you that you could go."

"Dang! Can't I ever have some fun? All I ever do is play basketball. It sure would be nice to do something different sometimes." Evelyn walked over to Ricky with much anger.

"You listen here boy! You ain't got to play no basketball. Until you learn how to clean up your room, you ain't going nowhere."

Then Ricky lunged out at his mom. What a mistake? "Well mom, if you had not fired Miss Rosie, my room would be clean all the time." SLAP! Evelyn slapped Ricky upside his face and with the slap accompanied some pretty stern words.

"You better tend to your business, do you hear me boy? I said do you hear me?" Ricky quickly looked away from his mom.

"Yes Ma'am!" I could tell he was so embarrassed. Evelyn continued.

"Matter of fact, you can go to your room right now and clean it up. That would not bother me at all. And another thang, tell them fast tail little girls to stop calling this house. Also, I already told Bentley that he would not be cleaning your room up so you better handle that responsibility."

I felt sorry for Ricky, but there was clearly nothing I could do. He left for his room. I looked on rather helplessly as Evelyn and I headed for my car. I had to broach the subject with her.

"Evelyn, don't you think you were just a little rough on the boy?" She immediately got defensive with me.

"J.R., I don't need you telling me how to raise my son, okay. We need to talk about other matters so trust me, you don't even want to add more on the plate than you already have to consume…don't even go there."

You think she had to tell me that twice. I don't think so. I tried to help Ricky out but I had to leave well enough alone. Evelyn and I got in the car and then she began her attack on me.

"Okay J.R., I am anxious for you to tell me why you cheated on me. I expect you to come correct too." Whoa! I did not expect for her to just jump right into it like that, but I had to get this conversation over with.

"Actually Evelyn, I went to Georgia and made a serious mistake because I allowed this woman to come into my room and we just got lost for the moment." Evelyn stared into my eyes the whole time I was talking.

"Well, moment seems inaccurate as you managed to produce a child out of the event. So J.R., have you seen the child yet?"

"No Evelyn, I have not seen the child."

"So J.R., what is the plan with this child out of wedlock?" I really did not understand where Evelyn was going with this question so I just kind of played it by ear, so to speak.

"Evelyn, what exactly are you asking me? I mean, I have accepted my responsibility and I think I should take care of the child. I really don't have any feelings for that woman. It was really just an accident."

"J.R., please stop calling the sexual collaboration of two people an accident. There was no accident. Instead, I think it may have been an unfortunate incident that you very well could have prevented."

Okay, Evelyn was absolutely right, although the tension was starting to irritate my last nerve.

"You are right sweetheart; it was such an unfortunate incident. I want you to know that I clearly learned my lesson and I've been completely true blue to you ever since."

"So J.R., what was it about this woman that made you cheat on me? I mean, was she special? Evidently she must have some quality or feature that I don't possess."

Oh boy! This was getting just a bit far fetched. How do I tell her that it was just a one night stand and nothing else? It was a fluke and I allowed myself to stoop to that level. Hey, I still contend that I was not married at the time. I realize what I did might be conceived as wrong in many folk's eyes, but it was not an act of infidelity; I wasn't married at the time. Can somebody please holla if you hear me?

"Evelyn, she had no feature that you do not possess sweetheart. I just placed myself in a no-win predicament and I lost."

Evelyn's mind was working overtime, as her thoughts could not be contained. *He must think I'm some kinda fool if he think I'm just gonna bite on that bone. Men think women are so stupid and dumb.*

"How so J.R.? How did you place yourself in a no-win predicament? I mean you go to work everyday and so running into women must be an everyday occurrence. Are you telling me I should not trust you on a daily basis?"

Evelyn displayed a piercing rage-type anger; you could see it written all over her face. She was really trying to shake me. Her thoughts were more volatile than any loaded gun.

J.R. must think I'm stupid, trying to belittle his night of cheating; it wasn't simply a mistake or accident. He got the wrong farm girl up in here. Talking about a no-win predicament. I wanted to say to him, nigga, that's the reason I can no longer trust yo ass anywhere you go. I'm not buying into this so-called no-win predicament. If he was smart enough to realize all that, he should have been smart enough to rid himself from the temptation. I wonder whether or not he is still seeing that hoe. That old saying that a thief always returns to the scene of the crime is definitely a possibility when sex is involved. This child care center better be all that or else.

"Evelyn, please believe me when I tell you this: you can trust me forever and a day sweetheart because I swear to you, I will never, ever cheat on you again. Since I have been married, I have been the happiest man alive. You can quote me on that Evelyn."

"J.R., once again, I just need to know that you are not going to be trying to live the lifestyle of a player. I really don't care how much money you got. Money does not move me."

"Evelyn, first of all sweetheart, please forgive me. Will you forgive me?"

I pulled up into the driveway of the building that I just bought for Evelyn. She was looking all around and for the first time, got a look at her new Daycare Center. You should have seen the expression on her face!

"J.R., this is nice! Wow! I can have a big marquee on the front of the building with the huge words, Evelyn's Drive Through Daycare." Then, she looked at me and I believe I saw some of that anger beginning to dwindle.

"I forgive you J.R. for now, but you must understand that it won't be so easy to forget this incident. That tendency will drive my moods every now and then. J.R., just so you know, I do not tolerate infidelity. I can do bad all by myself, and I refuse to be a victim of someone cheating on me. My mom surprised me by saying that I should treat your premarital excursion like a bachelor's party. But, you see, I got to deal with the fact that there is a child involved. That will make it extremely difficult for me. I will try though, with all my might."

Evelyn made me feel somewhat relieved. I understood that it would be more difficult for her to forget what had happened. I could tell that she really adored this new building. I've got to admit this was a great move on my part. I cannot have a woman like Evelyn at home with too much time to think. I need to ensure that she is working and mentally pre-occupied, so she won't get on my last nerve. Hey, I know the married men out there who are shackled down, strapped at the wrists and ankles, with dog chains around their neck, know exactly what I'm talking about.

Marriage is like a game of chess. You got to keep her busy so she won't be free to roam up into your business. Somebody please holla if you hear me.

Evelyn and I checked out the entire building and you could tell she was really excited. I had devised a business strategy for her day care center over a month ago. It was designed so parents could drive through, drop their kids off, and then drive back through and pick them up. We also had future plans to have a transportation service for those parents who desired their children to be picked up and dropped off at their homes. I thought our plans and intentions were great until she startled me with the next bit of information.

"J.R., I really love this facility and you know who I think

will be an excellent manager of my day care center, Teralyn?" I almost tripped on my feet when she said those words.

"Evelyn, awhrahm, you think that would be a smart move? I mean mixing family into your business like that, could be dangerous. Do you think Teralyn would be qualified to manage such a facility? You do realize that these will be with upscale customers who reside primarily in the Merrick Park community?"

"Sure J.R.! She just needs to work on her communication skills like I did, but I think she would be good in the position. My plan is to work with her and then train her into the position."

"But Evelyn that could take a lifetime. I think she needs to work on more than just her communication skills. An English course alone does not teach leadership."

"J.R., what exactly are you trying to say? Are you calling Teralyn slow?" I hesitated to reply, but my thoughts had no respect of persons. *That's exactly what I'm saying. She is not only slow, but rude, and comes across like a bull in a china shop. She would run customers away with her ghetto-fabulous attitude. Of course, I was not about to tell Evelyn that now.*

"No sweetheart, I'm not saying that she is slow. I just think that type of job might be over her head for now. In time, she could grow into the position, but you don't want her to detract from your business. I would be more inclined to hire a Caucasian manager at first. The primary reason for this selection would be to build up your customer base here since it is located in a predominantly white area. Therefore, the initial face of your company, until you develop a strong customer base, should be

Caucasian."

"Hold up now J.R.! Is this my business or yours? Let me know right now because if it's mine, then I make the decisions and you can stay clear and allow me to do just that."

"Of course it's your business Evelyn, but I am just trying to make certain the business gets off on the right foot. That's all I'm saying. You must hire certified child care providers and I would like to think that you would want a manager running the business with a college degree and have the experience necessary to step right in and run this operation."

"Oh, so you trying to say that just because I don't have a college degree I can't run this business? Are you trying to insult me J.R.?"

"Evelyn that is not what I am saying. I'm just trying to say that I would think that you would want to have a person in the position that could assure or ascertain success when it comes to working with the demographics of this area."

Evelyn and I were still walking and talking. My phone started ringing and the caller ID indicated it was from the mayor's office. I took the call and walked out to my car.

Directly after I finished coordinating my calendar with the Mayor's secretary, I remembered that I had to call home. I wanted to make certain that Bentley was taking care of getting the house ready for a very romantic night with my wife. I dialed the house and Bentley answered the phone.

"Bentley, how is everything looking? Did you get the roses?

"Yes Sir, Mr. Carter! I got five dozen roses as you

217

requested."

"Bentley, here is what I need for you to do. I need rose petals leading from the front door to our bedroom. I want the five dozen roses on a nice pedestal in the bathroom and I want rose petals leading directly to them. Do you follow me Bentley?"

"Yes Sir, Mr. Carter! I do follow you."

"Okay, I need to be real quick because Evelyn is about to walk out and join me. I also need some bath water ran and make sure that it is about ten degrees warmer than room temperature. I want plenty of bubbles and I want them nice and fresh and glistening like diamonds. Bentley, use my Forever Stay Bubble Bath formula. That makes the bubbles stay around forever and they never dilute in the water. Please mix in some Arm and Hammer Baking Soda and some Epsom salt. Bentley, I want you to have some shrimp and steak tips nicely chopped and saturated with caviar sauce. Please separate the shrimp shells from the shrimp; I want to feed my baby with very little effort. Please prepare her favorite salad the way she likes it. Make sure you have that nice bottle of Merlot chilled to perfection, ready for her immediate consumption. Bentley, are you there?"

"Yes Sir! Everything will be ready for you two."

"Now, I want you to go into my private stash in the guest bedroom quarters and get a movie CD entitled Romancing Her Panties Off. It's a triple X throw down movie."

"But Sir, don't you think that's a little too raunchy? You want a romantic atmosphere and not a smutty atmosphere."

"Bentley, I thought you were gay. How are you going

to tell me what type of atmosphere to create?"

"Sir, although my sexual orientation may be different than yours, I pride myself on being romantic and I know what a woman likes."

I thought to myself, *he got some nerve with his gay behind.*

"Bentley, have you ever seen the movie?"

"No Sir, I have not, but I don't think a triple X throw down movie would be appropriate for the occasion."

"Bentley, I loosely use the term triple X throw down. Actually, the movie is about a man romancing a woman and the first forty-five minutes are the best foreplay moves I have ever seen or imagined that a man can provide a woman. Then, the last forty-five minutes has the best gut wrenching, bone chilling, hair rising sex that I have ever seen in my life. All I want you to do is to have the CD playing as soon as we walk into the bathroom. Don't play the sound, but I want the visual on my huge screen bathroom television. Are you with me?"

"Yes Sir, I am totally with you."

"Next, I need you to get the right music playing as soon as we open the bedroom door. Please have them arranged in the following order: (1) One of Those Days by Whitney Houston, (2) I Need Some Me Time by Heather Headley, (3) LaToya Luckett's Torn and then mix in some Barry White, Luther, and Ronald Isley. I need their hottest lovemaking songs.

Also Bentley, make sure the aroma candles, with the forest river brook scent, are burning. As soon as Evelyn and I go into the bedroom, I want no interruptions, any whatsoever. Please hold all phone calls because we will be shutting down for the rest of the evening. Bentley, can you make all this happen in the next, say, hour and a half?"

"I most certainly can Mr. Carter. I just need to get the movie CD and place it in the CD player, and arrange the requested music. Everything else is pretty much elementary."

"Okay Bentley, Evelyn is about to come to the car so I need to bounce."

"Excuse me Sir? You need to what?"

I forget that Bentley really does not understand our slang. I need to be patient with him because he is too proper for our time.

"I need to get off the phone Bentley. I will call you later."

"Okay Mr. Carter! Do call me when you are about five minutes out."

"Check that Bentley. Evelyn is coming now so I need to get off the phone. I'll holla later."

I quickly got off the phone as Evelyn approached the car. I jumped out the car, ran to the passenger side of the car, and opened the door for my baby.

"J.R., this is a very nice building. I must admit you did well and I am very proud to be the owner of this facility, way up in Merrick Park. I got to come back and take pictures and show momma all of this. Then again, I need to wait until the marquee goes up that says Evelyn's Drive through Daycare. I can't wait to shop for office furniture. Okay honey, what was it that I was mad at you about? I can't quite remember."

Chapter 23
I Need Some E Time

Wow!   Evelyn got so wrapped up into the new building that she practically forgot all about the reason we were deep in heavy discussion. After we left the furniture store I quickly drove home so that I could romance my wife.

When we arrived, Evelyn quickly noticed the rose petals that led up to the front door. I parked right in front of the house and took her in that door.

"J.R., what is that all about?" She pointed at the rose petals. I acted very clueless.

"I don't know Evelyn. I guess we need to go inside and see what's going on?" She looked at me with a very sly look on her face. She was anxious to see what was going on. We rushed inside and she saw the rose petals heading towards the bedroom hall. Bentley greeted us at the door.

"Good evening Mr. and Mrs. Carter. Your bubble bath awaits you."

Evelyn turned to look at me. She was all smiles. Of course the mother instinct within her made her inquire about Dominance Nicole.

"Bentley, how is my baby doing?"

"Ma'am, she is sound asleep and well taken care of."

Evelyn went to take a peep at her and I went along; she was lying there sleeping so peacefully. Then, Evelyn was anxious to follow those rose petals.

I got to admit that Bentley earned a definite pay raise. When Evelyn saw the roses, she just started glowing like a Christmas tree with lights, while sniffing the freshness of those roses. The bathtub water was beaming as though

Bentley had sprinkled diamond pieces throughout. The huge screen television showcased a man that was intimately caressing the thighs of his lover. The music started off with Whitney and her song, *Just One of Those Days*, played ever so smoothly throughout the room. Bentley did good!!!

The aroma in the air made you feel as though you were on the riverside of a canyon. The food was elegantly prepared and perfectly contained and preserved in an exquisite warmer. I watched Evelyn as she admired the work of art and the atmosphere that Bentley had made possible.

It was now my time to contribute to this evening's festivities. I slowly and gently caressed Evelyn's shoulders as I positioned her to watch the movie that was very stimulating.

The man on the screen had laid his woman down and buried his thick two inch wide lips into her tender most area, as she laid their with her legs spread wide open. The man had been gently sucking the entire surface of the woman's most tender area on her body and his thick lips covered all of that real estate. The woman was gently screaming as the man delicately used his tongue as though it was a surgical instrument. His head was buried beneath the woman's thighs and he was enjoying every inch of her tender most parts.

I told Evelyn to let me undress her and caress her. And then I gradually took off Evelyn's silk sweater, her corduroy pants, and then her bra and panties, keeping her focused on the television screen. I slowly and delicately guided her into the bathtub.

Then, I had Evelyn lay back in the tub in her most

comfortable position. I stood there totally naked in front of her and I served her like I was a paid waiter. As the bubbles accented the water, I fed my woman shrimp and steak tips.

I mixed her favorite salad with the entrée and then I served her favorite Merlot wine. The atmosphere was similar to being on a romantic, deserted Island, all alone, just the two of us.

After feeding Evelyn, I scrubbed my baby with a really soft wash cloth. I made sure no part of this lovely piece of real estate was left untouched. I told her to just relax and let me do all the work. The feeling was such a cleansing for me as well. When I was done, I held Evelyn in my arms. As we lay there in each others' arms, I kissed her and reminded her how much I missed these moments. I told her how much I loved her, how complete I was with her, and shared with her my commitment.

Then, we quickly bathed one another and kissed with the passion that would set a forest on fire. I led her out the tub and dried her off with the nice super soft towels that Bentley provided.

I led Evelyn to our bedroom and then I further set the stage for taking care of my business. I positioned her on her knees with her back towards me. Then, I gave Evelyn my famous and rarely performed ice cream scoop.

While she was on her knees in the doggy style position, I grabbed her buttocks, parted those waters and stuck my tongue out as far as it could go. Then, I slammed my tongue between those butt cheeks, hitting all of her lower to upper parts.

First, I would whisk my tongue over those parts very softly and slow and just whip from the bottom to the top. I would repeat this action on numerous occasions until I heard her moan with irresistible passion.

Then, I would slow my scoop to a speed of slow motion while allowing my tongue to sink into her lower pitted area, in search of that special part of her body. With my tongue and juicy lips, I played with that special part and sucked and slapped it around with my tongue and lips and Evelyn's entire body was jerking, shaking, and experiencing spasms like never before; she bellowed out sounds of surrender.

I even managed to gently get that heart of her sexual pleasure between my lips and tongue and gently rubbed it, sending Evelyn to total submission as she shouted out with uncontrollable sounds.

"Ooh babeee…I can't ta..take… it anymore.   ohh… ohh…ohh….God that feels so good!"

The J to the R was just getting started. I gently and slowly stroked my tongue up and down her little bump while dipping my tongue into her pitted areas both lower and upper.   For each area, I would try and stuff as much of my tongue as possible and then wiggle it from side to side. Evelyn could not handle it as her body shook from multiple orgasms.

Next up, I sat in a chair and I had Evelyn sit on top of me with her face towards mine and her legs on top of mine. We practically consumed one another in the most loving way.

"Oh J.R.! You feel so good inside baby. Oh...I forgot how great this felt….oh baby."

"I miss being inside you baby. You know you been depriving me for awhile now."

She was already ablaze as she started bouncing while

using her legs to lift her bottom. It's a good thing the chair was so sturdy because home gurl just got buck wild on a brotha. I had to lay the lumber like it's never been laid before. Phew!

"Oh baby my legs are getting so tired, but I don't wanna quit. It feels so good honey. I don't wanna quit J.R....oh...oh...oh..."

I started lifting Evelyn up by her hips so I could help her legs out. Them extra push-ups and weight training was paying off royally.

"Oh J.R., you done got bigger...oh yeah...oh yeah."

I took my sweetheart on to everlasting Loveland as we both came in unison like members in a choir hitting a note. We met each other there and embraced as we continued to sit in that chair. We were both out of breath and tired in the most pleasurable way. Nevertheless, I had to share my words.

"Evelyn, I want you to know that I love you baby. I apologize for ever doing anything to hurt you. When I'm on the road, I think about you, when I'm at work I think about you, when I'm not with you, I'm craving to be with you. I sometimes feel so scared because I want to breathe you because you are so much a part of my spirit. I am so proud to share a child with you honey."

Evelyn just laid there in my arms and rested her head on my broad shoulder as she dozed off to sleep. I put my honey to rest in bed and cuddled up around her, protecting her with my body. I gave a soft and gentle prayer to the man above, thanking him for blessing me with my wife and newborn baby.

"God, I really do thank you for blessing me in all areas of my life."

Then afterwards, I slept like a drunken sailor, snoring louder than jet engines roaring from an aircraft. Life was so good in the Carter house.

Chapter 24
Can Proven Facts Lie?

Jewel was in the office on a very early Wednesday morning. She had gotten several email messages from her former fiancé, Sidney, who was now completing an investigative assignment for her. Sidney's investigation team was rapidly developing into a formidable and reliable investigation force. He often boasted as to how professionally accurate his team could be regardless of the task. Sidney's professional goal was to make a name for his unit within the arena of Homeland Security.

As Jewel read the email revealing all the hidden facts, she became disgusted. She was so unbelievingly surprised that she called Sidney on the phone.

"Sidney, I was just reading your email. I find this so ridiculously impossible. I would not think any woman would go to such extreme measures. Are you for certain that your guys are not making a huge mistake?"

"Jewel, I can see how you may come to that conclusion, but my team has fully investigated every lead before deriving to this conclusion. We have all the facts before us Jewel and the facts don't lie."

"I guess I am so flabbergasted over all that I'm reading. I cannot believe that a woman would go to such extremes to get a man or to attempt to bribe a man."

"Jewel, I think the reason why you are having such a problem with the results is that you are somewhat brainwashed. In your mind, men are the only deceivers, liars, and cheaters. You really do think that all men are dogs, and that we do all the dirty work to screw a woman and not vice versa."

"Sidney, are you speaking for all men or are you

speaking in reference to yourself? You can try and defend all men, but please don't try defending yourself. You got caught in the act so let's just leave well enough alone."

"Now you see Jewel, that's what I'm talking about. All you saw was the conclusion and the act. You don't know whether or not I was set up." Jewel started to get uncomfortable with where the conversation was headed.

"Sidney, don't even go there. J.R. is a saint compared to you and your doggish lifestyle. I'm surprised about all these actions regarding J.R., but you were too busy in New York and you know I'm telling the truth. Let's not even have this conversation anymore okay? I want to keep our interests on a professional level. How soon can I get the full report on this investigation?"

"Jewel, you can get the report today. Why don't we meet for dinner somewhere and I'll bring the report. That way we can have a nice meal and continue this discussion. It'll be my treat!"

Jewel was definitely not trying to meet with Sidney on a personal basis. Her intentions were purely professional.

"Sidney, how about one of your employees hustle the report over to my office immediately because major decisions will flow from this report." Sidney blew in the phone as though he was frustrated.

"Darn Jewel! What's it gonna take for you and I to get back together? I have apologized over and over again. Why can't you just forgive me and let bygones be bygones? I still love you and you know that. Don't think for one moment that your new boyfriend, Corey, can bring you the happiness we once shared. I know you still care for me which is why you supported me relocating to the area."

"Sidney, I supported your relocation to this area because I knew you could really do well professionally and I have never been wrong before, have I?"

"No dear, you have been right on cue, but what about us?"

"What about us? There is no us Sidney. I got to run, so please have one of your folks drop the report over to my office immediately. Your payment will be in your business account by close of business today. Great job by the way!"

"Now Jewel! Don't you feel bad that this guy is not anywhere near as guilty as you concluded him to be? I mean, the guy got set up tremendously and he made some foolish mistakes."

"Sidney, that's what all you men do. J.R. is still not innocent. However, he is just not as guilty as he appeared to be. Nevertheless, I still blame him for cheating."

"Jewel, the guy was not even married yet, for crying out loud."

"So what Sidney? You see that's why you and I are not together now. You think you can cheat all you like up until marriage. Well, guess what, you had the wrong woman in mind if you thought that I was gonna continue to be a fool. Good day Sidney and once again, great investigative work. Your funds will be in your business account. Bye bye!" Click went the phone.

Then the phone rang again within a matter of seconds. Jewel answered the phone immediately, although she knew it was Sidney calling back.

"Hello."

"You know you got some nerve hanging the darn phone up on me Jewel. It's not like you and I didn't spend several years in a relationship. I really don't like the way you have been treating me and I am demanding that you treat me with respect. Then again, at least treat me with professional respect. After all, our team did just uncover the mystery of your boss and his alleged cheating behavior. I am really serious Jewel, and I demand respect from you. Are you there?"

"Sidney, I have given you more respect than you deserve and you can certainly believe that. I commended you on the work that your firm did with the investigation details. But now, I really do need the report right away. This investigation has been my focus for quite sometime." Sidney started blowing on the phone as though he was getting really impatient.

"Jewel, I realize that you are very busy, but I'm just asking if you and I can get some time when your pace slows down. I'm really serious Jewel. I know I messed up before baby, and I am so sorry. Please believe me when I tell you that I am still madly in love with you. Can I get just a little bit of time real soon?" Jewel was listening to Sidney but, she really was not planning on bulging.

"Sidney, I don't see that happening anytime soon. I told you before you came here that our relationship was done. Please honor and respect my wishes by keeping what we have on a professional level. I do have a man in my life right now and we're very comfortable with our relationship. I don't want to do anything to jeopardize it."

"Jewel, what about us baby? What about my love that I vowed to you before I ever knew who you were? Come on Jewel. I didn't come back here for the work. I came back here for you. I have not treated any woman in my life like I did you."

"Sidney, you were not faithful to me. I cannot overlook

your infidelity. Now, Houston is full of some of the finest women in the world. I'm certain that if you were to make yourself available, you could probably find a number of women who might tolerate your lifestyle. I just can't do that."

"Jewel, I'm not the same, sweetheart. I learned so much from being stupid. I really have turned over a new leaf."

Jewel was not really interested in hearing Sidney beg any longer. She was more concerned with what was in the investigative report and needed it to finalize this business with her boss.

"Sidney, I have got to go right now. You take care of yourself and we shall remain professional acquaintances. I got too much on my plate right now to even focus on the past. Take care of yourself."

Jewel was slightly sensing some guilt and she had to deal with the battle of the mind. *I really hated that I had to be so cold to Sidney, but he certainly was cold to me when he elected to cheat around on me like he did. He may in fact be a different person altogether, but I cannot chance ever engaging myself in a relationship with him again. I'm certain he will find someone here in Houston real soon anyway. There just comes a time when a person has to just move on.*

Chapter 25
The Mix

Loke had finally returned to work. The wounds from the shooting incident caused him to miss a lot of time from work. He walked into his new office and found several messages on his desk. He also noticed that he had several telephone messages that had not been played. While reviewing his messages, he ran across one that really startled him.

"Loke, that first meeting was a mere warning. The next one will result in your death," said the voice on the answering machine. Loke immediately had concerns. He knew from his previous experience with death that he had to take more direct precautions in the future. He got on the phone as a result of the message.

"Hello, this is Lola."

"Lola, I just wanted you to know that your lover, Michelle, has left me several threatening messages on my telephone. She is really starting to concern me."

"Loke, she was my lover, but that is no longer the case. Why don't you report her to the police?"

"Well, I'm not afraid of that crazy woman. She better watch it or she will catch me on the wrong day. I will hurt her in a very brutal way."

"I can't believe you have not already turned her in. For crying out loud man, she almost killed you. What man in his right mind would not report to the police someone who almost killed him?"

"Lola, you need to stop acting like I brought this situation upon myself. If you wouldn't have challenged me with that stupid bet I wouldn't have even been in the situation for your lover to attack me. You deserve part of the responsibility for her ridiculous behavior."

"Loke, perhaps I need to refresh your memory. I invited you to a threesome because it was my fantasy."

"What's your point?"

"You knew I was already in a relationship with Michelle. It was you who promised to rock my world in such a way that I would never return to Michelle."

"Did I handle my biz or what?"

"Well, you did just that! You did, in fact win the bet. I never thought any man could ever love me as good as my lover Michelle."

"I rocked your world gurl, had your head spinning, took your butt to the moon and convinced you to kick your lesbian lover to the curb. Still, I did not expect her to come after me like she did. I was just doing what I normally do as far as sex is concerned. I just bring it like that."

"Oh, so are you trying to say that we can't develop anything from the relationship? I stopped seeing Michelle with hopes of seeing you on a permanent basis Loke."

"Hold up Lola, I did not say anything about seeing you permanently. I was just doing what I do. I'm not looking for a wife or anyone like that. I must also tell you that I have a special person that I am about to live with."

"So! Is that why you have not been returning my phone calls? Do you really have someone serious in your life? I thought you told me my stuff was the bomb, remember that? You even told me that you really enjoyed being inside of me and wished you could have this for a lifetime."

"Lola, that was all pillow talk baby. I mean, I can accommodate you every now and then, but that's about it.

I told you I was not trying to get serious, but our thing together was merely a sexual fling."

"Loke, you are a liar. You told me that you loved everything about me and that if I stopped seeing my lesbian lover, you would take me to another level and the two of us could be a serious item. Now that I have broken up with Michelle, you are changing your tune."

"Lola, I am not changing my tune. We can be a serious item ...serious enough to be kicking it every now and then. Once again, I do have a potential love interest and I really don't want to upset that chemistry. She kind of came along unexpectedly after I got out the hospital. She was there for me Lola. I mean, you never once came by the hospital to visit me, did you?"

Loke was lying about Teralyn. She was not really there for him, but that sounded like an excellent selling pitch to convince Lola as to why she was his current special lady.

"Loke, you don't understand. I was devastated when I found out what happened. I did call in and speak with the nurse on several occasions, but I could not bring myself to seeing you. I felt totally responsible for what happened to you. I was not only afraid for your safety if I came to see you in the hospital, but I was also afraid of what Michelle would do to me. She's crazy, I tell you."

"Okay Miss Lola! Fix it however you choose to."

"Loke, you don't know this woman. After what she did to you, she threatened to kill me if I didn't come back to her. That's why I called the police and had a restraining order placed against her. I just hope the authorities will keep her away from me. You need to come forward and report her to the police. She needs to be arrested and put away so we can both get on with our lives without fearing for our lives."

"Scared? Lola do you think I am afraid of this woman? You must be crazy. I am not scared of that dike. She best stay clear of me before I do something serious to her. I don't play now Lola."

Loke was obviously putting on a front as his thoughts captivated the true essence of his feelings. *Then again, Lola might be right. I need to come clean with the cops and let them know that I got caught up in a lover's triangle and they need to arrest that crazy hoe. Especially since she has been calling my office and threatening to do more harm. Oh well, guess I need to let the cops know that she was the one who came to my office and waited for me to depart and shot me like she did. Of course they will ask me why I did not come forward at first and I will tell them the truth...I was embarrassed by the overall incident and I did not want to admit that some stupid woman took me out like that.*

Lola continued to explain her point to Loke

"Loke, I hear your every word, but you were practically locked up in the hospital for a minute and you don't need to be underestimating Michelle. I am ever-so-careful when I leave my house and find myself constantly looking over my shoulders. If I don't feel safe going somewhere, I just don't even take the trip. You need to be real careful until Michelle is behind bars. I mean, she is capable of killing both of us at a whim. You of all people should know this."

"Yeah, thanks for the advance warning," said Loke in a very sarcastic tone.

"Did I tell you about the time that she clobbered this guy at a club after the guy kissed me on my cheeks? I'm telling you Loke, the woman is a powder keg."

"Lola, it's kind of funny how you did not tell me all this prior to us engaging in that threesome. I mean, it was enough that I had to stomach her trying to sex your body right in front of me. Nevertheless, I knew she did not have what you craved and that's something no woman can provide."

"Yeah right! Like you did not enjoy her loving me down in front of you. I saw how she made you all excited. And what is it that I craved so much for?"

"Please woman! You know I don't need to even answer that question. Besides, you got plenty of it from me when I turned you out, upside down and every which way but loose. I told you I would have you leaving that trick once I got done with you." Loke started laughing as he concluded those words.

"So you bragging about your little performance, huh?"

"Little is not the word to use when describing me baby. I gets the job done and you know this. By the way, what do you have on right now?"

"Why do you care? I'm still in bed with a tee shirt on."

"Really? Wow, what I would pay to be that tee shirt right now."

"Oh really! I have on the real short tee shirt that goes halfway down my stomach. What do you have on?"

"I'm at work Lola. What in the world do you think I have on? I have on a white shirt, blue tie, and dark blue dress pants."

"Can I take your clothes off over the phone? That sounds like fun to me. It's been awhile since I undressed a man."

"That might be possible if you let me taste your

thighs."

"You can taste anything you like," said Lola.

"I can. Awh, suki suki now! You know when I start I don't like to finish until I'm done. You remember them loud sounds you made as I brought down the wood. Are you feeling me about now?"

"I'm not feeling you yet, but I would love to start feeling a brother. What next after you taste my thighs?"

"I will taste those thighs of yours by planting my tongue firmly between those veins of yours and licking very gently at first and then licking real hard. Can you feel where I'm coming from?"

"I'm trying to feel where you are going my brother. Keep on talking and tell me more and stop asking me so many pointless questions."

As Lola was talking on the phone, Loke heard this noise in the background that sounded like a real cheap battery running some device.

"Lola, what is that noise I'm hearing in the background?"

"Huh? Ahm, what? What, ahm, noise?"

Lola's voice was getting lower and sexier as her tone had dropped down like she was on the receiving end of a nice, juicy pipe.

"Lola, you can't hear that loud battery sounding noise? What the heck is that I'm listening too?"

"Oh…oh…oh.…just shut up and keep on talking Loke. Oh papeee…. babeeeeee! Ohh…"

"Lola, you mean you are actually servicing yourself while talking to me on the phone. You are a trip."

She kept on making those loud humming like sounds as though she was under total submission to my voice.

"I'm…using….my…..silver bullet keep tal….king ba…by. Oh goodness! Ohhh!..uhhuh..uhuh......get it baby….get it baby…."

"How am I supposed to get anything over the phone?"

This is so embarrassing to me. I am not used to a woman using my voice over the phone to get her rocks off. I have never been down this road before. Normally, I'm the one causing all the commotion. She needs to realize who she is dealing with. I slammed the phone on the hook, and said to myself; *my name is Loke, not joke. She gots to go.*

Chapter 26
Marked Cards?

Jewel spent countless hours reading over the investigative analysis report Sidney's team had comprised. She just couldn't bring herself to believe that her personality had undergone these tumultuous mood swings. Without even consulting me, she verified the data contained inside the report over and over again.

Her process had taken over a week, and she still had not consulted me on the findings of the investigation. There was a section in the report that Sidney had neglected to mention. She felt this information was crucial to the outcome of the report. Therefore, she would have to talk to Sidney again. Thus, she picked up the phone and did just that.

"I figured you would be calling me back after you got the report."

"Sidney, this is much more serious than I could have ever envisioned. What gave your team the gall to investigate to this detail?"

"Jewel, we did not do a formal investigation on anyone with exception of that Mayberry woman. We, instead, did a comparative analysis of the various blood types involving all parties."

"I need to ask you one more time if your results in your report are totally accurate. Sidney, if the implications of your study are correct, there could be major repercussions and serious discoveries that could literally threaten innocent relationships."

"Jewel, I stand firm on the evidence gathered. We did a sure-fire study on the blood types and the blood that flows in our veins does not lie."

Jewel was too floored to even respond. She did not realize that she had a serious battle on all fronts. As soon as Sidney finished his words, Jewel was deep in thought. *I cannot believe Doralee would stoop to such level, but then I also find it difficult to believe some of the other stuff in this report either. I won't challenge Sidney just yet but until I do my own personal investigation, I really cannot take a chance and put any stock and value in this report. The facts just don't add up and I really know that certain people are not capable of doing what the report implies.*

"Jewel, are you still there?"

"I'm here Sidney. I'm just inundated with all this newfound information."

"Once again, funny how the truth can be so revealing to where everyone involved becomes analyzed to some degree."

"Sidney, is there absolutely any possibility that these tests are inaccurate?"

"Jewel, unless the hospital made a mistake with the blood types, the tests are not inaccurate. I'm sorry this information has taken you by such surprise. Just remember this one fact about all people. We all have skeletons in our closet."

"Sidney, I want to go a step further and contact the hospital folks who processed the blood work."

"Jewel, you do what you must do; I know how stubborn you are about finding the truth. I'm also sure that you're gonna check out the hospital as well as the other key information listed on the report. After everything is said and done, I am willing to bet you that you'll derive at the same conclusion our company reached. I tell you, we're right on target."

"Sidney, you do know me well. Let me go now and conduct my own investigation. I'll be in touch."

"Bye Jewel."

Directly following the phone call, Jewel got busy! She was on a personal mission to find out the real story. She never thought in all her wildest dreams the investigation would net so many implications, and certainly not the number of concerned parties. Jewel was as thorough as they came.

She traced every step of the investigation. She traced how Sidney's team gathered all their information and spent three days turning over every stone relative to the findings. After researching this report and finding that it involved all of us, to include, Doralee, Evelyn, Jamie Randella, Dominance Nicole and I, Jewel had firmly arrived at her conclusion.

Unfortunately in her mind, she had reached the same conclusion that Sidney's investigation team had presented to her.

Thus, she needed to respond accordingly to the information gathered. However, prior to acting upon anything, she tasked Sidney's investigation team with another job. Her phone conversation to Sidney did surprise him to some degree because she had another task for his team to perform.

"Sidney, I want to know every time that Doralee traveled at the company's expense. I want to know her involvement with the Hispanics in this area. I want to know how often and where she visited when she came to this area. I want to know exactly how many times her and J.R. really did collaborate and where. I want to know every woman J.R. has been with since he has been in Houston.

I want to know the when and the where. I want to know every time Evelyn went to Dallas after she married J.R. I want to know where she went when she visited Dallas. I want to know who has ever visited her here in Houston and I want to know everywhere they went. Are you comprehending Sidney? I want to know everything that I can about Miss Evelyn. I want to know more about Ricky's father. How long has he been strung out on drugs? Has he contacted Evelyn? Have they met since she's been married? What, if anything, have they been involved in? I want all the details and all the juice Sidney. Do you fully understand where I am coming from? I want that information and I want it yesterday!"

"Wow Jewel! If I didn't know any better I would think that you're taking this a bit more personal than usual and this is more than just a professional interest. Why unravel all that stuff on your boss and his wife? Why do you care about Ricky's father? You sure act like you have personal interests in this matter."

"Sidney, just leave all the extracurricular thinking to me. Get me the facts and I will go from there. You understand my request?"

"Jewel, I perfectly understand your request. I just hope you will be able to appropriately process the information once you receive it. My team will take care of this job."

"Thanks Sidney and please call me once you get all the details. I got to run now, bye bye!"

Jewel got off the phone and began to focus on the data that she had already received. In the meantime, she devised a strategy of her own.

She made reservations to fly into Atlanta and proceed

to Stockbridge, Georgia to visit Doralee Mayberry. She made no mention to anyone about her trip with exception of having the secretary book her flight. I was too engrossed in my real estate commission report and my delivery presentation to the mayor.

Nevertheless, Jewel was determined to resolve any issues relative to Doralee Mayberry.

She arrived in Atlanta on a Friday morning and after getting a rental car, made her way out to Stockbridge, Georgia. She was headed to see Doralee Mayberry in our business office there. Upon arriving at the office, she was greeted by the secretary who was surprised at Jewel's unannounced visit.

Although the visit was sudden and unexpected, Doralee's secretary cleared her boss's calendar so Jewel could have some time with her. As soon as she made Doralee aware of Jewel's visit, Doralee rushed out into the office area where Jewel was patiently standing.

"Well, what a surprise? How are you doing Jewel? Please feel free to join me in my office."

Jewel just stared at Doralee and did not say a mumbling word until she walked into the office and waited for her to close the door.

"Well Jewel, what have I done to deserve such a visit?"

"Doralee, let me get straight to the point. I have received some startling news about your manipulative efforts involving Mr. Carter. As a result of your foul play, you are fired. You have until 4:00 today to clear out of this office, and if you do not clear out by then, the authorities will have you kicked off these premises. Here is your one month salary which is all you will be getting from this company. Effective immediately, you will have no further contact with Mr. Carter and his family. And if you do, you will be reported for criminal investigation regarding your bribery attempts involving Mr. Carter."

Doralee just stared at Jewel with a shocking expression of disbelief on her face. Her mouth was wide open and her eyes outstretched as though she had been informed that she was sentenced to prison for a certain crime.

"I'm sorry but I don't understand why I am being fired exactly. I had an affair with Mr. Carter, but it was a consensual one and so why should I be fired? J.R. and I are lovers and if anyone should be fired, he should and not me."

Her words inflamed Jewel to instantaneous anger. Jewel's next words were about to flow out of her mouth like a double edged sword.

"Doralee, you and J.R. were never lovers. You were nothing more than a one night stand. To add insult to injury, you drugged J.R. with your prescribed medication and Viagra by mixing it into your special Italian wine where you made him totally defenseless and lethargic. Don't you dare stand before me like you have been innocent with your setup of Mr. Carter. You planted your leads all around Mr. Carter so you could get to him. I have no doubt that you two did what you did on a consensual basis, but you took it to unprecedented extremes. By the way, there is a difference between consensual sex and drugging someone to where they become nothing but obedient to your every command."

Doralee was well schooled at appearing innocent while knowing she was as guilty as Charles Manson.

"You don't understand. Mr. Carter lured me to his hotel room after our interview. He wanted me badly and his desire for me was written all over his face. I was very professional during the interview, but I felt his eyes undressing me. I gave him what he wanted and ultimately needed."

"Don't even flatter yourself. You sent low wage leads after Mr. Carter. You enticed him into sleeping with you and then you held that over his head so you could blackmail him into hiring you for this position, and then giving you astronomical pay bonuses."

Doralee just stared at Jewel in sheer amazement as to how she clearly knew all the facts. Doralee was somewhat intimidated.

"But, you don't understand. J.R. is still the father of my baby girl. You can't undo a born baby. He needs to own up to his child support and fatherhood responsibility."

"Let's just see about that Doralee, since you brought her up. Let's talk about how the baby's blood type does not match J.R.'s by any stretch of the imagination. Shall we talk about the sperm bank that you visited to procure the seed for your child? Let's talk about how you realized that J.R.'s foolish unprotected sex with you did not impregnate you. Instead, you wanted to blackmail him for life by getting yourself pregnant via the sperm bank route. You are clearly a disgrace to all women."

Doralee's face sunk towards the ground as her shame was exposed. She could only place her hand to her forehead and look down towards the floor.

"This is not the truth. I did not go to any sperm bank whatsoever."

Jewel anticipated her denial and she was as patient as

a rattle snake was about to devour her defenseless prey. Thus, she smoothly removed a report from her purse and conveyed to Doralee the signatures of the sperm bank and her signature was highlighted. Doralee got quiet and walked away from behind her desk.

"Now, I suggest you back up and stop trying to deceive people with your foolishness. Once again, vacate the office and you better not ever attempt to make contact with anyone in the Carter family, ever! If you do, you won't be so carefully warned the next time. Do you hear me Doralee?"

She nodded her head as though fear had totally overcome her body.

"I hear you and I understand."

"Good! Now, start vacating the office and don't make any attempts to return. I hope you're smart enough to have saved some of that money over the year, because you're going to need it. I also hope you'll be a better mother to that child of yours than you've exhibited as a woman."

Jewel grabbed her papers and began to walk out of the office. Just before she walked out the door, Doralee made one last request.

"Jewel, I suppose it would be asking too much of you if I asked for a job recommendation and used you as a reference for future employment."

Jewel didn't even dignify the question with a response. Instead, she just walked out without even looking at Doralee.

Jewel was relieved to know that all was not too bad for J.R. She was glad to know that all he had to overcome was the cheating and that the baby, Jamie Randella, was not his child at all. She was very anxious to catch her flight back to Houston so she could meet with J.R. and inform him of everything that had taken place.

She knew he would be ecstatic to know that Doralee was fired, did not share a child with him, and would be ultimately out of his life for good. However, she elected to refrain from addressing certain other segments of the investigation report.

Chapter 27
Time to Get Off

Jewel, you have got to be pulling my leg. You mean to tell me Doralee drugged me and made me seem helpless. Then, she went to a sperm bank and got impregnated? What woman would go to that extreme to bribe and manipulate a man?"

I was having a serious conversation with Jewel. She had flown back from Houston, and found me at home chilling as Evelyn and Teralyn were away in Dallas attending a business meeting concerning her daycare center.

"J.R., Sidney's team did an excellent job tracking down all of Doralee's sources. For instance, they tracked down the doctor who legally prescribed to Doralee some liquid medicine that would relax and calm her nerves."

"Jewel, please tell me you are lying. You have got to be kidding me."

"No J.R., the truth has been exposed. She must have loaded that wine bottle with the majority of her prescribed medication. I was too impressed with how Sidney's team tracked down every trace of her actions, although she had performed these actions over a year ago."

Jewel seemed excited for me. I was excited as well. Regardless of what I was told, I didn't want to appear overjoyed in her presence because the fact still remained that I did have sex with Doralee. Thus, I felt a need to mix the pot up with Sidney's name in a natural kind of way, eventually. I just had to ask the question in a very subtle manner.

"Jewel, I am still in a state of shock here. Why would Doralee do such a thing? What would possess her to play such a dangerous game? Whoever would think that a woman could mastermind such an operation?"

"J.R., it just goes to show that you cannot put anything past a woman; especially a woman that you don't even know."

"But Jewel, more impressive was how Sidney's firm brought about all the answers. Shoot! The LAPD should use him to investigate Tupac's death." Jewel chuckled slightly.

"Now Jewel, does this mean that you and Sidney are back to dating again?"

"J.R., Sidney and I will never date again. I am pretty much done with him."

"But Jewel, what if you are wrong about Sidney? What if he made poor decisions like I did and winded up into an affair like mine?"

She started raising her hand and nodding her head as to cut me off, but I continued to talk.

"You do realize that women would do anything to attract a high profile attorney like Sidney? I mean, he could be more innocent than you realize."

"J.R., I am not about to get into this conversation about Sidney. His case is totally different than yours. He was caught red handed and was not drugged nor tricked into getting in the sheets. He practically initiated hooking up with the woman I caught him with as well as the other women he started seeing."

"Jewel, are you really certain about all that or are you speculating?"

Jewel got an expression of anger on her face. She looked at me as though I was insulting her.

"J.R., please speak solely for your circumstances

because you really don't know about mine, okay. I am not trying to relive those moments regarding Sidney. He confessed to me about all the women he had been sleeping with, after he was busted."

"Well Jewel, isn't confession a good thing?"

"Confession is a good thing J.R., but don't make it everything and don't you get too comfortable in thinking that you did no wrong regarding Doralee Mayberry. I don't care how drugged you were, you had no business in a room with her. Don't be flaunting around me like you were totally innocent."

"Wow! My bad Jewel. I can only say that you are absolutely right. Regarding Sidney, I am so very sorry about the pain you had to experience."

"J.R., I am not about to let no man dictate my happiness. You all are too wishy washy for me anyway. One moment you are in love and trying to spoil a sister and the next moment you trying to hit everything moving. I am just learning to keep you all on a certain level." Jewel, seemingly was sharing with me her inner most perspectives on a brotha.

"Now Jewel, what's going on with you and Corey?"

"J.R., I got to go. I really did not plan on talking with you about the men that I have been dating. Corey is Corey. He has his issues just like the rest of you all. We still date, but we are no longer on a serious track."

While Jewel was talking, Loke called me on my cell.

"Hey man! What's going on?" I said.

"I should ask you what's happening. I got your message. You still want to go out and get lit up?" Jewel grabbed her purse as she prepared to leave.

"Loke, hold on okay. Jewel, you ought to come and

hang out with me and Loke. We gonna hit a nice club, dance the night away and get lit up. You should come and join us."

"J.R., I am not about to go to any club after flying all day. I am gonna get my papers and get out of here. When will the Mrs. be back?"

"Oh, Evelyn and Teralyn won't be back until late tomorrow evening." I started to walk with Jewel towards the front door.

"Now J.R., don't do anything foolish tonight at the club. You still need to realize that you are married now, until death do you part. Do you hear me?"

"Jewel, come on now. After I have been in such torture over the past year for my foolish decisions, I am not about to go and get back into some more trouble. Trust me girl, I have learned my lesson."

Jewel stood at the door and just looked straight into my eyes as though she was analyzing me. I walked her to her car.

"Okay J.R., I'll see you in the office tomorrow. You and Loke have a nice time, but please be careful. You got my phone number if you need me."

"Jewel, I'll be out with Loke. We just gonna hit a club or two and have a good time. This will be my first time going out since I been married. It's all good. You take care of yourself now."

"Okay J.R., I'll talk with you tomorrow, bye bye."

Jewel left the house and went straight to her car and drove off. I walked back into the house and I started back talking with Loke.

"Loke, I was just seeing Jewel out. What time you gonna come by and pick me up?"

"J.R., I'll be over in about 30 minutes. I really don't want to stay out too late because Teralyn called me and said that she may be coming back on the red eye."

"Loke, don't let her infringe upon our party time man. You should have told her to go ahead and stay the night and return on tomorrow with Evelyn."

"Hey man, I hear you J.R., but I miss my boo and I can't wait to see her."

"Whatever man! I bet as soon as we hit the club, you going to forget all about her Loke. I know you way too well man."

"Look man! I'll be over real soon. Let me get my playa look on and I'll see you in a few minutes. J.R., please remove your entire ankle and handcuff marks man so it won't be so obvious that you been in lock down, ahahahahaha!"

"Yeah right man! I'll see you in a few, later!"

I took a quick shower and threw on my nicest threads. Before I could splash on my Versace cologne and slip on my Cole Haan shoes, Loke was ringing my door bell. Bentley, of course, opened the door.

I was so excited about the outcome regarding Doralee. She was done, gone, out of my life and I never felt so free over the past year than I had right now. I walked into the living room and there Loke was standing and talking with Bentley. I was so happy to see Loke, so happy to be free, and just happy to be happy and alive.

"Yo Loke, you want to drive or do we need to get one of my security guards to drive us?"

"No way J.R.! We don't need any security man. I'm driving my ride. It's all good my brother. How does it feel to be free?" Loke shook my hand and we exchanged our typical brotherly hug and started laughing.

"Man, I feel real light my brother. Those heavy burdens have truly been lifted. Jewel really did an outstanding job getting the details from Sidney." Loke stopped walking towards the car and quickly asked about Jewel.

"Sidney? I thought he was out of the picture a long time ago. Didn't you tell me that she caught him cheating on her and she sent that brother packing?"

"Exactly! But the brother packed and came straight here not long afterwards and started up his investigation firm."

"I know you definitely ain't mad at a brotha," said Loke.

"I know that's right! He led the investigation that uncovered all the details as to what Doralee had done. He really did a great job man. I mean, for instance, I knew that when I was with Doralee after I sipped on that wine, I was a different brother. It's almost as if I literally transformed into a different person. You know I could press charges against her man. This woman drugged me with some Viagra and with some type of relaxation medication that made me a follower with a lot of steel downstairs, if you know what I mean."

"Hey man, I know exactly what you mean, but I would leave well enough alone. You don't want to be wrapped up in litigations with this crazy slut after she done almost ruined your marriage. I say just leave well enough alone and press on man."

"Loke, I do agree with you. However, Jewel does insist that I do have grounds to have this woman arrested and brought to court under serious charges."

Loke and I hopped into his truck and he drove off as

we headed for the club to get our groove on.

"Jewel is an attorney J.R. I would expect her to take that position. However, you need to do what's right for you and your family's peace of mind my brother. Let the stress go man. Now, let's kill this serious talk, get ready to go up in here, and sniff some honeys' perfume. U feel me?"

As Loke and I arrived at the club, I wanted to make certain that we had the same intentions in mind for the evening.

"Now Loke, I just want to make sure we are both on the same page. I am not trying to get laid or anything like that. I just want to have some fun, get a little lit, and that's it."

"Playa, why you even going there with me? I know you married now and all that jazz. Hey, if you don't want to, we don't even have to go into the club. We can go to my house if you like and just knock down some cold ones. It's really your call."

"Naw Loke, let's go ahead and party. I may not even know how to act nowadays, but I just want to have some fun. Besides, who knows when Evelyn will be out of town again?"

"You got a point there J.R."

"Don't misunderstand me! By no means am I saying that I can't get out when she is home. I'm just thinking that with all the issues that have emerged over the past six months, it's probably better for me to get my groove on with her out of town."

"J.R., you are preaching to the choir my brother. Once again, do you want to do this or not? It really does not matter to me."

"Loke, let's do this man. Besides, I need the break.

Let's represent."

Loke and I finally walked into this club called Houston Nights. It was an upscale club that attracted only upscale customers in a very ritzy part of town in west Houston. Loke and I walked into the joint as though we had papers on the place.

Less than five minutes after we walked in the club, this terribly fine sister walked over to Loke. I mean, baby girl was bouncing in all directions …and I mean from head to toe. I was quickly knocking down a Hurricane with the triple shots.

"Fancy seeing you here," the woman said as she basically whispered in Loke's right ear. Loke quickly turned around with his guard up like he had seen destruction in the flesh.

"Michelle, back up off me now before it gets ugly up in here."

"Man ain't nobody pushing up on you. I just want you to know that I ain't completely finished with yo trifling self."

She pointed her forefinger into Loke's chest while talking and he knocked her hand away.

"Back up off me Michelle. I'm not gonna warn you no more."

Michelle stepped back off Loke and walked away with some threatening words.

"If I ever see you in public again, that's yo ass!"

Then she walked off with the nicest twitch and the nicest bounce that a woman's butt could possess. I quickly had to inquire about Michelle.

"Loke, what the heck was that all about?"

"J.R., that's a long story man. I'm not even trying to talk about that confused dike tonight."

"Confused dike? Loke, why you gonna hate on the woman like that man?"

"Woman? Don't let her looks fool you. She is not a woman by any stretch of the imagination."

"Loke, what did she do, turn you down or something?"

"Not at all J.R.! I'm trying to tell you that she is not a traditional woman. She likes women."

"What? So you are trying to tell me that she is a dike?"

"That's exactly what I'm telling you. I'm about to press charges on her crazy, hood-like behind. Anyway, I don't want to spend the rest of the night discussing her J.R. She's the one responsible for my chest wounds."

"What? Did she hire somebody to do that or what?"

"No. She did it herself."

"But Loke, why would she do that? Hey man, what did you do to her?"

"See J.R.! It's not even like that. I bet her girlfriend that if she got a piece of me, she would never return back to her lesbo friend. So her girlfriend invited me for a threesome and I had to represent, u feel me?"

"Loke, you mean to tell me that you screwed around with babes that are involved with dikes? Come on Loke! How stupid is that?"

"See J.R.! That's why I'm just telling you man. You are too quick to judge me. This was just a one time good deal. I just told Lola that if she got the right kind of loving from a real man that she would never go back."

"Well Loke, did she?"

"Hey man, if she would have gone back, I would not have been shot up like I was and that stupid incident would never have occurred."

256

"Loke, you mean to tell me that you turned this gay woman out to where she gave up the life?"

"Yo man, what kind of question is that? Better yet, what kind of expression is that? What did you expect? You know what J.R., you do not understand that you are in the presence of a legendary playa. I pride myself on knowing how to break any woman down to her knees and have her begging for more. You see a guy like me is really too much for just one woman. U feel me?"

"Man please! There is not that much loving in the world anymore. Look at you out here dodging the threats of some gay woman. I am no longer feeling that playa lifestyle my brother. You need to get out while you can. These crazy women out here will eat you alive."

"J.R., I can see you feeling that way, but it was really your stupid actions that brought about all that drama in your life."

"Loke, you don't think trying to break up a gay relationship is being stupid?"

"Heck no, man! That mess is an abomination to God anyway, according to the preacher."

"What preacher Loke?" Loke acted real timid all of a sudden.

"Oh man, I forgot to tell you. Teralyn and I went to church one Sunday."

"Oh really? I literally begged you to go to church with me, but you never would."

"Whatever man! Anyway, you should be glad that I even went, whether it was with you or Teralyn."

"Hold up playa! I am glad that you went to church. I'm just saying that I guess I had to have a package like Teralyn to get you to go to church with me."

"Come on J.R.! Don't even believe the hype. As far as turning Michelle out, I was helping God out." I just started laughing as I was knocking down my drink.

"Oh, so you were mixing God into your actions huh? Don't go there Loke. Your actions were purely selfish and you know that."

"Hey J.R., on a serious tip, you're knocking down them drinks way too fast man. You are about to set yourself up for a serious hangover if you keep drinking at this rate. You know, one day I really do need to teach you how to drink."

Loke quickly looked down at his watch.

"J.R., it is now 8:30 so let's try and be out of here about 10:00 so I can go home and rest up for my boo."

"What boo is this? You got Casper the friendly ghost coming over? Ahahahaha....ughh!"

"I see you got jokes. Actually, I told you that Teralyn was flying back early tonight. By the way, she is planning on moving in with me tonight. That's just between us J.R."

"Loke, are you crazy or what? You don't even know her like that. Why the heck is she flying back tonight anyway?"

"Hey man, I don't know what happened, but I got the impression that she and Evelyn had a falling out. You know how it is man; sisters do that every now and then."

"Loke, I know how it is. I questioned Evelyn as to why she was gonna make Teralyn the manager of her company. She has absolutely no experience whatsoever and she wears her emotions on her sleeves."

"J.R., are you certain about that? I mean, Teralyn has not said squat to me about her being the manager of Evelyn's daycare business. Matter of fact, the two of us were thinking about going into business together."

"Oh really? What business were you two thinking about starting up?

"J.R., don't laugh man. I actually did some research and it is really a very lucrative industry as long as you run it right. This is a prime location for this type of business. Teralyn even wanted to bring her best friend Shaneequa from Alabama and make her a part of the business as well."

"Loke, what exactly are you talking about? Industrial, retail, government type work or what? I'm curious."

"To some degree, depending on how you look at it my brotha, I'm talking about all the above. Primarily, we were planning on opening up a strip club man."

I almost choked off my drink when I heard that.

"Loke, you are a dentist dude. What does running a strip club have to do with dentistry? You do not want to tamper into that industry. Trust me man! That is more of a headache than you can handle. I bet Teralyn got you interested in something that bazaar."

"J.R., just think about it man. What a great way to recruit honeys and then you can make money off of their sexploits."

"Loke, we won't even labor in this conversation." I immediately signaled to the bartender.

"Hey boss, can you get me two more Hurricanes?" I quickly turned to Loke.

"Loke, you want another Bud?"

"J.R., you need to slow down playa. I'm good. I don't need another drink. Matter of fact, I'm done drinking." Loke quickly turned away from me as he got distracted by what he saw.

"Whoa! Check out that fine honey over there man." I turned around to see who Loke was talking about. I could not believe what I saw. There was Veronica and boy was she looking like a million dollars. I quickly started draining my drink because I felt the temptation of Veronica hit me hard. Before you knew it, she strutted her way over to where I was sitting at the bar.

"Well, hello handsome. May I have this dance?" Loke quickly intervened.

"Hey luscious, you got to be the finest woman in the house? I almost dreamed about you last night." Veronica extended her hand to meet Loke's hand.

"I'm doing fine, thank you and how, may I ask, did you almost dream about me last night?" Loke did not stop at trying to capture her attention.

First of all, my name is Loke, short for Latrell Oliver King. I almost dreamed about you because had I met you on yesterday, I would have dreamed about you last night. Baby gurl, you have got it going on and I mean that with all the energy I possess."

Veronica looked at me and smiled, and quickly interjected her thoughts.

"Wow! With a line like that, you should be selling houses too."

"I tried but I got fired for ripping too many folks off." Loke started laughing and quickly corrected the comment.

"I'm just joking Veronica. I'm a dentist by trade." Veronica responded back to Loke and then continued to talk with me.

"It sure is nice to meet you Dr. King. J.R., you told me about Loke. He's your best friend and partner, right?" I was sipping that Hurricane real fast as I was diligently trying to escape from reality, while also staring at Veronica.

"Show you right, show you right Roni."

The alcohol was gradually kicking in and I was certainly feeling the flotation. Loke quickly intervened again.

"So Veronica, you already knew me? Before yawl go and dance, where did you meet J.R.?"

"J.R. sold me my first house." Veronica grabbed my arm and began to pull me out of my chair. I slightly stumbled and Veronica noticed.

"J.R., are you okay? You seem a little tipsy." I was feeling somewhat high, but I did not want to admit that to Veronica.

"Roni, I…I'm fine. Let's go shake a leg." Veronica and I hit the dance floor. While I was dancing, Loke met some hottie on the dance floor and started getting his groove on. Loke was smiling like he had just won the lottery and I was fading fast, but I was not going down without a fight.

Chapter 28
Business or Pleasure?

Evelyn and Teralyn were staying at their aunt's house in Dallas. Evelyn elected to stay there rather than stay at the convention center hotel because she took Dominance Nicole along with her.

The business convention had come to an end and Evelyn did not choose to fly out on late Friday night as Teralyn chose to do. However, prior to Teralyn's departure, she and Evelyn did have their share of friction with one another.

Evelyn had met a visitor in the living room area of her aunt's house on Friday evening. She expected the visit, however she was still surprised at the overall outcome.

She had just put Dominance Nicole to sleep, and Evelyn had just tucked her into bed. Shortly afterward, her aunt yelled upstairs to tell Evelyn someone was at the door asking for her. She seemed very excited as she ran down the steps.

"How are you doing?" She gave the visitor a big hug and he hugged her back.

"I am doing fine Evelyn. You look more beautiful now than I have ever seen you look before in my life."

"I must admit, Sam, you are looking so much better since the last time I saw you."

Evelyn's thoughts truly conveyed her inner most treasures. *My goodness! Do I even know him? He has really cleaned up and is looking so fine! Wow! I am starting to feel real uncomfortable.*

"How is my son doing?"

"Ricky is doing real well. I spoke to him earlier. He is at another five star basketball camp in New Jersey."

"Wow! I understand he really knows how to play basketball. Too bad I never really tried to teach him the game."

"Well, you would never know by the way he plays. One would think several folks have taught him the game."

"Can we talk about us? I really do miss you and Ricky too."

"Sam we can discuss us, but please keep in mind that I am a happily married woman right now."

"Evelyn, are you sure you did not marry that guy on the rebound from recovering from our relationship? I mean, you guys did get married rather sudden, and you and I were battling some pretty serious issues over seeing my son."

"Sam, I am not meeting with you to discuss my marriage. You were strung out on drugs and really doing bad. Now, how have you been coming along? I can tell you are not strung out anymore as you are looking good."

"Evelyn, what about what we had?" Evelyn immediately got fidgety as she began to shuffle her hands.

"Sam, what we had, we had."

"Evelyn, you are in serious denial!"

"Sam, I will not discuss the past right now."

"Evelyn, we will need to discuss the past someday. Can I see the baby?"

"For what Sam? You have nothing to do with my baby."

"I hear ya Evelyn."

"Sam, I'm sorry and I really don't mean to be short with you. It's just that…"

"I understand. You are happily married now and I guess that's the way things will be."

"That's right Sam! That's exactly the way things will be. Now, how are you really doing?"

Sam just stared at Evelyn and he felt deep down that she was not being realistic. Then again, he knew he had to comply with her demands if there was any chance he had of getting back into her life.

"I'm doing real well. I am feeling good. I been clean now for about 11 months and I am even working at the local dry cleaners downtown. I have really learned a very valuable lesson."

"Well, your son is really taking off. He's excelling academically and getting lots of attention in the basketball arena. He's such a great basketball player, ranked as one of the top high school players in the nation."

"I had the pleasure of seeing him on television and I must admit that he really touched me. Watching him made me want to do right."

While Evelyn was talking to Ricky's dad, Teralyn walked downstairs and did not even recognize Sam. She just kept staring as they were both standing up in her aunt's living room. Upon realizing who the stranger was, Teralyn decided to join them.

"Sam, is dat-chu?" Teralyn walked into the living room with her hands on her hips. Sam just barely looked at Teralyn and spoke to her.

"Hey T, how are you doing?"

"I'm doing well Sam. You sure look like you doing real well too." Evelyn intervened in a blatantly rude way. Teralyn tried to talk to Sam, but she felt shunned by her twin sister.

"T, Sam and I are having a private conversation, if you don't mind."

"Wow E, don't be so rude."

"I'm not being rude. That's why I'm asking you to give us some privacy. Can you go check on Dominance Nicole?"

Teralyn got totally upset, knowing that Evelyn was treating her that way in front of both their former lovers.

"No, you go and check on Dominance Nicole yoself. Being business partners don't mean I gots to obey you 24/7. I ain't always gotta be at work."

"Never mind then Teralyn, I will check for myself. You just want to show yo butt off in front of Sam." Evelyn quickly ran upstairs while Teralyn was left alone with Sam.

"Guess you don't know me no mo?"

"Of course I know you T. I just don't think we should be too vocal around Evelyn."

"Ont know why not. It's not like she didn't know you and I were knocking boots." Sam started whispering real low.

"See T, I really don't know if she knew."

"She knew Sam coz I told her after she got pregnant wit Ricky. You wuz jest too drugged out to notice da signs."

"Must I be reminded of my drug infested days? I'm a different man now."

"I see dat-chu is, in more ways den one." Teralyn started giving Sam the elevator stare going up and down his 6 foot 4 inch, 230 pound frame. Teralyn was still really feeling Sam. *Phew! Sam is still fine with dat cute Chris Brown like smile, caramel taffy brown skin, and dat nice muscular body. If he won't a druggie, he clearly could have da richest women taking care of him. He is dat fine. Make a stranger want to say, what-cho name is?* Teralyn's thoughts became rudely interrupted as Evelyn came back downstairs.

"Dominance Nicole is sound asleep so T, you can be excused now. Once again, this is a private conversation."

"E, you don't gots to be so snotty bout thangz. Ain't nobody tryin to push up on yo baby daddy. I wonda how much privacy you need nigh dat-chu married anyway, or did-ju forget?"

"T, get out my business. You ain't my momma so step, okay. I thought you were planning on catching the red eye back to Houston. You only got a few hours to do that. I suggest you get to stepping."

Evelyn raised her right hand with the thumb standing up to emphasize the stepping comment. Teralyn really got pissed off by that comment. She just stared at Evelyn and then stared at Sam. Then, she got up and handed Sam a card, but Evelyn quickly slapped her hand.

"No you ain't gonna disrespect me like you have done through the years. I allowed you to sleep with Sam back in the day because I did not want him cheating with any other hoe, but those days are over twin sister."

"Dem days should be ova coz you married nigh, but I guess you done forgot about Mr. J to da R."

"T, carry yo butt wherever you going and mind yo own business. I'm serious. I'm starting to wonder if I want to make you the manager of my daycare center or not. You got too many issues surrounding you."

Teralyn picked up the card that had her number on it. She was trying to give it to Sam. Sam just stared as though his hands were tied. However, he did take a deep stare down Teralyn's chest as she bent over in front of him with her melons all loose and bouncy.

"Fine E, I will see you in Houston. Do I need to take my niece wit me so she won't be exposed too early to her cheating mom?"

"Forget you T! Once again, mind yo own business and you need to get to stepping if you gonna catch that red eye."

Teralyn went upstairs with vindictive anger. She was not expecting to see Sam, her one and only lover during the time that Evelyn was pregnant with Ricky. Seeing Sam made her lawn moist and her nipples hard as he used to screw her britches into a fade, back in the day. When she came back downstairs, she went and stood straight in front of Sam.

"I shoulda known you won't no good. You told me you wuz done wit E and when you got back on yo feet you would only seek a relationship wit me. I wonda what changed yo mind."

Evelyn quickly came over and grabbed Teralyn by her arm. Teralyn quickly jerked her arm away from Evelyn.

"Let me go E. Dis ain't got nuttin to do wit-chu. Yo lying baby daddy told me he waz done wit-chu. I jest want his explanation. You'z a married woman nigh so dis shouldn't be any of yo bizness."

"T, you need to stop tripping like this girl. Stop embarrassing yourself. You go ahead and find your own man and stop leeching off me for men. I'm asking you kindly to go ahead and leave right now."

Teralyn just stared at Sam and he just stared back as though he owed her no explanation. Teralyn was so embarrassed and could not believe that Evelyn was acting as though she was still single. Nevertheless, she got her bags and had her cousin take her to the airport. She was determined to move out of Evelyn's house and move in with Loke who was expecting her tonight around midnight.

Chapter 29
Back At the Club

Veronica was so surprised to see me high and wired. It didn't seem to matter to her. She just seemed so pleased to see me. I'm certain she had numerous questions, but she definitely did not pose any. I was sinking fast from the alcohol that I had been drinking and I was truly enjoying every moment of the party atmosphere.

I've got to admit, I was pretty much plastered. In fact, I was so drunk that I did not even recall Veronica leaving for the night. Nevertheless, Loke did inform me that Veronica left word that she would call me tomorrow. Loke was anxious to leave the club so he could get home and get ready for Teralyn. I was so drunk that he had to help me walk to his truck. I was trying to sing some rap song as we were departing the club.

"J.R., you are so funny man! I did not expect you to bring me so much laughter tonight. I have never seen you this drunk. You are a trip. I don't know how many of those Hurricanes you knocked down, but boy are you wasted."

I was hearing Loke, but I only heard patches of words from him.

"What?...Where?...What hurri...hurricane is coming dis way?...When? We need to, awhrah, se...seek shelter, don't we?"

Loke started cracking up and laughing real loud. Then, he was quick to correct me.

"J.R., I did not say anything about a hurricane coming this way man. I was talking about all those drinks you had. You are a trip man. You are too funny."

Loke just started laughing again real loud as he had his left arm hooked around my right arm so he could help me walk out to the parking lot. When we got to his truck, he could not believe what his eyes clearly saw.

"Oh No! Dyaaammm! This is so crazy. J.R., that lesbo done slashed all four of my truck tires man. Dogg! I can't believe this, man! Dogg!"

He let me go for a minute and I was trying to open the car door as I was clueless as to what he was talking about. Loke kept on expressing his anger.

"Now how are we supposed to get home man? AHHH! I'm gonna get that dike. She will pay for this man." I started pulling money out my pocket to give to Loke.

"Hi...how much do I owe? and fo...for what?"

"J.R., put your money back in your pocket man. I can't believe that you still walk around with all that kind of money. You don't owe me anything. Dang! You too drunk to even know what I'm talking about."

"You k..keep th..thin..king I'm to...too drunk...now...I knowz...what...t..t...time it iz."

Loke called for a tow truck on his cell phone and then he grabbed my cell phone and brought up the numbers to my security folks.

"Carter Security," was the reply to Loke's call.

"Hey, is this Thomas or Walker?"

"This is Thomas Sir. How are you?"

"Well, I'm jammed up right now. Mr. Carter and I need for you to come and pick us up at Houston Nights. Do you know where that is?"

"Most definitely Sir. We got the electronic connection to Mr. Carter's phone which kind of tells us where he is at all times. He just had that system implemented now for about a week and it works like a charm."

"Awesome Thomas! Can you guys please come and

pick us up? I have a tow truck also set up to get my truck."

"Sir, did your truck break down or something?"

"Well, not exactly! It's sort of a long story, but I would appreciate it if someone could come and pick us up."

"Of course, Sir. You will have a pick up within fifteen minutes. Are you guys in the parking lot of the club?"

"Exactly Thomas! We will be standing near my truck in the front parking lot of the club. Thanks for the help and I'll see you later."

"No problem Sir! Help is on the way."

Loke got off the phone and clamped my cell phone back on my belt. For some reason I thought he was a stranger trying to steal my wallet so I swatted at his hand and then swung at him and fell to the pavement.

"Dude, you are seriously tripping. Now, I'm gonna help you up so don't get up swinging at me again. I'm with you big guy and I am not a stranger trying to take anything from you. I tell you, if it was not for you and your funny state of drunkenness, I would be some kind of upset over my tires being slashed."

Loke was talking to me as he helped me stand up after I fell. I misunderstood him again.

"Rrr..really..what fires are com...com....ing... he....here?...We need to hurry up man. Why we still waiting any...way? What-chu do....ahhrah...run out of gas?"

I started laughing and so did Loke.

"No man. You are cracking me up."

Loke started talking to a few honeys that were walking by outside the club and of course they noticed his truck's tires were slashed. I tried to keep quiet because the alcohol was messing with my head.

Finally, the tow truck showed up to take Loke's vehicle to the nearest dealer and Loke also called the Houston Police Department to report the lady in question. He arranged for an appointment with the authorities on tomorrow as he did not want anything to distract him from being home for Teralyn.

As soon as I got dropped off, Bentley escorted me to my bed and helped me get undressed, and he appropriately laid me down to rest. I was out cold in a matter of minutes.

Later on throughout the night, I was awakened by Evelyn. I was still not sober, but I felt her warm embrace caressing my body. I think she tasted my toes and stuffed them into her cold, wet mouth. I thought I would explode for a minute. Then, she just started tasting her way all the way up my leg.

"Oh my....oh....Evelyn you show feel good. I can't do much right now be...because my head ain't co....cooperating. I love what you are doing to me."

Evelyn did not say a spoken word, but her lips and tongue and wetness from her body did enough talking for me.

She seemed to enjoy the taste of steel water which was actually still soft water because my big head won't totally in synchronization with my little big head. Nevertheless, the feeling was so great that I just laid out and let my woman take care of me. She seemed to have parked downstairs and was not about to move, as she was getting plenty of neck exercises by going up and down it seemed a thousand times. I was not about to complain. Then, she moved forward and gently bit my nipples in a sweet slightly painful way. Afterwards, she whispered in

272

my ear.

"I want to screw you so bad J.R. I saw yo pants jump when you first laid eyes on me. You wanted dis stuff, didn't ya boy?"

I just started laughing uncontrollably as Evelyn was tickling me with her words because she has never talked like that before.

"Qu….quit playin Evelyn!"

I started laughing again and then she leaned forward and suffocated me with her melons.

"Whoa! Them thangz done got larger. I didn't know the baby brought all that."

I tried to suck those nipples, but I kept missing as she was focused more on insertion and penetration of her body right on top of steel water.

When she finally did place steel water into that awaited resting place, she seemed so tight at first. Nevertheless, she went to town riding me like I was a white pony. She pretty much straddled me down and I grabbed those melons for leverage and before you knew it, she was screaming my name in a very countrified kinda way.

"I'ma get all dis daddy….oh my…dis pudding tang iz yo's daddee…..OOWEE… OOOOWEE."

I was really too wasted to notice that Evelyn had really went on much longer sexually than she normally had and she also said a lot more words, but I was fading in and out. She just laid there with her head in my arms. I tried to rub my woman's hair, but she kept moving my hand and would not let me touch her hair. Evelyn must have gotten her hair done in another style and did not want me to mess it up. It was pitch black in our room and we could barely see each other's body.

About five minutes later, I fell out cold. I was sleeping like a bear in hibernation. Evelyn laid right there in my arms which is where she belonged.

The night was such a comfortable ease for me. I slept like a little baby with no responsibilities. Heaven must be at my grasp because I felt like I was resting with the angels. Thank you Lord, for all the peace in my life.

Chapter 30
Caught In the Crossfire

Saturday morning gradually rolled around like it never had arrived in my past. I was asleep and knocked out cold when the drama of my life resurfaced, but this time seemingly beyond my control. I awakened to a loud voice that totally confused me as I gradually responded to my wife's voice.

"You trifling piece of dirt, get out of my house right now Teralyn. J.R. you are nothing but a liar and a cheat. I want you out of my house too, right now."

I woke up to Evelyn's loud shouting voice standing over me and when my faculties came around I was in bed, butt naked with Teralyn. Evelyn evidently saw me lying in bed and all cuddled up with Teralyn whereas I thought I was all curled up in bed with her.

In my mind I was as innocent as OJ; well maybe not OJ, but perhaps Michael Jackson; well maybe not Michael, but I was in all truth as innocent as I could be. Although I was as innocent as I was, Evelyn was not trying to hear me at all.

"Evelyn, please understand sweetheart, things are not as they appear." I looked at Teralyn with a look of how could you and she just got up and started getting dressed.

"Shut your lying mouth J.R. You are nothing but a dog and, Teralyn you ain't nothing but a hoe. I want both yawl out my house right now. I am serious."

"Look sweetheart! I was out cold last night and all I remember is being out with Loke and having some hooks. Although I cannot explain how in the world I winded up in bed with Teralyn, you must know that I did not plan or arrange this."

"Right now, I don't even want to hear your mouth so please shut up talking to me. I am so disappointed in you. I mean, I'm not surprised by Teralyn's atrocious acts because she is so accustomed to coming behind me to pick up my men."

"Screw you Evelyn! Ain't nobody gots to go behind you for nuttin. I'm not even interested in yo cheating husband. He da one dat begged me like Sam used to. I jest wanted to get his beggin butt off my back."

Evelyn quickly attacked Teralyn as she was talking noise and getting dressed. Evelyn hit her upside her head and commenced to giving her a sista gurl beat down. I quickly intervened and separated the two, all butt naked. After I separated the two, I quickly put on my underwear. Then Evelyn continued.

"I want both yawl out my house now. Teralyn you can fly yo trifling butt back to Alabama right now. I am so sick of you and yo little hoe tendencies."

"Evelyn, ain't studdin you. If you eva lay anotha hand on me, I will kill yo ass. I don't play dat!"

I intervened again and Teralyn began to walk out.

"Teralyn, before you leave, can you please tell Evelyn the truth? I have not been after you at all for any sex. You are not telling the truth and you know it. I have never been after you, but you have been tossing your salad all up in my face from day one." Evelyn quickly intervened.

"Please, both of you just get the hell out. I don't want to hear either one of you talk."

My eyes were locked dead set on Teralyn as I was trying to understand everything that had happened. I must admit the last act I remember was going on the dance floor with Veronica at the club. I really could not take my mind to remember nothing much past that.

"Evelyn, we must talk baby because I insist that I am innocent. There is no way I would be clear of the Doralee Mayberry crisis to turn around and do something this stupid. You got to believe me baby."

"Innocent like you were with Doralee in Georgia. J.R., I am sick of you and I won't continue to be married to you because you are a cheater."

While Evelyn and I were in discussion, Teralyn had quickly exited into the guest quarters to get her other belongings. She immediately called Loke and asked him to come and pick her up right away, as I continued to try and talk to my wife.

"Evelyn, let's don't do this baby. You and I have come so far in such a short period of time. Please find some strength in your heart to give me another chance."

"J.R., I should have left you when you cheated on me with Doralee. I am sick of you to the limit. Now, if you don't leave this house, I will because I refuse to remain in the same house with a cheating husband. I just refuse to do it."

I stood there and stared at Evelyn as she was so sincere with her words. I looked out the window to my bedroom and I thought about the trouble my life had experienced. I really could not take my mind past dancing with Veronica at the club and I was trying so hard to remember everything else.

In all actuality, I was really unsure as to what really happened last night. I started to resent the fact that I even went out on last night. I knew that Loke should have some answers.

"Evelyn, I am so sorry baby. I'm sure we can get the

answers to what happened in time. I do apologize for not knowing exactly what happened. All I ask is that you remain in this marriage baby. Remember our vows, until death do us part sweetheart." She came over and started jabbing her finger into my chest.

"Nigga you gonna sleep with my twin sister and then have the nerve to throw wedding vows at me. Get out of my sight J.R. I am dead serious. If you don't leave this house, I will and I mean every word of that. If I have to leave, my kids are all leaving and we won't be back."

"Evelyn, where the heck am I supposed to go? I tell you what, I'll just sleep in one of the guest bedrooms until you are ready to talk and discuss this incident."

"J.R., I want you out of this house. I don't want to smell your cologne, hear your voice, see your dog tendencies, or any parts of you. Get out or I will. Once again, if I leave, my kids are leaving too and I mean right away. The choice is yours you cheating, slimy dog. I can't believe you were stupid enough to bring your cheating behavior into my house, much less our bedroom."

"But Evelyn, you got to understand...." She quickly interrupted me.

"I'm not understanding nothing else, but you getting out right now. I'm done with this relationship. At least Ricky's dad was more faithful than this."

Evelyn stormed out of the room and I stood there in my underwear. I sat down on the bed and attempted to retrace every activity of the previous night. Nevertheless, I could still not take my mind past the fun I had with Veronica. I still couldn't remember anything past the time I had with Veronica. I immediately called Loke to talk to him, and to see if he could help me out.

"Hello."

"Loke, you won't believe what's going on man." I heard Teralyn talking in the background.

"J.R. let me call you back. I'm in the process of taking my boo home man. Remember I told you Teralyn was moving in with me?" Oh my goodness! She already packed and left and headed to Loke's house.

"Loke, I really don't advise that man. You and I need to talk as soon as you get some time. I'm serious man. I need to talk to you about what happened last night. All I remember is dancing with Veronica and that's it."

"J.R., I'll call you back man. Let me handle my business first and I'll get back with you."

"Hurry up Loke because you need to talk to me before you move Teralyn into your house."

"J.R., you are already too late for that. I'll call you later man. I got to move her in and then I got to handle that business from last night. You remember?"

Loke hung up the phone. I really did not know what business he was talking about from last night. I started to check out my other options as to where I could stay. I was somewhat too popular to just stay in a local hotel and I really did not want people knowing my business.

I definitely could not stay at Loke's place since Teralyn was staying there. I thought about just holding my ground with Evelyn and refusing to leave. However, I did not want her leaving this house with the baby and also shaking up Ricky's current state of affairs. That alone would be too much for me to worry about. Furthermore, Ricky would not be back from camp for another week. Thus, at the present time, I did not have to worry about explaining anything to him. On second thought, at least Evelyn would still be here at the house, as opposed to going somewhere else. Then, hopefully, things would simmer down and I would be able to talk with her when she was ready. I could create a business trip out of town, but I don't think I want to be too far away in case Evelyn decided to jump ship. Here I go again stressing up a storm. Why does my head hurt so baad?

Chapter 31
It's Just Me against the World

Wow! I tried calling Loke again, but I got no answer. However, I needed to talk to someone. I sure would love to talk to Julie, but I would be embarrassed to tell her everything. Thus, I had to call on my stalwart, my solja at war, my gurl Jewel. I called her work number because she was expecting me at work for the purpose of going over my presentation with her.

"J.R., hold on." Jewel answered the phone as usual. She was always there for me.

"Okay J.R., how was last night? I see you survived the club."

"Jewel, I'm headed your way. By the way, I need a place to stay for a few days. I would stay at Loke's place, but I can't. I don't want to stay in any hotel for privacy reasons."

"J.R., what is wrong with your house? Is there something I need to know?" I could tell Jewel was in a good mood.

"Jewel, I'll give you the details when I arrive. I just need a place to stay for right now."

"J.R., you know you are more than welcome to stay at my place."

"Jewel, that's fine, but only you and I need to know that."

"Really? Darn! There goes my idea of making a radio announcement." She started laughing.

"J.R., I understand completely. I'm anxious to hear what's going on."

"Okay Jewel, I will see you in a little while. I am on my way, bye bye."

After I finished talking to Jewel, I took a quick shower and packed some clothes in a suitcase. I also stopped in to see Dominance Nicole who was once again sound asleep. I touched her face and kissed her while she was in the bassinette. Bentley walked in as I was kissing her forehead and he whispered gently to me.

"Hi Sir, she has been sound asleep. How are you today?"

"I'm doing fine Bentley. I got somewhat of a headache, but I'm doing okay for the most part."

"You seemed really lit on last night, I might add."

"Bentley, did you see me on last night?"

"Yes Sir! I practically put you to bed Sir."

"Are you serious? I somehow do not remember that at all."

"I pretty much heard you sleeping afterwards like you had not rested at all in this house."

"Bentley, do you recall when Miss Teralyn came in the house?"

"I sure do Sir. I helped her with her suitcase."

"Did you take it to her room or what?"

"Sir, if you are asking me if I saw her when she walked into your bedroom, the answer is yes. I was shocked as to the lack of clothes she was wearing."

"Really? So, how did that come about?"

"Sir, you were snoring so loudly when she opened the door that it could have set off a fire alarm."

Now see, that told me quite a bit. I was knocked out sleeping and Teralyn came into my room to get her groove on. As much as we seemed to hate each other, why would she even think of doing such a ridiculous act? I went on with my conversation with Bentley.

"So Bentley, as far as you know, I did not lure her into my room."

"If you did Sir, it was done prior to her arrival to the house. She did go into your room as though it was a planned event."

"Thanks Bentley, I really do appreciate the information."

I soon became very sick and stressed out. Nevertheless, I was curious as to whether or not Bentley knew what was going on.

"By the way, do you understand what is going on?"

"Yes Sir! Miss Evelyn caught the two of you in bed together and she has asked both of you to leave. I tried to wake you up Sir as Miss Evelyn had security pick her up from the airport. However, for some reason Miss Teralyn told me to get away from the door and that everything was fine."

Oh no! I could not believe what I was hearing.

"You mean to tell me that Teralyn knew Evelyn was coming into the house and she just told you to get away from the door?"

"Yes Sir! I was thinking there was some type of a game being played on Miss Evelyn. However, when she went in and responded, I was shocked to find out that there wasn't a game. To this moment, I really did not understand why Miss Teralyn seemingly wanted Miss Evelyn to walk in on the two of you." Bentley had quickly earned his worth in gold with me.

"Bentley, I need for you to repeat this same information again at a later time, okay?"

"Sure Mr. Carter. I can only repeat the truth Sir."

"Bentley, that's all I care about, is the truth. I got to

run now."

I rushed out of Dominance Nicole's room and I went back to the bedroom and noticed that Evelyn had locked the door. I knocked on the door hoping that she would open it so we could straighten this whole situation out, but she wouldn't. She just began shouting at me through the door saying, go away, and finally I did leave.

I headed directly to work. The drive was almost nonexistent as my mind was pre-occupied with what may have happened last night. After I arrived at my work facility, I went straight to Jewel's office and saw that she was on the phone.

"Evelyn, I cannot believe this. You must be joking."

Apparently Jewel was already talking to Evelyn. She was giving Jewel her version of what happened which I'm certain would only be just that. I sat down in Jewel's office and waited patiently for her to finish talking to Evelyn.

"My goodness Evelyn! You poor thing. Gosh! I feel so sorry for you. I can't imagine how that made you feel. I want you to know that I will be here for you. Please don't hesitate to call. I implore you to get some rest before you make any decisions whatsoever. I'm praying for you sweetheart, bye bye." Jewel hung up the phone with Evelyn.

"J.R., somehow I don't think it's a good idea for you to stay at my place. Do you realize your wife is about to leave you? She said she caught you sleeping with her twin sister. Now J.R., I informed her about the Doralee setup but I cannot explain this incident."

"Jewel, I was asleep and Teralyn came and got in the bed with me and seduced me. I thought she was Evelyn and I bit real hard."

"J.R., come on now. You are trying to tell me that you could not tell between your wife and another woman in bed?"

"Jewel, you got to understand I was out cold. I'm not even certain as to how I got home from the club."

As I was talking to Jewel, I got a call on my cell phone from Loke.

"Hello Loke. Let me call you back."

"Hey man, don't even bother. I can't believe you got so drunk as to go and rape your sister in law and my woman. You should be ashamed of yourself."

"Loke, what in the hell are you talking about?"

"J.R., I want to know right now. Did you rape Teralyn? I'm demanding some answers out of you right away. How could you have gotten so drunk as to do something so stupid?"

"Loke, I did not rape anyone."

Jewel stared directly down my throat. Then, she just looked away nodding her head.

"J.R., you got real drunk and did a lot of things that you did not realize. For instance, do you remember feeling on the butt of about three women at the club?"

"Loke, Please tell me you are just kidding man. I have no recollection of that at all. I do not go around feeling on a woman's behind."

"Well J.R., that's exactly what you did and on one occasion, you got slapped so hard that you fell to the floor."

"Loke, please tell me that you are joking? I don't remember anything like that."

"That's exactly what I'm trying to tell you. You did some stupid acts and you don't remember any of them.

How can you be so certain that you did not fondle Teralyn so much as to rape her?"

I thought about what Loke was saying. I do know that there was evidence that I had released the hounds because of the residual substance on my thigh that I noticed before I stepped into the shower, prior to getting dressed and leaving the house. Nevertheless, I figured that the residue was from me being lured by Teralyn while in my sleep. All I knew was that I did not remember what happened. To make matters worse, there was no condom in sight.

"Loke, I don't think I could ever rape anyone and I know for certain that Teralyn is making that up."

"J.R., you need to be concerned because we are headed to the hospital and she has already mentioned the fact that she would be pressing charges against you."

"Pressing what?" I instantly lost my temper.

"Man, please cease the madness! Bentley told me that she came into my room while I was snoring up a storm. You need to check that hoe at the entry doorway of liars' anonymous."

"J.R., I don't appreciate you calling my woman a hoe now. My only point to you is that you need to be aware of the severity of rape. If she takes you to court and brings you under charges, you could be facing 25 years to life in prison." I continued to stew. I started shouting at Loke on the phone.

"I ain't going nowhere because I didn't do anything. The fact that I can't remember does not make me guilty."

"How do you explain the dry flow of stream that was coming down her thigh? If you did not rape Teralyn, yawl did exchange some deposits."

I became very silent as I really did not know what happened on last night. All I recall was the fun that I had at the club dancing with Veronica.

"Loke, I think we need to talk later because I am too confused to address your questions."

"J.R., you better come up with some answers real fast dude because if she presses charges against you, I don't think it will be pretty. I will try and keep her from doing that, but you need to understand everything that is going on right now."

"Loke, she can press all the charges she likes, but I feel very confident that I did not rape her. She needs to stop tripping right now."

"All I'm trying to say J.R. is that you were not totally aware of everything you did. Now, on a side note, I will have serious problems if you two had any sexual relations. Sometimes I wonder if you were really attracted to her like that because sometimes on the other side of displayed dislike or hatred is covert attraction."

"Yeah, whatever Loke! I have never been covertly feeling anything towards Teralyn, okay. Can I give you a call later? I'm at the office with Jewel right now."

"Do what you must do J.R. I just hope our friendship can sustain this round."

What in the world was Loke talking about? Hey, I got to deal with one stress at a time. However, I had to respond to his childish comment.

"Loke, don't go there man! We should not let women disrupt our friendship. This is all fabrication from someone like Teralyn. You need to be able to read between the lines."

"J.R., you need to be able to hold your liquor and not

do stupid acts when you get a little alcohol in you. I'll talk with you later, but you need to realize that Teralyn and I are rapidly becoming a serious couple. I hope I don't have to choose."

I really could not believe the words that I was hearing. Loke doesn't even know Teralyn that well. He's been down with me from startup. I was not about to even address these hurtful words. He will eventually see the light.

"Loke, I hear ya man. Let's chat later on. Bye." Jewel quickly began her line of questioning.

"J.R., what is this rape crap all about? Is Teralyn accusing you of rape?"

"Jewel, she is lying up a storm. There is no way in the world that I raped that hoe."

"J.R., is it true that you even had sex with Teralyn?" I quickly thought to myself, *I guess it's take out aim fire on J.R. day. I really did not know the answer to Jewel's question as I was out cold, but I had to say something.*

"Jewel, I don't even remember going to sleep. Bentley had to put me to bed."

"J.R., that is ridiculous. I really don't understand why you would drink so much to where you would lose your common sense. Do you have a drinking problem or what?"

"No Jewel, I do not have a drinking problem okay. But Jewel, check this out. Bentley said that Teralyn came into my room late in the night while I was drunk and asleep. Bentley also told me that he came to knock on the door when he saw Evelyn returning. He said that Teralyn ran him away from the door when he tried to alert me of Evelyn's arrival. It's almost like she wanted Evelyn to see her in bed with me which really makes her highly suspicious."

"J.R., this is very bizarre at best. I am confused and I can't even imagine how confused Evelyn would be if she knew all the details. Right now, she is talking about making plans to divorce you. Have you spoken to her about these obviously, premeditated schedule of events?"

"Jewel, she won't even talk to me. What else must I do to prevent a divorce from happening? This would be a total mistake on her part."

"J.R., I recommend that you give her some time to gather her thoughts. In the meantime I encourage you to comply with her requests for now and don't do anything that will set her off."

"Set her off Jewel? Did you say set her off?"
I stood up like I was ready to throw something at the walls in Jewel's office.

"I'm about to set something off up in this mug. I did no harm last night, but I went out and got drunk and now I'm potentially facing frigging criminal charges for an act that I know I did not commit. I woke up and Evelyn automatically assumed that I had been sleeping with her sister. Jewel, I am getting tired of all this mess. You know, if Evelyn wants to leave me over some stupid stuff like her sister tricking me, then Jewel, I refuse to beg any further. I'm serious."

"J.R., sit yourself down and be calm for a minute. Your wife has a very legitimate reason to be upset and confused, okay. She just saw you in bed with her twin sister. You need to be more sensitive to her feelings at this time."

"Jewel I am very sensitive to her feelings, but it just seems that I just got out of the Doralee Mayberry crisis and now I have been tossed straight into this crisis. My problem is that I wish my wife would somehow trust me."

"J.R., you are asking an awful lot from her. You just need to be sensitive to what she has just gone through; a pregnancy, shocking news that her husband cheated on her just prior to the wedding and supposedly has another child, and now returning home finding her twin sister in bed with her husband."

"Jewel, I did not screw her. It did not go down like that."

"Shut up J.R.! You were too drunk to even know how it went down. If you had not gotten so darn drunk you would not have placed yourself in such a predicament."

Jewel was absolutely correct in every way. I truly regretted getting so drunk that I could not imagine all the events that were going on. Now, I got to get through this crisis. I must admit that I am not gonna give up on my wife. I am truly in this marriage until death do us part. Then again, if she leaves me, I probably deserve it with all the crap I've taken her through. I will give her the time she may need and hopefully she will conclude that I love her, and that's really all that matters.

Jewel and I continued to converse and then eventually she convinced me that now would probably be a good time for me to go home and take a break away from the state of Texas. At first, I did not agree, but after further thought and study, I totally agreed.

Therefore, I had my secretary book me a flight the next day to Ocala, Florida. I really needed to get away from the madness for a couple of days.

Chapter 32
Cousin Mike Breaking Off Something Proper

Since Evelyn wanted me out of the house, I figured I'd take some time off and fly home for the weekend. Besides, I needed to get my home front battery charged. Therefore, I flew home to Ocala, Florida. I arrived into town and once again, there was no one there to pick me up at the airport.

I could have sworn that my mom said that Cousin Mike would pick me up at the airport. Anyway, I thought to myself, *ain't no telling where Cousin Mike is.* I was slightly ticked off because, once again I had called in advance to let mom know I was flying home and she told me that Cousin Mike would be there waiting for me. After numerous calls home to try and track someone down to pick me up from the airport, I finally just rented a car.

I do recall that when I called home to let them know I was coming, mom seemed rather eager to see me. She did mention, however, that dad was home and he was upset with me. Mom did not know the full story about dad and what had transpired over the telephone between dad and I. I was not about to disclose my dad's private life, having experienced the fruit of my own sinful harvest.

However, I had to anticipate that dad had put a twist on the realities that actually occurred, regarding what he and I last talked about. Besides, I'm the one that should really be upset. I peeped his card and came to the conclusion that I was supporting his playa activity with another woman or other women.

To think that I was sending him all that money that he said he was using to buy mom things and knowing that he was not, really zapped my little joy light tremendously.

This really did upset me, and the more I thought about it, the madder I got. Then again, I was also hurt to know that my dad was cheating on my mom.

At first I thought dad was jealous because he felt that I had bought them a new house and new car all to satisfy mom and not him. Dad always felt that they did not need either, but instead he wanted money. Well, I guess I could now clearly understand why.

I pulled up to my parents' house which was located in a cull de sac on Clearview Circle, a really nice suburban area in the northern part of Ocala.

I was terribly shocked at first as I noticed the grass had not been mowed, it seemed for days. The garage door was up and there were boxes and cluttered junk all over the place.

To make matters worse, their house stood out like a sore thumb! All the other houses on the block were very well maintained, and this one looked as if it had been deserted for months. You should have seen the way the lawn looked.

I was truly embarrassed as I drove into the driveway. Dad's huge truck was parked out front of the house and mom's new BMW and her old Audi were in the driveway. There was also a seriously beat up looking Pinto parked in the driveway.

I immediately got busy as I pulled up in the long and wide driveway and parked behind my mom's old Audi. I went into the garage and started straightening up the garage.

All of a sudden, I heard some distinct sounds coming from the house. I opened up the door to the kitchen that led to the garage and there was the culprit.

Cousin Mike was getting busy with some woman in the kitchen. I walked in at the wrong time.

"Make me write some good checks baby. What's my name baby?" Cousin Mike said.

"Oh..oh..oh..oh...oh..yo name   is...Mike.... bounce dem checks baby."

The woman was darn near out of breath as Mike was hitting her backside in the center of the kitchen floor, located at the island.

"Naw....that ain't it....what's my name baby?"

Mike commenced to spanking her as he was humping uncontrollably.

"It's big Mike baby....yo name is big Mike. Spank me harder baby. Please!"

The woman was barely able to speak, but nevertheless Mike spanked her real hard.

"That's right gurl! Say it louder. You know that turns me on...say it louder."

"Oh..oh..oh...it's big Mike...big Mike....big Mike... bounce dem checks baby."

"That's right momma...whoa...I'm bout to bounce dem checks all over the house."

Mike was pumping about as hard as he could from the doggy style position. The sound was so loud as he was clearly hitting it hard.

"Oh...big Mike....big Mike.....big Miiike....."

I could not believe what I was seeing. Once again, Cousin Mike was in my momma's kitchen with one of his women leaning over the island as he was knocking her from the doggy style position. I had to bring his atrocious activity to a halt and I did not care about the fact that they were naked and seemingly about to come.

Well, I was nice enough to at least let them reach a climax, but as soon as they did I chimed in with vehement anger and displeasure.

"Oh you pullin it out of me baby...it's getting ready to pour up in dis mug......oh...awwh," said Cousin Mike.

"Dat's right big Mike...let it rain boo...let it rain....come on big Mike...bounce dem checks harder baby...Oh Jesus....Lord God above....Oh Jesus...Oh Lord.......Oh thank you Jesus...thank you Lord! OHHH!"

As painful as it was for me to watch, I stood right there and watched. This woman was practically praising God as Cousin Mike was wearing that backside out. It got worse. Cousin Mike, after coming, immediately slid down on the floor between her legs and made her sit on his face.

"Oh Mike! I love it when you lick me down there baby. God! It feels so good. You really know how to finish me off baby. Phew!"

Cousin Mike was licking and tasting her like a hungry man had found food.

Afterwards, he quickly stood up and she commenced to finishing him off. She came to her knees and ate him like he was her desert. She was sucking and tasting like she was a hungry Hebrew slave. He just stood there looking down at her with his arms all folded while maintaining such a proud look on his face as though he was posing for a camera shot. He even started pumping his muscles and making sounds like he was the Incredible Hulk. Mike was a trip!

I could not believe that they did not see me standing there looking as pissed as I did. Directly after they finished, I made my presence known.

"Mike, you know if I was a murderer and thief, I could

have easily killed the two of you."

They both jumped as though I really scared the two of them.

"J, what it be like man?"

"What in the world are you doing carrying on this way in my momma's kitchen? I mean you all up on the island and everything like this is your house? You should be ashamed of yourself."

I stood there looking at Cousin Mike and his lady friend all to realize that they were still naked. Mike was quick to speak to me again.

"J.R., how you be man? I was supposed to pick you up from the airport. Auntie Em said you were not arriving until late tonight. Ya plane landed early didn't it?"

"Mike, the plane did not land early. I was scheduled to arrive at the time it did and you failed to pick me up at the airport and I guess I can see why."

"Oh no J.R.! It's not that serious man, trust me. Yo man, did you get those new Jordans for me?"

"Mike, can yawl like put some clothes on please? I mean spare me the agony man okay."

His friend obviously did not hear a word that I said as she stood there in her glory and unashamed of the fact that she was naked and caught in the act.

"I'm sorry my name is Sharon. It is nice to meet you and I have heard so much about you."

She extended her hand and because I knew where her hands had been, I was not about to touch them. I waved her off.

"Hi Sharon, my name is J.R. and it is nice to meet you too, but certainly not under these circumstances."

I looked away from her body as I spoke to her. Then,

she just continued talking to me. Why did it seem as though she was talking for days?

"I have heard a whole lot about you and how you are so nice and everythang. Matter of fact, Mike said that you owned half of Disney, that you were about to become the new mayor in Dallas, Texas, and that the Dallas Cowboys wanted you to play for them because you were so good. He said that everythang you touched turned to gold and God was really in your life."

She just went on and on ...my goodness! She just kept on talking for days and none of the stuff that she was saying was true about me. Have you ever met someone and they just started talking to you and carried on with their own conversation as though you were actually talking back to them? Well that's the way she was on that day.

Cousin Mike was just standing there listening under a great degree of shock until his cell phone rang. He started gently whispering as though he did not want to be heard. I could hear him easily as I tuned Sharon out.

"I got-chu boo. You know I love you gurl. Jest let me handle some biz and I will call you back. By da way, how is my stuff? I know you know what I mean gurl. Hehehe!"

Mike started laughing and then Sharon turned to him in anger. Now, how in the world she kept talking to me without skipping a beat and heard everything Mike said on the phone, I will never know.

"Nigga you know you got some damn nerve talking to anotha hoe after you just finished making love to me."

She reached and knocked the phone out of his hand and it hit the kitchen floor and broke. Mike got upset.

"B---h, I know you done lost yo mind. It better not be broke or you will buy me anotha one. I'm serious."

"Who you talking to? Are you forgetting who bought you that phone? You better recognize!" Mike bent over to check out his phone.

"Who were you talking to Mike? That betta not be that trifling hoe Chakita or I'm gonn know somptin."

Mike was busy trying to put his phone back together and stood up with anger in his eyes.

"You don't be telling me who I can and cannot talk to, you uneducated bimbo." Sharon immediately responded.

"Oh no you ain't gonn call me no bimbo up in here after you jest finished rockin my world. Nigga I will scratch yo brown eyes right off yo face. Do you hear me?"

She walked up on Cousin Mike like she was ready to attack, while twitching her shoulders from side to side, lifting her right hand up in a clockwise motion and snapping her fingers. Cousin Mike shoved her and nearly sent her to the floor.

"You betta stay up off me gurl. You don't know me like dat, to be walking up on me and talking dat nonsense. I will kick yo ass and throw you out my aunt's house naked if you don't shut the hell up."

Sharon started rapidly moving towards him as to counter attack. Like a fool, I got between her and Cousin Mike and raised my voice real loudly.

"Calm down yawl. This will not be going on in my mom's house. If yawl must fight, then take this mess outside because it won't be going on in my mom's house." I caught a slap right upside my right jaw as Sharon was trying to be like Mike; Mike Tyson that is. I held Sharon and told Cousin Mike to leave the kitchen.

"Mike, go in the room and put some clothes on for crying out loud."

"Naw J.R.! She done pissed me off. Don't nobody tell me what to do, a no good skeezer."

He started walking off and then he turned around quickly to leave a message for Sharon.

"Yo coochie won't all dat anyway. The gurl on the phone, her stuff knows how to hold me down and you can't even compete with her."

Mike started walking out the kitchen as Sharon was trying to evade my grip as she was swinging and trying her best to reach Cousin Mike. I held her for awhile until she calmed down.

Then, about five minutes later, I released her. After I did, she totally surprised me.

"You want some of dis stuff?" She started holding both her boobs and pointing them out towards me.

"You can get dis if you want it and I mean all of it. I just love the way you held me in your arms and I could feel yo thang get hard."

I had no idea what she was talking about and I definitely was not about to go there.

"Sharon, put your clothes on. It ain't that kind of party okay."

"Well J.R., if it ain't that kind of party, what kind of party is it? I like that strong grip you had on me. It kinda felt good."

She started putting her hand on my chest and I grabbed her hand. I was not about to have this conversation with Sharon. Then, out of the blue, my mom and dad drove up into the driveway.

"Sharon, you have got to get out of here. Go and get dressed real fast." She panicked with fear.

"But my clothes are in Mike's room. I don't want to go

near his cheating ass."

"Look, you got to go somewhere okay." I screamed real loud for Cousin Mike.

"Yo Mike, you need to let Sharon put her clothes on because mom and dad just pulled up. Hurry up man, I'm serious." I turned to Sharon.

"I'm sorry, but yawl got to be adults. I will go outside and detain my parents, but you need to get dressed real fast. My mom does not play that."

I went outside and spoke with my mom and dad. Dad was very stern looking like he was mad, but mom was glad to see me.

"Hey mom, hey dad, how are yawl doing?" I hugged both my parents.

"Hey boy, how long you been in town," said my mom.

"I actually just got here a couple of hours ago."

"Son, whose car is that? You didn't have to get no rental car again with all these cars we got here at the house," said dad.

"Well dad, nobody picked me up at the airport so I just got a rental car."

"See what I mean Em?! I tell ya! That boy wastes more money than the president and MC Hammer both."

"J.R., I told Mike to pick you up at the airport this afternoon. Why didn't he pick you up? Where is he at anyway? He told me he had your flight number and everything," said my mom.

"Awhrah, Cousin Mike? Well, see now, awhrah I think he was busy. Yeah, that's right. He was busy mowing the lawn."

My dad started looking around for the lawn mower.

"J.R., what lawn was he busy mowing because this

lawn has not been touched for quite sometime." My mom quickly interjected.

"Honey, Mike was supposed to have mowed the lawn. He keeps saying he laid down some seeds and he was waiting on the good grass to come through and then he was gonna cut it."

"Did I say he was mowing the lawn dad? Oh no, what I meant to say was that he was going to mow the lawn and something happened. I believe he thought it was gonna rain so he was going to wait and do it later."

Both my dad and mom just stared at me. Then my mom started wondering why I was acting funny.

"J.R., we ain't had rain for days here. We been in a drought. Did Mike feed you that bull crap? He jest be trying to get out of work. Where the hell is he at anyway and whose car is that in the driveway?"

"I think Mike is sleep in the house. That car there is my rental car."

"Boy, have you done lost yo mind? Em and I can recognize a rental car with the rental car tag on it. We talkin bout that piece of junk right there."

My dad pointed to what was apparently Sharon's car.

"Actually, I really don't know whose car that was. I been out here trying to straighten up a little and I just went to get some water out the house." Oopps! I said those words and I realized that I did not have any water with me. Mom began to question me.

"J.R., what is going on? Why are you acting so weird? I know you too well boy. What is going on with you?"

Then, before you knew it, the front door to the house opened up and Cousin Mike was pretending to see his visitor off. He was talking real loud so my parents could here him, but it sounded so fake to me. I had to hold my breath from laughing at the boy.

"Miss Jones, thanks for the lesson on Jehovah witnessing and maybe the next time I'll be interested in buying a good book or two from you."

"You welcome Sir and thank you for taking the time to hear my offer."

Sharon was leaving out the door and she just waved to everybody, got in her car and drove off. My dad was staring at her as though he wanted to tear into her juicy butt and my mom was looking at her as though she was confused. Then, my mom hit my dad upside the head with her purse.

"Em, what was that for?"

"You know what that was for? You staring at that girl like yo eyes were laser radar or something."

"I was just, awhrah, making certain she was leaving, and that's all."

"You know one thing you and yo son have in common is that when yawl start to lying, you always stuttering with that awhrah stuff. It's a dead give away."

Sharon drove off real fast and then my mom lit into Mike as we all headed into the house.

"Mike, who in the world do you think you fooling? Ain't no Jehovah Witness gonna be coming up in my house in daisy dukes and a halter top. I know you ain't having no woman up in my house."

"Auntie Em, she's a Jehovah Witness, fa real doe!"

"Shut up lying boy! Ain't no Jehovah witness gonna be walking around here like a hoe. That woman won't no Jehovah Witness and you know that."

"Auntie Em, I'm serious. She was jest talking to me

about how God created the universe and stuff. Tell her J.R., you met her when you pulled up in your rental car."

See what I'm saying. Here we go again. Cousin Mike needed me to bail him out because he knew that my mom and dad would kick him out their house if he was running women up in there. Now, he got me out here lying to cover for his broke behind. Both my mom and dad stared at me without batting an eye.

"Well, I must admit that when I did pull up, I did hear her calling on the name of the Lord and stuff. She seemed to really enjoy praising his name." My mom turned her head and approached me closer.

"J.R., what are you talking about? What name was she calling on?"

"You know mom! She was calling on Jesus and stuff and praising his name."

"Do Jehovah witnesses acknowledge Jesus honey?" My mom turned to my dad and posed the question to him. He was brutally honest in his reply.

"Em, I don't know. Don't get me to lying. You know I don't know Jesus from Buddha." She turned and looked back at Cousin Mike.

"I don't think so. J.R., you need to stop trying to cover for Mike and Mike you need to pack yo bags so you can return with J.R. to Houston. I'm tired of yo non working, hoe chasing behind. I told you I did not want any women in my house and you continue to disobey me whenever I leave my house."

"But Auntie Em, come on nigh. That's not true at all."

"Stop lying Mike. Do you know how much hair I done cleaned up in yo room and in this house. I'm the only woman that be's in this house and my hair don't be shedding like these weave haired women that you be bringing to my house. Pack yo bags and get out." My dad just looked and made no comments.

"But mom, Cousin Mike can't come with me right now."

"J.R., you told me you would hire him. Are you trying to tell me otherwise now?"

"No Ma'am! I just got too much going on right now. I'll send for Cousin Mike at a later time, but not right now."

We continued the discussion for sometime and then mom finally agreed with my plan. My plan was just that, as I really had no intention of bringing Cousin Mike to Houston just yet. I had too many bigger issues to deal with.

Later on that evening, my dad and I finally talked. He still denied ever cheating on my mom and he wanted me to act as though I did not hear the conversation over the phone between him and that other woman. I listened to dad and I was not about to be confrontational.

Nevertheless, he still wanted me to give him some more money. My dad was truly a trip!

Chapter 33
It's Like That Huh?

About two days later I had returned from Ocala and I was informed by Jewel that Evelyn had gone out of town. I was somewhat nervous, angry, and upset because she took Dominance Nicole and did not inform me. In addition, she would not answer any of my phone calls.

Loke was acting really funny as he had been truly stricken by the poison of Teralyn. He would not return my phone calls I had left him. I refused to visit him at his house because I did not want to deal with Teralyn.

When I found out that Evelyn had left town, my plans were to stay at the house until she returned. I did notice that she did not pack or carry clothes that would indicate she was gone for good, which made me feel somewhat better.

While waiting, I finally got a call from Loke and for some reason he wanted me to meet him across town at a store called Tuesday Morning. I was confused initially by his unique request; nevertheless I met him there.

We went into the store and Loke was shopping around like he had never seen discounted items in his life. I mean he was shopping up a storm, buying item after item. I was definitely not in a shopping mood. As I watched him shop, I began to notice that Loke was very evasive.

"Loke, what's going on with you man? Why didn't you return my phone calls? Is there something I need to know?"

I was walking down the aisle and watching Loke act as though he was a kid in the candy store.

"J.R., not a lot has gone on man. I just been real busy and on top of that, my woman really don't want me interacting with you anymore."

I could not believe what I was hearing. I was certain that Loke had to be just joking.

"Loke, we are grown men and we don't let women dictate who we take on as friends. I am not really interested in hearing this stupid stuff about Teralyn."

Loke stopped walking and looked at me with a serious look on his face.

"J.R., I know you may find this hard to believe, but I am really falling in love with Teralyn. I am so close to asking her to marry me."

"Loke, are you sure you are not being manipulated by her?"

"Come on J.R.! Teralyn has really been good for me. I mean, since she has entered into my life, I have completely shut down my activities with other women. She is the one I want to spend the rest of my life with. I'm about to surrender my playa's card."

"Loke, take it from me man, don't rush into marriage. You really do need more time to get to know Teralyn. She is not even on your level if you don't mind me saying that."

"J.R., you and I probably won't be meeting like this again man. I have already been told by Teralyn that I need to make a choice. It's either you or her. I regret to tell you that I must do what a brother has to do."

I could not believe that I was standing here hearing my close partner and friend basically telling me that he was no longer interested in being my best friend any longer due to a woman.

"Now Loke, you know we are thick blood and we can't afford to let any women separate us."

"J.R., Teralyn is not just any old woman man. Now,

she agreed not to press charges against you for rape if I agreed to conclude our friendship. I'm actually looking out for you by taking the higher road."

"Loke, are you serious? Are you trying to tell me that you will no longer be my boy because of this lying tramp?"

"J.R., don't refer to my fiancée as a lying tramp."

"Loke, you know what I mean, okay. Fiancée? Wow, you sure do strike fast."

"Actually J.R., I did not strike as fast as you did."

"Well, I guess you might have a point there."

"J.R., on a more serious note, Teralyn said that Evelyn was still involved with Ricky's daddy. Supposedly, the trip to Dallas was all about that."

"Loke, I don't believe that. Do you really think that Teralyn's words have any credibility with me? Remember, I'm the one she's lying on by saying that I raped her. I just think Teralyn is making that mess up."

"J.R., you can believe what you will my friend. Hey, on the real, I just wanted to tell you thanks for everything and I hope the best for you and your family."

"So Loke, it's like that huh?"

"J.R., it's like that man. I'm gonna check out and purchase these items. You take real good care of yourself man, okay."

"Loke, you do the same. It is really unfortunate that our friendship will come to an end over a woman. I would have never believed the likelihood of that happening in a million years."

"Well J.R., the bible says that a man should cleave unto his wife and leave his family."

"Don't start quoting any scriptures to me man. You don't even have the correct correlation. If you want to end our friendship because of your hoochie momma, you go ahead Loke, but you just remember this; you will need me before I will ever need you."

"J.R., you don't have to get all melodramatic with me."

"Naw Loke, you go ahead and step! I'm out!"

I walked out of Friday morning or whatever the hell the name of that store was and I was very upset. I could not believe my best friend was going to drop our friendship all because of Evelyn's trifling sister. I was so disappointed in Loke; after all I've done for him. He had some nerve to even go there with me.

Anyway, as I departed the parking lot of that store called Tuesday Night, I got a phone call from Jewel and she told me that she was going to meet Evelyn. I just listened and I refused to comment for the time being. I was just too upset for any remote form of conversation.

Nevertheless, I had hoped that wherever they met, Jewel could possibly talk some sense into Evelyn's head. As for me, my best course of action was to go home and just wait patiently for the results of their conversation. I was emotionally tired and worn out from everything that was taking place in my life. While I had retreated like a soldier that had lost the war, Jewel proceeded to meet with Evelyn.

When Jewel drove up to meet Evelyn, she was surprised to see Evelyn as happy as she was, talking on the phone.

Jewel anticipated that Evelyn would be depressed, but she did not appear to be that way at all. They met this time at a coffee shop near downtown.

"Hi Evelyn, how are you doing?" Evelyn was still talking on the phone and then all of a sudden she got off the phone when she recognized Jewel.

"Hey gurl!" Jewel spoke to Evelyn again.

"How are you doing Jewel? How is business?"

Their unique, mystique, and collective looks made the two of them look like high class divas. Evelyn wore dark black shades where you could not see her eyes. Jewel wore brown tinted shades where you could barely see her eyes. Jewel and Evelyn went and sat on the outside of the coffee shop and began to chit chat.

"Jewel, I have given much thought to this situation and I must admit that I don't think I can do this anymore. I have not spoken a word to J.R. since the last incident in our home. Jewel, I just don't think I want to continue in this relationship. The last thing I want hanging over my head is the fact that my trifling twin sister had the nerve to sleep with my husband, and the gall to do it in our bedroom. I have racked my brains as to why I should stay and honestly, the negative reasons outweigh the positive ones."

"Evelyn, you must realize that marriage within the early years is very challenging at best. I can't speak from experience, as I have never been married, but I do know what my mom and dad went through. You guys have not been together that long."

"Well, that is what I mean as well. Over the period of one year, I've been cheated on twice, led to believe I was the only love in his life, and found out that he may have been a father to another woman's child. Now, I'm being told that he may have raped my twin sister. Now, I'm certain he did not rape her, but he did sleep with her. So, to the woman who is hurt, which is worse? It is what it is."

"Evelyn, are you still in love with J.R.? What do the

words until death do us part mean to you?"

"Jewel, I'm not even for certain anymore. I am probably still in love with J.R. at this time, but what does love have to do with it? I think J.R. is still busy and I really don't think he has brought an end to his ways with women."

"Evelyn, as an outsider looking in, I would not suggest terminating a marriage that is so fresh off the tracks. I just don't think you have given your marriage enough time to work. For as much as J.R. is bad, he is good."

"Jewel, you look me in my eyes and give me three good reasons why I should remain in this marriage after that nigga has slept with my twin sister."

"Evelyn, once again, whatever happened to the vows that you pledged to keep? Remember, I was your wedding planner and I coordinated the entire ceremony. As a participant of that process, the most influential words I recall from your wedding vows were until death do us part?"

Evelyn stared speechlessly at Jewel. Jewel continued to express her viewpoint.

"Okay, first off, your husband has a brilliant business mind. Let's look at what he is responsible for producing. He pushed me towards practicing criminal law again at which I have found new life into the profession. He has also helped me develop my business mind, which I didn't even know existed. He encouraged Loke to start expanding his dentist offices and to expand his oral dentistry work, and he has since flourished from J.R.'s inspirational influence. He helped fulfill one of your dreams by acquiring your daycare facility and helped you get on track with your lifelong dream. Should I even dare to mention his fatherly affection toward Ricky and the manner in which he has inspired him both educationally and athletically? Don't forget the community efforts and his brilliant work on the mayor's executive staff and city council?"

"Jewel, this is all business though. I am not in this marriage for the money and I realize many may believe otherwise."

"Who cares what others believe Evelyn? You are the only one that matters. Speaking of money, I can name over fifty million green reasons why you should not leave J.R. As he develops these properties and sell them, his overall worth will definitely increase tremendously beyond that figure."

"Jewel, once again, I am not so motivated by money."

"Evelyn, I have had boyfriends that possess cheating minds and hearts and trust me, J.R. does not fit the type. He is not the cheating type and you need to recognize that."

"Jewel, he may not be the cheating type, but he does manage to be in a cheating position quite often."

"Evelyn, J.R. has been a great father to Ricky and I am certain he will be a great father to Dominance Nicole as well. He may have made a mistake here or there, but J.R. is really a good man. Don't walk out on a good man."

"I don't feel like I'm walking out Jewel. I feel like I have found a man who can't seem to be happy alone with me. However, I do realize that J.R. is good for both Ricky and Dominance Nicole."

Jewel, took off her shades and just looked at Evelyn.

"So you say that your basis for your leaving J.R. is due to him cheating, and money has no significance

310

whatsoever on your decision."

"That's the absolute truth Jewel. For it is not about money for me, I'm only interested in his loyalty and commitment."

"Oh really Evelyn? I take it that you have been totally loyal and faithful to J.R. since the two of you have been married?"

Evelyn began to really get nervous as she began to start scratching her hands.

"Sure I have Jewel! You know that yourself."

"You know what Evelyn, I thought at one time I knew, and then I've suddenly realized that I really don't know anything about anyone. I want you to know that I have been noticing more and more the physical features of Dominance Nichole."

"Jewel, what's your point? This is about J.R. and not about Dominance Nicole."

"Evelyn, that's exactly what I thought until I began to notice how Dominance Nicole looks more and more like Ricky."

Evelyn twisted her head while snapping her fingers in the air with her smarty pants expression.

"Dah! What you expect? That's his sister."

"Oh I realize they are brother and sister. It's just somehow amazing that they are so much alike in facial and body characteristics."

"Jewel, I really don't understand your point. I really did not come to discuss Ricky and Dominance Nicole because they have nothing to do with my current relationship with my husband."

"Evelyn, I beg to differ with you. You see, they have everything to do with your current relationship with your husband. The point that I am making is that two kids only look exactly alike when they in fact have the same mother and father." Evelyn really started to get upset. She was getting very angry at Jewel.

"Jewel, what in the hell are you trying to say?"

Evelyn took off her shades and stood up from the table. She started breathing real heavy as though she was very nervous. Jewel also stood up from the table, placed her shades back on, folded her arms and just stared at Evelyn.

"Jewel, I really don't appreciate what you are trying to imply."

"Evelyn, I am not trying to imply anything. Let me give you this information." Jewel reached into her purse and pulled out a piece of paper.

"So what Jewel? That's just a hotel receipt. That piece of paper does not prove anything."

Evelyn shoved the receipt back at Jewel and it fell to the floor. Jewel humbly retrieved the receipt from the floor and put it back into her purse. Then she removed another document that would clearly upset the course and flow of their conversation.

"Well Evelyn, I thought you would be just a bit more graceful during this portion of our conversation. The hotel receipt merely establishes a time reference. This information actually tells the story."

Evelyn nearly snatched the document from Jewel with high anxiety to see what was on the paper.

"What are you talking about Jewel?"

Evelyn was getting more and more angry. Then, she examined the document that she snatched from Jewel. The document was genuine and official and it caused

Evelyn to calm down and listen to what Jewel had to say. Evelyn slowly sat down as though her body was crumbling and she placed her right hand underneath her chin as to hold it up, while looking so pitiful, and still staring at the piece of paper. She immediately developed that *I'm busted* look on her face. Jewel proceeded to drop the law.

"Now Evelyn, should we not start this conversation over again with more truth and honesty? The document reflects that J.R. could not possibly be the father of Dominance Nicole on the basis of their blood types. The receipt conveys the time period as to when you and Ricky's dad had a hotel rendezvous."

Tears began to flow from Evelyn's eyes. She was totally busted.

"Jewel, all I can say is that it was an honest mistake. I did not know that meeting Sam and loaning him some money would result in going to bed with him."

"Excuse me Evelyn? Did he force you to go to bed with him? I mean because if he did, you can easily bring him up on charges."

"No Jewel, he did not force me."

Evelyn was crying like a little child that was denied privileges.

"Evelyn, if the purpose of your meeting with Sam was to give him money, why would you feel a need to do that in a hotel? That's typically not the meeting place for transacting money, unless we are talking prostitution activity which we are clearly not."

"I don't know Jewel. I just did. I just did."

Evelyn was crying as though she was ever so sorry and under intolerable torture. Jewel did not let up.

"Truth of the matter is that you agreed to go to bed

with Sam and you hid behind pregnancy as to why you would not sleep with J.R. when in all reality you could not sleep with J.R. because of your feelings that you currently have for Sam. Am I telling the truth Evelyn?"

Evelyn was crying and fighting the tears as they were gushing from her eyes. Her reluctance to answer the question confirmed the very fact that Jewel was speaking the truth. Jewel had handkerchiefs in her purse, but refused to share them with Evelyn.

Evelyn was totally helpless, embarrassingly busted, and full of pain and torture as Jewel was dropping the law down like cold winter rain. She articulated blow by blow everything that happened almost as though she was there and had an insight as to all the activity that had occurred. Her one on one performance with Evelyn would have clearly convinced any courtroom jury to bring back a verdict of guilty beyond reasonable doubt.

"Yes! You're telling the truth," Evelyn finally confessed.

"Okay, I thought maybe there was some value in starting this conversation over again and on the right tone. Now, as I see it Evelyn, J.R. is the actual loyal and committed one in this relationship. He loves you and no one else."

Evelyn buried her face in her hands as she continued crying. Then, she resurfaced and expressed her emotions.

"Wow Jewel! Why do you care so much? If I did not know any better I would think that you were interested in J.R."

Jewel looked down and away from Evelyn and tilted her shades before she left words that resulted in a jaw dropper.

"Reason number four Evelyn as to why you should not leave J.R. If you leave J.R. over some trivial mess like your trifling sister sleeping with him, he won't be around for your return."

Evelyn wiped her eyes and stared at Jewel with her mouth open as though there were more revelations to come.

"Jewel, what are you trying to tell me?"

"Evelyn, if you take your little happy butt and leave that fine man behind, you can best believe that he will be mine by time you return. That is not hearsay, theory, nor fiction, but that's a fact!"

Evelyn's jaws dropped further apart and she just stared at Jewel like she had just told her the most shocking news she had ever heard. She stroked her hair and just looked at Jewel with amazement.

"So Jewel, it's like that huh?"

"That's right Evelyn! It's exactly like that. Now, you carry ya little happy butt home to your man and forget about this leaving nonsense. As for me, I'll be submitting my resignation papers to your husband in the morning as I'm resigning my position with J.R. and as Ricky's agent. I can no longer witness another bitter, ungrateful, and clueless woman stressing over a man of the highest and brightest quality as that of your husband."

Evelyn continued to stare in amazement as she wiped her eyes and looked at Jewel as though she might attack her.

"But Jewel, are you gonna tell J.R.?"

Evelyn seemed woefully concerned and very scared at this point.

"Tell J.R. what Evelyn? That the baby he is so proud

315

of and believes he had with you is really not his. Tell him that you cheated on him with Ricky's dad not long after you married him?"

Evelyn started wiping tears away from her eyes as they formed up again. She could not say a mumbling word. Instead her eyes did all the talking as Jewel fully understood.

"Evelyn, you go ahead home to your husband. I'm not about to tell J.R. about your infidelity; nor will I mention that Dominance Nicole is not his child. That is your job."

"Jewel, can I please ask you just one more question before I leave?"

"No Evelyn! J.R. and I have never had an affair nor would either one of us contemplate such. We really were like brother and sister and we really were great business partners. That was the extent of our relationship. Now, did I answer your question?"

"Yes Jewel, you sure did."

"You take care Evelyn and please don't be so quick to throw stones the next time, when you privately live in a glass house."

Evelyn stood up, put on her shades, and left without saying a word. She knew exactly what she had to do at that point. She left the coffee shop and didn't stop until she reached her home. She had finally come to her senses and realized home is where she truly belonged; home with her dearly beloved husband, J.R.

Author's Closing Comments

Hey yawl! I just wanted to take the time to thank you for supporting my work.

Many people did not feel so inclined to encourage me when I embarked upon this writing career. Even some family members instantly hated on me and turned their backs on me, but little did they know, they fueled my fire!

Make no mistake about it, for I am a struggling author trying to get out the gate.

Nevertheless, the generosity that you have shown as my fans has clearly improved the odds. I thank you dearly from the bottom of my heart and I can assure you that you will not find another so humble, appreciative, while yet hungry for the satisfaction of providing my fans the greatest entertainment within this venue.

Be on the lookout for my kid's novel, *Broken Ankles*, which is soon to hit under my kid's pen name, Raywill. Also, next up, I owe you *Salty Roots*. Stay on the lookout for my comedy thriller, *The Author*, where I talk about yawl as fans. Yawl are a serious trip in a very humorous kind of way.

In addition be on the lookout for my poet Jerome Redd whose poetry book is about to be dropped in the latter portion of the year. Once again, I thank each and everyone of you for your time and support! I also want to thank my editor, ghostwriter_67@yahoo.com

Peace!

Galuminatti

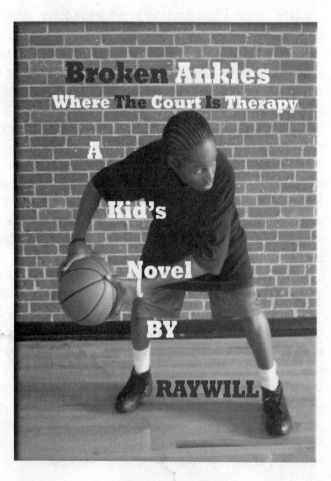

Broken Ankles
Where The Court Is Therapy

A

Kid's

Novel

BY

RAYWILL

COMING SOON